D1478230

THE FERAL GIRL

Nick Alimonos

Books in the Aenya Series
(in chronological order)

The Feral Girl
Ages of Aenya
The Princess of Aenya

ACKNOWLEDGMENTS

I would like to thank my devoted and lovely beta readers: Hynde Belahsen and Heather Zanitsch, for their never-ending support and encouragement throughout this long, arduous journey. I would also like to thank my amazingly talented illustrators: Heather Zanitsch, Alexey Lipatov, Vinogradov Aleksei, Oscar Paludi, and Jasmine Alimonos.

Tyrnael
Northendell
Dark Hemisphere
OCEAN
Potamis
Yefira
Nimbos
Ukko Mountains
Hedonia
Gulf of Sarnath
Wildwood
800 km
Thetis
Thalassar
Aea
The Black Coast
Makria
Kratos
Shemselinihar
Graton
The One Sea
Nibia
AENYA
2000 km

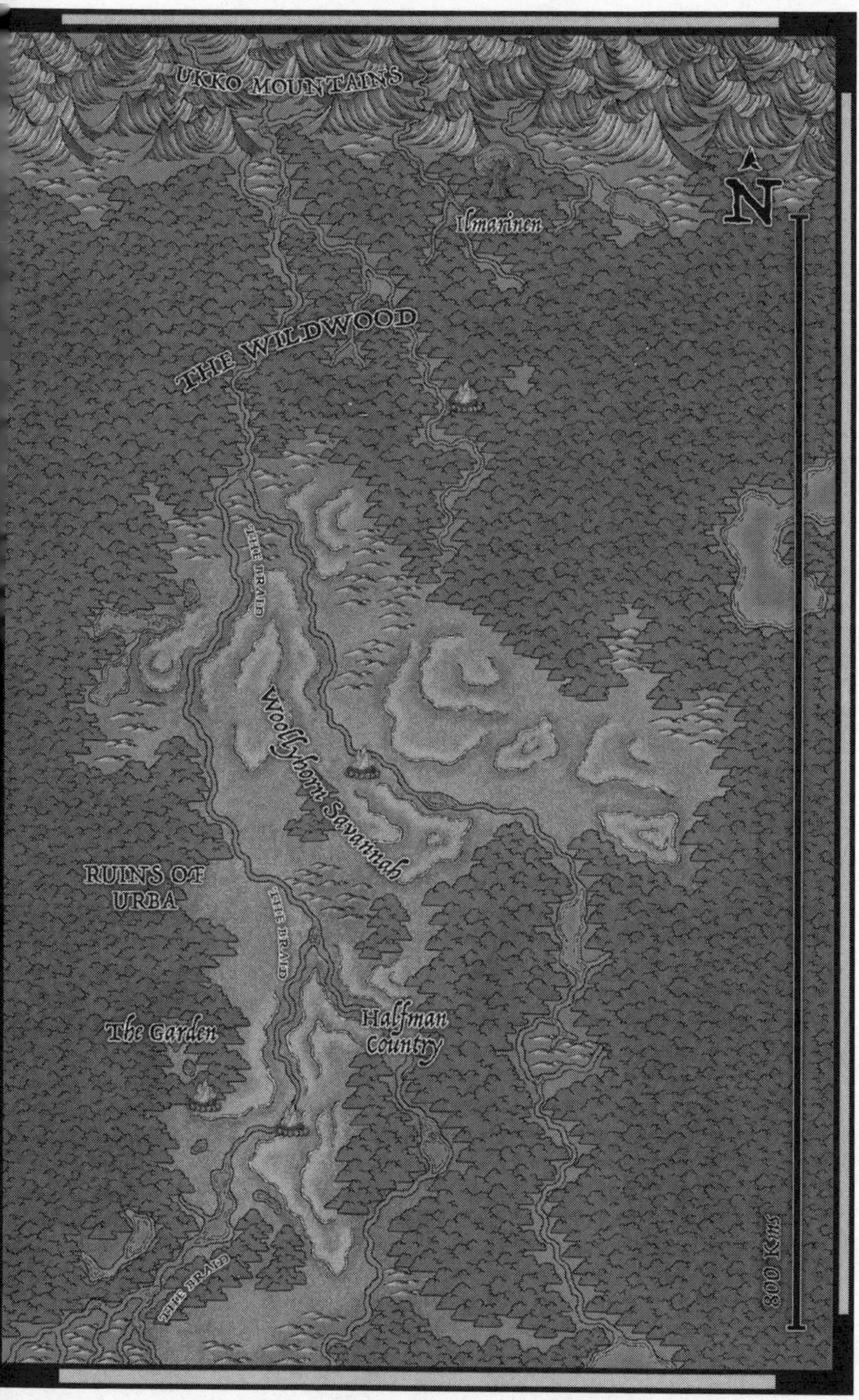

UKKO MOUNTAINS

Ilmarinen

THE WILDWOOD

THE BRAID

Woollyhorn Savannah

RUINS OF
URBA

THE BRAID

The Garden

Halfman
Country

THE BRAID

N

800 Kms

"The lonely road is the longest."

—*Song of the Journeyman*

Thelana pulled at weeds until her knees ached and her fingers turned raw. She yanked the green shoots slowly from the roots, lest they grow back, and wrestled with the stubborn red stems with their thorny petals until her palms started to bleed. *Invaders*, Baba called them. Each of her brothers and sisters, eleven in all, was responsible for a portion of the field. Once, she asked Father why the invaders had chosen to sprout in such numbers when they never had before, but he gave no answer.

As the setting sun painted the mountains gray and purple, Thelana decided she had done enough work for the day so her father would not reprimand her. She brushed the dirt from her thighs and the muck from her soles, then started for the giant tree crowning the hill. *Old Man Oak.* It was the way home.

A plum tree stood along the path in a glade of swaying heathers and disintegrating dandelions. She loved the sweet flavor of the yellow fruit, how they popped in her teeth, and the season was suitable for their picking. But the soil looked parched, cracked at the roots like aged pita, and the barren limbs that grew from it shivered with nothing to offer her but kindling.

Supper that day left her stomach hollow and groaning for more. The boys had brought nothing home from the woods, so Mana resorted to her usual stew of carrots, oats, and potatoes, with a pinch of mountain salt and basil mixed in for flavor. The portioning was meager, and to Thelana, it tasted a little better than boiled water. Still, she knew not to complain, even when the younger ones voiced their displeasure. A stern look from Father— his hand raised— usually shut them up, turning their eyes to the contents of their bowls.

"All the gods ask is that we endure," he said. An old proverb, one he liked to repeat, but which had long lost its power to console. "A little patience," he went on, "a few days until the grain comes in, and your mother will have us a feast."

Borz, her eldest sibling, stood abruptly from the table. She could see his hunter's markings glinting in the firelight, the impressions of every animal he had killed running from his thigh and hip to his ribs. He was old enough to jump the sacred flame, take a wife, and start a family. But for the past two years, on each night of the Solstice, he made no effort to court any of the maids from the other families, knowing what it would mean to abandon his own. "I am to blame for this, Baba. But I will do better. We need to delve deeper. Two, or three days at most. There are great beasts in the far places. I've seen them. Game enough to feed us for cycles. But we must find the courage to venture further out into the Wildwood."

"No." Father's voice betrayed no emotion, his countenance like the stone golems littering the hills of Ukko. "You don't know the dangers of the world beyond our borders. Out there, you eat, or you are eaten."

"Our ancestors were proud hunters!" Borz countered, thumping his chest. "They weren't afraid. We can learn to do as they did."

"I don't want to hear any more about our ancestors. The Goddess will provide. Aenya has never failed us."

Thelana looked from one man to the other. Baba's face was flecked with gray and lined with the ravages of too many suns. His once broad shoulders were now sunken and the sinews of his body rounded like an overused spade. Her brother was who Baba had been, brimming with pride and passion and eager to prove his worth. As always, she sided with the younger version. How could her father be so stubborn? Too blind to see the changes to the climate? She shot from the table, leaving her bowl wobbling and half-empty, angered and wanting everyone to know it.

When all was dark, she lay across the fingers of Old Man Oak, watching the stars drift across the dome of Aenya as her siblings slumbered in the boughs below. Everything she knew of the world was Ilmarinen. The Ukko Mountains guarded the north, with its painted caves, cascading falls, and the Braid River flowing from it. Flowering valleys of orange and violet stretched from east to west. And an impregnable forest, the Wildwood, bordered their country to the south. *But there has to be more than this*, she thought. The embers of the gods came wheeling up from the horizon every night, only to settle back behind the Greater Moon by morning. From whence did such lights arrive and whither did they recede? To and from other lands, no doubt, lands outside of Ilmarinen, places her parents never told her of or did not know existed.

A commotion stirred her from her reverie. She crouched in the branches, listening to the voices rising to her ears. Her parents often argued in the depths of eclipse when they believed their children were asleep. She could hear them shouting at one another and knew that her siblings, the older ones in particular, were likely disturbed by the noise.

Baba's and Mana's disagreements always revolved around the same exhausted subjects. Her mother did not wish to worry the family, to let on how bad things were becoming, but Father insisted they prepare for the worst. Tonight, the same conflict rang through the timbers of the house. But something felt a bit different this time. Thelana could sense it in the unusually hushed way her parents were speaking. It was as if they were desperately trying to keep some secret. Then, her brother's murmuring voice added to the clamor, and she had to hold back a gasp lest she be discovered.

Why is he there? He's never there!

She climbed the rope ladder from her bower, quietly as a huntress, peering through the arch of creepers framing the window into the main room. The clay chiminea blazed with a soft orange glow, illuminating the besom in the corner, the weeds growing through the floorboards, Baldr softly wheezing in his wicker bassinet. Mana and Baba stood in a deep well of shadow beside the dying flame, between their youngest and eldest sons.

Thelana could always tell how her brothers were feeling, whether they were cold or ill, or if they'd spent the afternoon daydreaming about one of the neighbors' daughters. But Borz betrayed no emotion but anticipation. He nervously paced the room, his small hairs standing in sharp relief in the dim blaze. The mirth in his face, which so often lifted her spirits, was absent. When his mother moved to embrace him, she could see the bloody rim of her eyes. It looked as if she had spent the night fighting tears.

The knock at the door startled the four of them. Thelana was unaccustomed to the sound and grew frightened. Father had built it only recently, to keep scavengers from their larder, but she could not imagine any animal making such a racket. It could not be anything pleasant, she surmised, given her brother's sullen expression. Then her mother, her face just as grave, tugged at her father's elbow, pleading. "Are you sure?"

Baba drew his fingers tiredly across the hairs of his face. His grooming habit had become less consistent, his beard more disheveled with every passing day. Now, a sudden intensity came into his eyes, and he adopted a harrowing appearance Thelana had never seen before. He possessed the face of a man who has tried everything, mulled over every possibility, only to find hopelessness.

"Bryseis, we've discussed this." He turned to his wife but was unable to hold her gaze. "The larder is empty. There is no other way."

The door reverberated again like a living thing, and Thelana considered what a strange thing it was having a door in her house. Ilma danced and dined and made love in open fields. Their rooms were partitioned, if at all, by curtains of ivory, amber, and lapis lazuli. While fences kept livestock from wandering into the woods, solid barriers prevented wild creatures from ransacking their stores. That Baba would have felt the need to fashion a *door* for their home suggested there were dangers to keep out.

The knock came a third time, more forcefully than before, and her mother turned faint. She looked as if she might topple, but Borz was quick to lend her his strength. Then Father reached for the grip.

The people entering the room dazzled Thelana's senses. They had to be *ilma*, she did not doubt it, the same kind of animal as herself. She could make out the meaty brows of their faces and the tuft of short-cropped hair growing from their apish skulls. And, while the men did not grow beards, she ascertained their sex from their broad shoulders and stubbled chins. But it remained to be seen whether either of them possessed navels, hairy limbs, or male genitals. To her eyes, they were like beetles from collar to abdomen, with the soft parts of their bodies hidden under reflective carapaces that bloomed with reds and yellows in the light of her parent's hearth. Most likely, they were ilma of a different sort. Their hides and the fittings for their weapons were too finely worked for her people to produce.

The strangers spoke in somber tones and only to Baba, gesticulating where language failed them. Mana receded into a corner all the while, as if she could not suffer their presence, and in like manner, they averted their eyes from where she stood. Thelana tried but failed to discover the nature of their discourse, but she was reminded of the Harvest Moon, when families from across the land gathered to barter for crops. Father was trading with them, she realized, haggling for a better deal, yet she could not fathom what her family might have to offer such people.

One of the men walked out, allowing a rush of cold air to swirl through the open doorframe, and Baldr began to wail. Mana lifted the boy to her bosom, shushing him, as the man returned carrying two heaping sacks. Baba pulled the knot from the bag, sifting a handful of grain through his fingers, as the two strangers moved to examine her brother. They looked over his teeth and fingers and heels, and every other part of his body, as if Borz were a prize hog, and Thelana understood, with a sudden tightness in her chest, that the men were appraising him.

They led Borz through the doorframe and her parents followed. Thelana crept down to the base of the great oak in pursuit, tiptoeing along the roots to the front of the house. She found them under the arbor, where fruitless grapevines grew in abundance, coiling about the posts and hanging down from the slats of the awning. Baldr straddled his mother's hip, clutching at the garland of flowers she always wore.

"What will we tell the children?" Mana was saying. "Don't they deserve to know? To say goodbye, at least?"

The situation was not unexpected, nothing her parents had not debated countless nights before. And yet, Baba chose his words carefully; whatever his answer, it could only be final. "Bryseis . . . the children . . . you know how they can be. Thelana especially. She has such a strong will."

"It's not too late to find another way. He is our firstborn son. My son. *Please.*"

Borz placed a finger under his mother's chin, caressing Baldr's soft, wispy hair with his other hand. "You've taught me to be strong, mother. Now you must find the strength to do what's best for the family. This is my duty, and I am not afraid to do it."

She tried to speak, to dissuade him from going, but could do nothing but break in his embrace.

The strangers became restless as the rest of their company awaited them in the distance. She could just make out the silhouette of a caravan, the fires flickering from their torches, beasts of burden tethered to wagons, indistinct banners rippling silently in the dark. Baba pulled his wife away, ever so gently, and the man who had appraised her brother now wrapped him about the waist in a long skin to hide his penis and scrotum and the parade of animal-shaped pigments—his many proud kills—encircling his hips. They were changing him, Thelana thought, covering his body to more resemble themselves.

Borz was led from under the arbor without a word of farewell, like an aurochs shackled to a plow. She wondered how her parents could bear to witness it, how her father could stand motionless as Mana quailed against him, her hair dashed across her face like a willow, as Baldr wailed and slipped from her thigh.

As the sight of Borz diminished, Baba twisted in the doorway, looking out into the deepening darkness. But he did not call out. Her father did nothing that night but wring his corded arms until his wrists reddened beneath his knuckles. Until Borz was no longer there.

Thelana should have screamed, chased after him, fought to save her brother somehow. A piece of her was being cut out and she could only peer from behind a wall and quiver. She knew the loss would fester in her for a lifetime, and yet she was helpless, a child paralyzed by uncertainty, who could but watch—watch as her life and everything she knew of the world unraveled.

That night, and every night thereafter, Thelana would ask herself why she had kept herself hidden, why she had been unable to stir herself into action. At the very least, she could have called out to him before he was led away.

The strangers were an enigma, entirely alien to Ilmarinen and her peoples' way of life. But they would not be the last to arrive. Stragglers invaded her homeland in the ensuing years, burdened by their belongings, many of them wounded, dying, and in desperate need of shelter. Most looked down upon her family, calling her *uncivilized*, *primitive*, and *naked*, words she knew to be condescending, if nothing else. Despite her father's admonishments, she learned what she could of the strangers, their habits, and enough of their language to barter, yet none of them knew her brother's whereabouts.

The Outsiders complained incessantly, like small children. They hated the food and the bugs and the lack of bedding, and walking anywhere without first shodding their feet was a constant ordeal. On hotter days, when they doffed their shells to reveal their underlying coats, their pale-as-milk shoulders cooked under the sweltering sun. Even as they looked down upon her people, and insulted them with names she did not understand,

Thelana and her siblings chided them, knowing what frail creatures they truly were.

But in the passing twilight, when the moons lay drowsily in the sky, Thelana could only think of her brother and of the men who took him. To Baba, the strangers were people in need, and he treated them as he would any Ilmarin from a neighboring farmstead. But for her, they were an invading species that came to occupy their beds and consume their food and rob them of their offspring. They imitated humans in every way, but ilma could never be so unfeeling, so greedy, to trade food for children. And in the dead of eclipse, when all lay slumbering in the arms of Old Man Oak, she conjured memories of Borz, imagining him as he had been that night, his pride stripped away as those things in the shadows prodded and probed him, muttering secrets with her parents, those men with the gaping holes where their hearts should have been.

No, they are not men, she decided. Only people with human faces. *Face People.*

DAY 40

"Goddess' blood!"

Her quarry raced ahead, its feathered legs kicking up pine needles, its elongated neck rising and contorting, its stubby tail vanishing between the ferns. Again she cursed. Even with her arrow in its throat, the bird continued to outmaneuver her.

She pushed through the brambles, led by a trail of frothy-pink blood, a crimson leaf, a wet stone. The chobo's three-pronged markings were becoming harder to find. Her supper was gaining ground with every ragged breath she took, and she could not afford to lose it over the hard roots of the trees.

Where are you now, you dumb bird?

Her spear was of worked ash, fastened by twine and molasses to a tip of chipped stone—an instrument of death in her hands—but useless if she could not get within reach of her prey.

She shut her eyes, quelled the heaving of her bosom to listen to the frightful stirring in the undergrowth, and sped off again. Her pursuit led her into a dense jumble of flora. Limbs of ash and juniper clawed at her sides, thorns snagged at her braid, nettles blinded her. She managed her way by the snap of twigs, and the knobby roots jabbing her instep, while the soft brush of scale leaves left the slick touch of moss on her feet.

Water flowed somewhere within earshot. She could sense it, the humid air settling on her shoulders. The chobo was likely tiring, losing blood, growing thirsty. Her prey was sure to stop for a drink, and she would catch it there.

She hurried into a sprint, following the report of water as the foliage cleared and the ground evened. Further ahead, the ridge sloped down into a valley, where the tumult of the stream filled her eardrums. *Good. The noise will muffle my approach.*

A copse of birches sprouted by the water's edge. She slipped between them, their slender boles offering little cover, keeping low as she crept toward the bank. Falls roared from a place she could not see. The gushing stream was like white webbing, dashing to froth against the rocks and spraying the air with mist. She knelt, her throat parched, her bones simmering. Pebbles of red and green and yellow glistened beneath her kneecaps. But the water was cold, blissfully cold under the scorching sun. She washed the sweat from her face and neck, drank deeply from her cupped hands, then retrieved her spear to resume the hunt.

The stream lapped against her calves in the shallows, stiffening her joints, while the undertow threatened to carry her away. She would need to maintain her footing, keep to the water's edge while crouching among the rocks to keep from being seen.

After less than a passing, she spied the bird standing by the bank, a short way from where she had started. She could hear its pained, wheezing breath from the hole made by her bow. Her arrow still protruded from its neck, like a feather gone astray, the bird having no way to remove it. It was a pitiable sight, dreadful even, but also somehow comical.

She watched the chobo dip its enormous beak—the bird's head was mainly beak—into the water. It showed no signs of alarm, seeming unaware of her presence. She waded into the depths to mask her sound, if not her smell, the stream swelling to her pelvic bones, the chill awakening her senses. Suspicion grew over the bird's large disc-shaped eyes, but it was too dimwitted or too weary to retreat. The current lapped against her belly, tugged at her every step, the slick moss caking the streambed threatening her balance. She resisted the urge to squirm as minnows darted between her ankles and nibbled at the fine hairs of her thighs. The chobo poked its head down for another drink, the continual loss of blood driving its thirst. She clung to the slippery edges of the boulder, paces from her kill, her spear fast in her hand, her heart pregnant with anticipation.

The chobo was taller than her by a head and would feed her for a cycle. But should it dash away, she knew she could not rush from the stream in time to catch it. And her arrows were spent. She had only the wooden shaft in her hands to rely on. But she decided against throwing it. If her aim were off by a hair, she would lose her supper for the night. She needed to get in closer. Shock the bird into inaction.

She sprawled over the rocks in a sudden burst, her movements muffled by the rumbling falls, the truncheon of her spear high overhead. The chobo's eyes were like shining drops of tar, lost in the scaly folds of its beak, and those eyes took immediate notice of her. But she was prepared, breaking over the din of crashing water with a ferocious cry. The bird stood paralyzed as the point of her shaft plunged deep into its body. She shuddered against the ensuing cacophony of honks and squawks and thrashing feathers, holding firm to the stony bit snagging its beak and vertebrae.

He just wants to live, like me, like any other animal would . . .

But it wasn't just any animal. It was her food source. She had to do as Borz had taught her. Act without feeling.

It's just a big, stupid bird, Thelana. A big chicken!

15

She tightened her hands about her spear, twisting down into the chobo's body with all of her weight, until the creature no longer struggled.

Her fury subsided, she found herself in a daze, bloodied feathers sticking to her bosom, the stream ebbing about her ankles. The chobo was limp, its neck lolling against its side. She removed her arrow and tugged at her spear, thanking the gods that neither was broken. Her fingertips, still trembling, were stained crimson. Remembering Baba's lesson, she apologized to the bird and thanked the Goddess for the sustenance it would provide her.

She had not eaten in days and could not wait to bring the meat to her campsite. But how was she to move it? She was alone, and the bird weighed more than she did. Two possibilities vied in her skull. She could cut the animal into pieces, which would take some time, or she could relocate. The stream promised ample water, but the moisture in the air would prove difficult for making fire, and attract biters come nightfall.

Forgetting herself and her surroundings, she neglected the swaying in the trees, the grumbling in the earth. A towering figure blotted the sky like a passing storm cloud, leaving a shaft of sun to blind her as she turned her gaze to the emerging King of the Wildwood. Apex predator of apex predators. *The Tyrant.* Its nostrils flared, damp cranial cavities sized to fit her skull, and a mouth to swallow her whole opened to reveal rows upon rows of serrated knives. She screamed, but not in fear. Once, she had been beyond terrified and had run into hiding. And she would no doubt hide from the Tyrant again. But today, she was pained with hunger. Today she was angry.

This is my kill! You can't have it! You can't!

The saurian's minuscule eyes—black and round as olives—took no notice of her. She raised her ash weapon and cried again, but her threats came to no avail. The Tyrant snatched her kill in a single bite, leaving the dead bird's lower half to dangle from its jagged teeth. But she refused to surrender what she had fought so long to keep, wrestling to tear a morsel from the carcass, if not the whole foot. She could be satisfied with a foot, anything to delay hunger for another night. Except the Tyrant was not one to share, and righting its enormous skull, she felt herself rising, following the bird into that monstrous gaping maw. Letting go, she fell hard into the shallow water as the saurian thundered off, satisfied with its poached meal.

A wave of dizziness passed through her as she regained her footing. She had spent too much of her energy pursuing the chobo, and now her insides were protesting. Dragging herself from the water, she wondered how she had managed to chase the bird so far across the forest. Hunger had driven her, she supposed, but now, she doubted whether she would have the strength to return to her campsite.

The Tyrant. She did everything she could to escape its notice, from hiding her scent to learning the pattern of its outings. Still, whenever she managed to kill anything bigger than herself, the Tyrant emerged to steal it away, leaving a ruin of vegetation in its wake. Two great hunters dominated the Wildwood, yet there was prey enough only for one.

Thelana started for camp, the sun skirting the tops of the trees, the earth turning dry under her feet. The forest was a living thing, and could turn into a bog after heavy rain. Darkness and moisture summoned insects, which she hated more than she feared. A sheen of sweat created a barrier against the smaller biters, but the sweet smell of her body lured the deadlier variety. The whine of the dragon mosquito, the flutter of a bird-wasp, the buzz of swarming fire-gnats, these were constant causes for dread. She was all-too familiar with their stings, after being unable to sleep on one side or another for close to a cycle. Even when the pustules shrank and the skin healed, some blemishes remained, until her body became like a canvas decorated by their mandibles.

The sun was melting into the turquoise disc in the east, casting bands of orange and yellow against the horizon. Eclipse was drawing near and she was still a good way from sanctuary. Monsters stalked in the gloom of night, she knew—nigh invisible under the moon's faint glow—hunters who hungered for supple flesh and bones easily torn apart.

Weary with exhaustion, her insides hollow and aching, she reached her campsite as the last colors of day dulled to shades of gray and indigo. A sudden gale greeted her as she entered the meadow she called home, the welcoming, all-encompassing arms of the camphor tree casting a long shadow across a mottled sward of grass and clover.

Her nightly ritual involved relieving herself at different locations, to mark her territory; starting a fire in the recesses of the camphor's roots; and scarfing down whatever she managed to scrounge up for the day. If she had the strength, she might whittle sticks into arrows, chip away pieces of slate until they were sharp enough for spearheads, or reinforce her shelter to protect from the rain. But tonight, her every sinew throbbed, and her spine and shoulders still hurt from falling into the streambed. Hunger was also taking its toll, blurring her vision, and turning her limbs sluggish and unresponsive. She could not hope to spark kindling in such a weary state and could only pray that the night keep balmy.

Olivoids paraded down the trunk of her tree. The oval-shaped beetles shimmered blackly in the dim light, and could pass for tiny fruits when they were not moving, but she was on to their ruse. She scooped them up one-by-one, dozens of tiny legs and yellow feelers squirming against her tongue, exploding in a pungent pulp between her molars. She hated the taste. But it was food.

She climbed methodically, her toes and fingers recalling every twist and knob in the camphor's bark. A makeshift cot of bamboo and beard moss awaited her at the top, thatched between the limbs a hundred feet in the air. When she first gathered the lichen for the padding, she awoke in the night with a terrible itch and a head full of bright red bugs. She learned to smoke them out the following morning.

Few predators could reach her there, where she lay her head to rest, and in the treetops, the winds gusted too fiercely for the biters to fly. Once, in the pitch of eclipse, she caught herself tipping over the edge, but even then, she never developed a fear of heights.

Like a bird in its nest, she inspected the curtain of leaves enclosing her arbor. The foliage kept her hidden from hungering eyes but grew wild in all directions, crowding in on her sleeping space. She tested the strength of the branches, which sometimes softened after a storm or were weakened by the white hungering bugs living inside them, then probed the hollows of the bamboo frame, finding her flint arrowheads, a knife cut from a saurian's tooth, and *the flower*. The orange blossom, the *ilm* her father had given her before she was sent away from home, was her most prized possession.

Taking up the small ivory blade, she carved a notch into the far stalk of her bedframe. Every notch represented a day, but as the elements eroded the green outer layer to its fibrous inner core, she could only hope to count the passage of time in her head. The cutting was more ritual now, something to prepare for sleep.

She eased onto her flank, her muscles no longer tensing, her body succumbing to the memory of prodding roots and thorns, and the river rocks battering her spine.

The last sliver of day receded, and the woods faded into shadow, until only the stars remained. She counted every flicker through a window of intersecting branches. The regularity of the heavens comforted her, for no matter how troubling her ordeals, the same constellations emerged night after night to greet her.

"Those are the gods watching over us," Baba explained to her once. "They are all sisters to one another. Each a mother to her world. Like the Goddess is to ours. Like Alashiya."

The stars moved in a great circle about Aenya, the way her people gathered about the Solstice Fire, and in those glittering arrangements, she could make out the Phoenix, the Archenelk, and the Horned Skull of the Taker. She remembered sitting on her father's lap as he pointed them out.

Was Baba thinking of her now? Were the crops yielding enough to feed her family?

Who was sick or wedded or welcoming a new child? She had only the past to look to, remembering how they played and laughed and danced.

Amina loved to scold us, to everyone's annoyance, all too ready for motherhood. She showed hair about her loins for years, but had yet to find her destined mate, despite her ceaseless yearning.

Anja. The boys fancied her the most, and she knew it. She never walked past still water without pausing to admire her reflection. Her hair was the color of sunshine, cascading like strands of gold from her nipples to her abdomen. She spent more time knitting garlands of heather, lavender, and jasmine than seeding crops.

Britannia was Thelana's co-conspirator, always bruised and looking for trouble and wanting of a bath. Mana yelled at her for roaming too far into the woods and tracking dirt into the house. Of all her sisters, Thelana missed Britannia most.

Aliaa was the know-it-all, familiar with every plant good for eating, healing, or that could make you sick. She collected bugs at her bedside, could tell you the meaning of the stars, and knew the secrets of letters. Thelana did not doubt that someday, Aliaa would go to live among the Mountain Folk, as a Keeper.

Nicola was scrawny, quiet, and prone to illness. She was born sick, and despite her parents' efforts, never managed to grow stronger. When the famine started, Thelana worried more for Nicola than anyone else in the family.

Then the boys. Laine and Vaino, the twins, forever bickering, always trying to outdo one another, their antics never failing to make her laugh. They hated fieldwork like the rest but were pressed to work harder than anyone.

Lodr and Heimdl could go nowhere without their tools, a chisel, an ax, and a cart for hauling logs. They had plans, those two, to build houses together, and when they were not planning, they joined Baba in the hunt.

Baldr was the last to be born. He was either too young or too proud to hide his erections. Mother never chided him for it, but we all laughed. Even hungry, even after days without eating, humor lifted our spirits.

Then there was Borz. She sighed and her body quaked with his memory.

They should have sent him out into the woods, not me. Thelana had known fourteen years, sixteen maybe—she was beginning to lose count—since escaping from her mother's womb. She was still a child, barely showing hair about the loins, scarcely old enough to jump the sacred fire. What did she know of survival that Borz had not taught her? She could never be as strong as he was.

DAY 43

The sun rested like a fiery bowl atop her back, blazed through her eyelashes, and the smooth stones seared her soles where she walked. She wiped her brow, her vision swimming in sweat, her eyes salty and stinging. The gods could be unkind but were not wholly to blame, for she had abandoned her sanctuary too soon, and the Eye of Solos was nearing its zenith.

Thelana was not ignorant to the way temperatures changed throughout the day, but with an empty belly and a mouth like a shriveled leaf, she could not have endured another passing sulking in her tree. The broader branch of the Braid was far to the west, so she headed for the smaller stream nearby, hoping it had not turned to dust with the coming of the dry season.

The heat found less purchase on her neck and shoulders when she stood fully upright, so she held her head high and exposed as she went looking for water. She kept to the shady path littered with maple leaves and pine needles and continued through the copse to a wide area she did not recognize. Young aspens towered all around her. She could not see past them and was at a loss from whence she had come or in which direction she had been moving. The striped boles of the trees possessed an uncanny symmetry, their slender shadows reflecting in perfect rows across the forest floor, and the deathly stillness of the wind lulled her weary mind, luring her deeper and deeper into the gathering of aspens until she was overcome by a sudden fear of losing her way.

All you have to do is sit. Sit and think your way out, Thelana.

She lowered herself against an old poplar, the smooth bark fitting between the blades of her back, a tangle of nettles below cushioning her buttocks. She prodded her brain for ideas, for any solitary thought, but her skull felt as hollow as her stomach—empty of everything but the hectic chattering of the crickets. They were complaining, she did not doubt, about this awful heat.

A lot of good that'll do you . . .

She sat with her face buried in her knees, her braid like a rope—a lifeline—in her hands.

Mana's voice sounded above the din of laughter, over the rushing, dashing, plopping waves. The lake was so clear she could count the pebbles along the bedrock. Her younger sisters were busy at play, hopscotching along the chain of rocks, as her older siblings, lost in the mist, focused on their grooming and bathing. Water cascaded down from a fissure in the granite beyond the bend, breaking into three separate falls, into *The Three Sisters*, as her people called it, marking the sacred place that none of the boys, not even Baba, were allowed to visit.

Only Ilmarin females were permitted to witness the Sacred Rite of Wo, when girls displaying hair about the loins came to offer their blood to the Goddess. Blood was the essence of life, without which no living thing could draw breath, and life given to the river was returned in the form of plentiful harvests and successful childbirths.

Here, Thelana was free to loosen the threads of her hair, and when after four days their blood was spent, her siblings' braids were entwined again, typically by a mother, an aunt, or a mentoring sister. Girls were done up this way before they were old enough to walk. The styling helped prevent infestation by parasites while keeping snagging thorns at a distance. But the braid meant a great deal more, defining her sex as much as her *noumena.* Without it, she could not count herself among the Ilmar. Females who let their hair grow wild and unkempt could not even be considered human. And it was her mother, always her mother, to whose loving fingers Thelana entrusted its weaving.

Mana . . . Mana . . .

The world came rushing back, and her mother's face shrank away, her firm but gentle smile; her reproving, yet reassuring, slate-gray eyes; every detail of her mother's features sinking, thinning to nothing in the flickering light. She woke to find an iridescent beetle gnawing at her thigh. It was pretty in its own way, changing from violet to crimson in the shifting light. She plucked it into her mouth and swallowed dryly.

Her head felt heavy, unmoored, like a plank of wood adrift. She straightened her knees and planted her palms into the leafy ground, each motion bringing spasms of pain. The sun god had abdicated from his throne as she slumbered, but his light remained, flashing between the slender aspens.

She shifted to her feet as a sudden gust rattled the leaves, stirring the small hairs of her body and rolling her braid across her shoulder. The air was warm and wet and sticky. She followed the stifling sensation into a tangle of flora, acutely aware of her surroundings. The clamor of life thrummed in her eardrums—the buzz and hum of flyers, the throaty croak of an amphibian, the rustling of waking hunters, the twitch of hidden prey. She had to be more than familiar with the noises each creature made. Mistaking a tree toad for a saurian could mean the difference between eating and getting eaten.

Frilled bracken bent against her knees. Jade-limbed nettles brushed at her sides. The grove enclosed her as she continued through it, awakening at her trespass. Every gnat nibbled at her ankles. Lizards darted from her steps. An azure moth went fluttering across her nose, carried up by the wind to a hyacinth bulb, its translucent wings folding in perfect mimicry of the flower's blue petals. The touch of the Goddess was omnipresent, guiding her, reassuring her.

The terrain grew into an uneven tapestry of crisscrossing roots, weeds, and pinecones, and she was forced to move more slowly and deliberately, her feet reading every subtle feature, every knob and length of bark, every prickling pebble, each crackling leaf and clover poking from her toes. Thorns proved more of a nuisance than a hazard, rarely penetrating the outer layer of her soles. And yet pain, she reminded herself, had its uses. *Pain sharpens the senses, keeps you alert, wakes you when you're feeling complacent.* Or so that's what Borz told her.

But the stinging sensation now shooting up through her instep set her brain on fire. She held back a yelp, having suddenly transformed into a one-legged, hopping creature. *What in the Goddess's name did I just step on?* Some angry thing with pincers, no doubt, squirming its last under her weight. But she did not pause to investigate it, refusing to lift her foot to examine the broken skin, assuming—praying rather—that a very large insect, anything with fewer than eight legs, had done the deed. A spider bite meant days, sometimes cycles, of misery.

She spotted a pear-shaped fruit, tantalizing her with its hues of orange and purple, but when she last ate what looked like an apple, she spent the night heaving out her insides. Strange fruits were a risk, as was the family of mushrooms growing from a cypress hollow not ten feet away. More than anything, she needed to sate her thirst, and fruit could only mean water nearby.

She found her way through the tangle of trees into a shallow depression. Brightly colored moss caked every rock and root, leading her to a ravine, where the earth was rich and black and stuck to her soles in clumps. But the bustling stream she remembered was little more than a trickle. She squatted over the embankment, her throat dusty and bitter, her fingers drawing handfuls of mud, but the water clinging to the topsoil disappeared with every desperate stroke.

This is so . . . unfair! I did everything I was taught! Everything Borz showed me.

She wanted to scream, but her voice was missing, dried out like the riverbed. All she could manage was a croak above a whisper.

"I did . . . everything . . ."

She clenched her fists at the sky, at the Goddess for allowing her to starve, at her parents for sending her out on her own. The outer world was cruel and unforgiving, and she did not possess the strength to suffer it longer. If only Borz or Baba were around to tell her what to do. Their voices—sounds of human speech—she needed it more than ever. But she could no longer rely on them. Could not hope for the impossible. She was alone and too far from home to return.

For some time, she lay there, half on her side and nearing oblivion, when a mound consisting primarily of mud and vines started up from the base of the ravine. She did not hesitate, sliding onto her stomach, her hand latching to the strange moving object. It looked like a small boulder, as broad around as her arms could reach, but was evidently alive. She flipped the creature onto its back, and it kicked at the air with its scaly legs, its head and tail withdrawing into its shell.

Sinking to her ankles in mud, her spine aching from the strain, she managed to drag the tortoise to the lip of the slope, where it plopped into the soft soil, nearly tipping her over. She brushed away the dirt and grass, revealing its ridged carapace, and considered how she might kill it. The tortoise could be skewered from the hole where its head poked out, but her spear lay forgotten in her tree. She then tried prying the shell apart, a hand clasping each side, but as she did so, a glimmer shone in the hollow of its collar—the tortoise's eyes—was it afraid?

No. I won't feel pity for you. I can't afford it . . .

Her strength spent, she resorted to stomping the animal to pieces, but its jagged outer edges would tear her feet apart.

A rock. I need a big rock!

The ravine was littered with them, rocks like giant eggs, smooth and round and yellowed with lichen. She picked one up the size of her head and hoisted it up above her shoulders.

"Please don't."

Nicola stood opposite the riverbed, her brown pupils shimmering from between her knobby cheekbones. "Please," she murmured. "Don't hurt him."

Thelana clenched her eyelids, not wanting to see her sister now. "Go away, Nicola. You're not really here."

"But why do you have to kill him? He didn't do anything to you."

"It's not about that, sis. I'm hungry. You know how that is." She waved her away and turned back to the tortoise, hoisting the rock again.

The tortoise extended its scaly appendages from its shell, and its shriveled head reminded her of her grandmother, the rare elder blessed to see beyond sixty years. Then it opened its jaws in a slow, protracted gesture as if speaking to her, as if pleading for its life.

"No!" Thelana cried. "I need to kill you. Don't you understand? Goddess knows you need to die so I can live."

Baba's voice rang out in a low, sullen tone, and she found herself in a field of heathers, pink stems moving in waves against her calves, the mountains of Ukko glistening whitely on the horizon. A twig of a girl no more than nine stood beside him, her ribs and pelvic bones jutting from beneath her sallow flesh like an unearthed fossil.

Nicola was despondent, pleading with Father, tugging desperately at his arm. A goat knelt between them on its haunches, strapped over a white stump, bleating meekly. Baba held a cudgel in his hands—a simple rock fastened to a tree limb—prepared to smash the animal's skull, his face lined with the ravages of many sleepless nights.

"But why do you have to?"

Thelana had never fully understood why he looked that way, so tired, so worn, so beaten down. *Defeated.* Baba had known no more than forty years, yet the last few seemed to count for decades. Now she understood why. When she lived in Ilmarinen, hunger was an everyday concern and the subject of most discussions. But actual starvation was a thing she could only have imagined, a distant yet ever-present threat, and her imagination had fallen short of the reality. And yet Baba knew, knew what it meant to perish when food becomes scarce, and he somehow managed to keep them from it. From the worst of all fates.

"Nicola." His voice was uncompromising. "I told you to stay in the house, didn't I? This isn't for you to see."

"But, Baba, Fleet didn't do anything wrong—"

"It's not about that. Now, do as I say and go home."

Thelana recognized the animal. She was more of a kid than a fully grown nanny, her horns just beginning to show like swollen nubs above her yellow-white brows. Thelana's family had been present for her birth, and Nicola had held her as a newborn, watched her sup at her mother's teat. They raised goats for milk, never for slaughter. But the world was changing, becoming colder, delivering invasive weeds that choked the life from the crops.

"Do as Baba says and come away, Nicola." Her voice remained firm. Unfeeling. And the young girl surrendered in her arms. Buried her face in her big sister's shoulder.

Baba stared at them as if noticing his daughters for the first time, his pupils crowned red, the whites turned hard and yellow by the sun. "I didn't want you here either, Thelana."

"I don't mind. I can help you do it . . . if you need me to."

"I know you can," he said. "You've always been strong. But I want you to take your sister home. Now." He faced slowly away and took up his cudgel again. Fleet no longer bleated, keeping limp and quiet under the ropes. Did she know she was about to die?

"It won't matter if you do it!" Nicola cried as she was led away. "I'm not going to eat her! I'm not! You'll see! I promise . . ."

Thelana tugged at her wrist. An immense oak awaited them in the distance. Home. "That's why you're so skinny, Nicola. You need to build up your strength or you're not going to make it through the high moon."

"But why does Fleet have to die so we don't? Why do our lives matter more than hers? That isn't fair." Fresh tears washed over the little girl's cheeks. Too great for her elfin face.

"It's just the way things are now," Thelana explained, bending to pluck a pink stem from the ground and tucking it behind Nicola's ear. "Now you look pretty." The small gesture was enough to convince her to dry her eyes and come away.

Thelana hated these visions, when she could no longer affix her mind to the present. It signaled the looming of the Taker. The arrival of Death. Her body was growing too feeble to sustain her in the physical world. Yet she could still spot the tortoise. It somehow righted itself and continued toward its hovel at the bottom of the ditch, gaining momentum as it edged over the slope.

Fleet had meant little to her. Thelana never mourned its passing, nor any of the beasts she helped Baba slaughter that year. Predators killed to survive. They did not pity. They did not feel remorse. And she was ilma, fiercest of predators, whose teeth was the knife, whose claws was the spear, whose hand was the rock. She loomed over the tortoise, the rock heavy in her arms, watching her prey make its slow escape, its stubby hind legs kicking futilely across the damp black earth.

She screamed, and the rock came tumbling down from her grasp. Followed by a single tear.

35

The Feral Girl

"I'm sorry, Nicola."

DAY 57

The brook led into the heart of the forest, to parts known only to the Goddess and to the curious animals peering from behind the rich jade foliage. She could sense the virgin soil between her toes, the trees striving to grow, breathing against her skin. Beneath woolly walking palms, past ivy-wrapped banyan trees, she lost herself to the overgrowth, to the smell of hickory and fallen rain. If she were to cry out, injure herself somehow, no voice would return her call. And yet there was solace to be found in isolation, in being so far removed from the world she knew. Without disapproving parents or worrying siblings. She went swift as her legs could carry her, driven by an intense need for discovery. There was a cadence to her movements, a rhythm she learned to listen for, leading her safely through the wood— through privet shrubs and prickling nettles slick with dew, over mossy stones and fallen logs wreathed in sphagnum, the shallowing brook dashing at her heels, her heart throbbing like a fire beneath her expanding ribs, her body unimpeded but for the wind and her jostling bow.

She halted suddenly, exhaling so deeply she was panting, her palms over her knees, sweat trickling from the tip of her nose. Gossamer threads stretched between the low-lying boughs, a ghostly, intricate spiral brushing against her waist and thighs, nigh invisible in the dim light percolating from the canopy of branches.

Stepping around the web was the most reasonable course of action. Even destroying it posed risks. A nest of infant spiders could break away, find purchase in her braid, attack her in her sleep. When she last ignored a spider's bite, her ankle doubled in size until she was forced to cut away the venom with her knife. Still, Thelana did not flinch from the sight.

All lay still but for the rumor of the creek gathering peat along the bank, and the graying maple leaves twirling and bunching at the crooks in the path. She took a knee to marvel at the spider's handiwork, the delicate latticework squared in a mosaic of light and shadow. The creature itself was a thing of beauty, with legs of indigo as thick as her fingers and a vibrant fractal carapace of red and blue and yellow. She grew more daring, the web oscillating with her breath as she drew near it, the dewdrops clinging to the weave shimmering like crystals. Yet the spider kept deathly still.

"Hello," she said. *Do you even see me?*

She thought she might sit and study the spider all day, waiting to see what it might do. But the peace she had so far enjoyed did not last. The gossamer lines shivered out of focus like the plucked cord of an olol. She could sense the tremor in her soles. A thunderous, crackling sound echoed from afar like an encroaching storm, disturbing the tranquility of the deep forest, rousing the hidden birds from their nests, jostling the pebbles in the creek. She wheeled around, searching past veils of ivy and hanging liana, but could see nothing beyond the trembling, heart-shaped leaves. The pounding repeated, a heavy, reverberating cacophony rippling through the earth.

It can only be one thing.

She started running as boughs came rending from their trunks, collapsing at her ankles. The forest opened to allow for the ingress of the Tyrant, its shining eyes hungrily surveying, its snapping jaws lined with knives.

She found a hollow in a collapsed tree, scurried inside it, and did not dare move. The log was unexpectedly warm and wet, home to a host of crawling, squirming things. Palmetto bugs plopped like heavy raindrops against her body, scurrying across her neck and torso. Centipedes as long as her forearms writhed across her backside. Still, she waited, resisting the urge to flee, to scream, to betray her existence in any way, bunched into a silent, quivering ball.

The Feral Girl

The ground boomed again. Branches crackled and snapped apart. Her eyes adjusted to the dim light seeping through the seams in the wood. She caught sight of it in narrow bands, watched its mottled hide pass slowly across her field of view, come so closely she could have touched it were she not confined. The saurian towered over the space where she had stood only moments before, sniffing after her scent, its cedar-thick tail bashing the poplars to kindling, the spiderweb pulsing with its footfalls. An errant step, and she would be crushed, log and all.

In the shadows of the log, the critters continued to multiply. They spawned from every niche and crevice, exploring her with their mandibles, goosing her flesh with their feathery feelers. The urge to bolt from her hiding place became more than she could endure. She could no longer keep still, convulsing at their touch, snapping at every creeping thing until their spiny exoskeletons oozed from her clenched palms.

A lifetime of misery came and went, before the quaking grew distant and subsided. She hurried from the hollowed orifice, dancing uncontrollably, smacking every parasitic organism suckling her body, tugging frantically at her hair to remove the last of them.

Ruin followed in the Tyrant's steps, leaving trees ravaged, water seeping up through the soil in the three-pronged shape of its feet. She wondered for how many years those banyans had stood. And if the spider survived, how many cycles would she need to spin herself another home?

The Tyrant was hunting. She could tell by the ravenous glimmer in its eyes, and knew she risked luring it back if she were to return to her tree unwashed and reeking of sweat. So she camped by the creek that night, her thoughts never straying from the saurian, realizing she could not remain long in those woods, that she needed to migrate to where it could not follow.

When sleep took her at last, she dreamed lucidly of her mother at her bedside, telling wondrous fables.

Ages ago, when the world was first made, the Great Mother descended from the Sky to grant gifts to each of her children. To the ilma, she gave her wits, and to the Rabbit, swift feet for running, and to the Spider, the craft of weaving. To the Tyrant, the Goddess gave sharp teeth for tearing apart his prey. But the Tyrant was unsatisfied, for he was proud and envied the Goddess's affection for the other animals, wanting her love only for himself. And so, he set about to devour the firstborn of Aenya, so that she would come to love him and him alone.

The beasts of the land endured great hardship under the Tyrant's hungry gaze. For seven times seven years, they endured his ferocious appetite until they gathered under the bodhi tree to send word to the Phoenix, who was Messenger between Earth and Sky, to beseech the Goddess's aid.

When Alashiya heard the pleas of her sons and daughters, she descended upon her unruly son in anger. But he joined his hands in repentance, and she took pity upon him and did not curse him, exhorting him to consume only what he needed to sustain himself and be contented.

But while the Tyrant promised to do as he was told, he did not remain faithful to his word, for his heart had turned black with the insatiable hunger of greed. And so, it was not long before he said to himself, "I will devour the entire world, and then there will be no one in it but me, and Mother will be forced to reckon with me and me alone." And for seven times seven years more, the Tyrant did just that, consuming every bit of the world as he desired, growing larger with every fish and fowl and beast he devoured, until swallowing the last of the tripe from the rivers and the last of the swallows from the trees.

When the Goddess saw what he had done, she flew down from the Sky in a terrible rage, and said to the Tyrant, "You are my son no longer. I banish you to the world's dark corners, to suffer forever in ceaseless hunger. Your arms I will make puny so that you will not even be able to scratch your own head. My curse will extend even to your children and all generations into eternity. I will make them flightless birds, witless and toothless. They will serve ilma, surrendering their eggs and flesh to be consumed, and as you have terrorized my children, so will your ancestors live in terror of all who prey upon the world."

DAY 60

The sycamore towered over the maples, aspens, and junipers, its roots like the knuckles of a great hand holding to the lip of the forest, reaching with copious boughs across the copse like a protective parent. Thelana clambered up the smooth white bark, her fingers finding purchase where there appeared to be none, finding limbs broad enough for her to stand every ten to fifteen feet. In Ilmarinen, she proved to be a gifted climber, reaching heights not even Borz could manage, mocking the worried gesticulations of her sisters as she pranced across the spidery treetops.

A sparrow's nest caught her eye. Five eggs, white with specks of yellow, lay in a mesh of sticks and leaves. She plucked the lot clean, swallowing them in single bites. They tasted of wood pulp and buried nuts. When the mother returned, she would find the nest empty, but Thelana pushed the thought from her mind. She needed her strength if she hoped to make progress.

The topmost branch swayed underfoot as she pulled herself over. She trusted her weight to the wood, her soles holding to the rounded limb like a bird's talons, a hand set against the sycamore's papery trunk.

The crowning sun bathed her world in fiery golds as the mountain air rushed over the treetops to tousle her braid and fill her lungs. Beyond the reach of the forest, a sprawling savannah met her gaze, an arid plain marked by ochre-hued boulders, tall amber grasses, and myriad craters mirroring the blue topaz of the sky. And the Braid River coursed through it like a silver thread, flowing southward toward a hazy, undiscovered country.

The day she started from home, she considered building a boat from reeds to ride the south-going current as far as it would take her. She had watched Lodr and Heimdl go about their woodcraft enough to know how it was done. But a boat would take days to complete, and a half cycle's walk from Old Man Oak, the waters of the Braid became violent. Fishermen, and boys with adventuring spirits, often drowned attempting to ford those rapids.

So she took to her feet, using the river as a guide. Life gathered about water, and the savannah was no exception. High above the slope, she spotted the striped gazelle leaping from the heath, and a field of dashing ziff further ahead. Such animals were rare sights in her homeland. The lumbering woollyhorn she knew from pictures made by her ancestors. When she and her brothers were camped by the Painted Caves, Baba had told them stories of the woollyhorn, how it grazed in the valleys of Ilmarinen ages ago, before the Goddess gifted them with the secret of animal husbandry, before the great horned beasts were driven away by hunters. But those illustrations failed to convey the animal's majestic scale, and if she had not noticed the birds nesting atop their spines, or the gazelle leaping from the sward upon which they stood, she might have second-guessed their size. The woollyhorn's bones could hold up a house, while the bony protrusion extending from its nostril could be used to dig out a canoe. If she were to kill it, if her spear could reach deep enough to split its heart, she could eat for a cycle or more and fashion tools for a lifetime from its horn.

She hurried down the sycamore, swinging, leaping, and hitting the ground in a shower of needles in her haste. Taking up a stick, she surveyed the valley once more, making a series of triangular shapes for the Ukko Mountains, an impression representing her treehouse campsite, another for the falls where she had hunted the chobo, and a fourth for the channel where she had killed the tortoise. The places where she crossed paths with the Tyrant she marked with X's. She finished the map with a series of vertical strokes dividing east from west. The Braid was the Lifeblood of Ilmarinen, bifurcating across the Wildwood into multiple tributaries like the skeins of a maple leaf. Given what she knew, the Tyrant's hunting grounds were limited to areas west of the river. She could avoid crossing paths with the saurian by camping along the opposite bank. But if she were to maintain her easterly bearing, the Greater Moon would blot out the sun, and she would find herself in the dark hemisphere, the land of bogrens. She did not know how far that place lay but was afraid to chance it. Her only course was to continue south along the Braid, where she hoped to find the Outside and other humans like herself. But keeping to the river was not without risk. Dangers abounded where water flowed in abundance.

Throwing her bindle over her shoulder, she crept through the wall of ferns toward the edge of the bluff. The escarpment sloped gradually toward the plain, then broke away, revealing a tangle of roots below. She sank to her heels in the rich soil as she continued down, clutching at the exposed undergrowth.

Where the forest retreated from the savannah, the change in the air was immediate in the loss of moisture on her lips, the hot wind brushing against her pores, the stones simmering under her feet. But the land was anything but barren. Spiny weeds shot up from fissures in the ground, nettles flourished in and around rock formations, and clusters of thorny green opuntia basked openly under a scorching sky. Flat-topped acacia trees provided shade, as did the baobab tree with its bulbous gray trunk and wiry branches.

She walked from shadow to shadow, careful not to scrape the tops of her toes, to the nearest crater. The water in the basin shone like rippling silver and smelled of freshly fallen rain, and finding it neither stagnant nor murky, she dunked her head and drank, before washing the sediment from the corners of her eyes and lips.

A girl emerged from the undulating pond. Thelana should have known the face, recognized her own body, but the cycles she had spent in the wild had transformed her into an animal without a name. Her soles were like an aurochs' hooves, black and hard and scaly, and her palms were callused and yellowed by old blisters. Her hair, the ruddy hue of peeled tree bark, was brittle and unkempt, falling from her knobby shoulders to her bony clavicle, ribs, and pelvis. She could have been mistaken for her twelve-year-old brother from the waist up had the mess of follicles between her thighs not hinted at her sex.

When the Mother of Mothers brought life into the world, the fauna and flora sprang from the Goddess's noumena. Somewhere in Ilmarinen that holiest of places could still be found, a sacred chasm in the earth, the origin of all living beings, the noumena of Aenya. Thelana had heard the tale many a time on the night of the Solstice, when the High Priestess acted out the Ritual of Creation, her dancing body painted with stars, the Hoop of Eternity flaming from her fingertips. The story served as instruction for all young women. *Bring life into this world.*

Thelana might have leapt the sacred fire by now, if she still dwelt among her people. Yet she wondered whether she would be permitted the rites, should she find her way home, if anyone would even want her for a wife and mother, a flat-chested, ungroomed girl, marred by so many scars and bruises. Borz had called her pretty once, had said her eyes glittered like the jade stones he collected from the mountain. What was she now? A wretched thing, no doubt, a feral creature transfigured by hardship. Perhaps, if she did manage to return to her people, she might scrub away the cycles, tend to her wounds, and do up her braid like a proper bride-to-be. She might then be recognized by her destined lover, and in wedlock, drop the 'a' from her name to become *Thelann or Thelannis*, as Mana, who was once called Bryseisa, became Bryseis.

A deep melancholy welled up in her eyes then, imagining her mother fussing over her joining ceremony. Imagining what could have been.

No.

She stoppered her tears with the heels of her palms, slapped the water to banish the frail-looking child from existence. Beauty meant nothing in the Wildwood. More than a mother-to-be, more than a waiting spouse, she was a hunter, a hunter of hunters. Only the swiftness of her feet and the sharpness of her wits mattered here.

Her mammoth frond contained her bow of yew, a clutch of arrows, the ivory knife she fashioned from a saurian's tooth, the fragment of a tortoise's shell, two hollowed coconut husks sealed with beeswax, and a stalk of bamboo no longer than her forefinger. She removed the cork from the first husk, pouring ash made from ground kindling into her palms, which she used to turn her skin a burnt shade of white; then, dipping her fingers into the fibrous shell of the second coconut, she applied a mixture of mud and plant matter, what her people called *koiob*. The streaking pattern was far from the elaborate henna her sisters used to beautify themselves, but she was not out hunting for boys. She proceeded to strap the ivory knife to her thigh, with her bow hung from her shoulder, leaving her bindle's truncheon in her hands. Glancing again at her reflection, she could no longer see the Ilmarin girl. A savage predator had replaced her, a white Smilodon in human form.

She tracked the scent of dung to a cloud of gnats; they were like flying bulbs the size of grapes, and the whir of their wings rattled her eardrums. One broke away from the bustling mass to settle in the wedge of flesh between her thumb and forefinger, leaving a bloody welt. She crushed it against her palm and sucked it down. The swarm now flowed in

and around her, covering her with bites. Any
other animal would have retreated from such
an onslaught, but she pressed on, shielding
her face with her forearms, advancing blindly
through the coalescing fog, wincing but never
relenting. She needed their treasure, the
waist-high pile about which they assembled,
the gift of the woollyhorn. Gagging for air, her
eyes watering from the stench, she snatched
up a handful and fled back to the water.

She doubled over, suppressing the urge to
retch, and as the instinct to empty her insides
subsided, she made for the tall grass,
concealed by her stripes and smelling of
dung.

The Braid broadened where the land lay
flat. A family of gazelle lolled nearby, in the
grassland by the ebbing current, no taller
than her hips in their coats of striped amber,
their majestic horns sweeping back over their
haunches. She peered through the stalks,
paces from where they stood, plotting every
step, bending not a stem.

Waiting.

Watching.

A tan-colored newborn crouched by its
mother for shade. Occasionally, the gazelle
lifted their noses to catch the scent of
enemies, but they did not depart from her.

The wind roared, blasting leaves into the
water, pulling at the curtain that kept her
hidden. The gazelles tensed, their limbs going
rigid, their eyes wide and alert. Moments

later, they lowered their heads again, resuming their leisurely frolic.

She slipped her bow from her shoulder, the fletching of an arrow balanced between her fingers, a second fixed in her teeth. Her ears filled with the tumble of water, the wind in the stems, the urgency in her heart. She made no sound as she nocked the twine of her bow. The angle was challenging. She would need to shoot over the grass and loose her obsidian tip in an arc into their spines. If she missed, they would be gone, and hunger would set in.

She wiped her brow, rubbed dirt into her hands, her fingers slick with anticipation. The grating noise of her palms was enough to spook them. They were beginning to move away, gazing uncertainly in her direction. Her heart battered her insides, turned her blood to fire, sucked the air from the hollow pit of her stomach. Finally, her bow snapped, sending an arrow whistling into the sky, but the gazelles went dashing away before the shaft could come down futilely, in a tangle of reeds.

Stealth could not avail her now. She sprang from the grass, hastily nocking a second arrow, as her prey bounded off, rising dozens of feet with every leap. Soon they would be out of range. She bent her bow again, more patiently this time. She would time her shot with their jumps. Use the wind to carry the killing blow.

Please, Goddess. Let me strike true.

A young female lay in the tussock, kicking spasmodically, trying in vain to remove the shaft from its body, her arrow penetrating clean through to its intestines. Thelana would end its misery quickly, pushing her weight into its stout neck with her knees while her dagger did the work.

She wallowed in the slaughter until, after an agonizing ordeal—agonizing for both of them, she thought—the gazelle surrendered in her arms, folding beneath her until it no longer moved.

Such is life and death. You are moving, and then you are not.

She plunged her knife into its ribcage, opening a cavity to fit her hand. Her syrupy fingertips dripped with crimson as the gazelle's heart made subtle jerking motions in her palm. She shut her eyes to the sight, knowing that if she could not muster the courage now, with her ferocity still surging in her veins, she would never find the will to do it.

Give me pardon, O great runner, for taking your life. Give me your speed, your alertness, your surety of foot.

She winced, offering thanks to the Goddess, her teeth soaked in blood. The muscle was slick and chewy but did not taste unpleasant.

Thelana huddled with her legs crossed over a nest of twigs, shielding the wind with her body, breathing life into her kindling. Some nights, the air blew too cold or too wet, but in the savannah, the infant embers took quickly, a small comfort in the all-encompassing darkness, a darkness so complete she felt herself swallowed, her flame but a candle glittering from the bottom of a deep well.

The featureless aspect of the night bore heavily upon her, adding weight to her loneliness. At least in the woods, the outline of the trees reminded her of people, and the voices of the sleepless birds and lovesick crickets suggested conversation. But all was deathly quiet in the plain but for the spitting flame and the humming of the wind.

She had only the flame for companionship. It answered her queries in crackling tones as she fed it, and in its dancing appendages, she saw innumerable stories play out. The *red flower*, her people called it, was another gift from the Goddess, bestowed upon the first Ilmarin, who passed the knowledge on to her children and they to theirs, and so forth, until Borz shared the gift with her. The flower's hunger was insatiable, growing the more it consumed. All creatures feared its appetite, but only the Ilmar knew its secret. The red flower brought destruction but also life, warmth, and healing. Bringing the flame into being was an art her brother taught her, and after a time, she developed a talent for it.

The headless body of the gazelle lay beside her, flayed down the middle, its flesh cut into strips. She had spent the remainder of the afternoon draining the blood and smoking the meat. Burning sage and lavender helped preserve the flesh while warding away the biters. But removing the head had been a trickier matter. She had had to work her knife in a sawing pattern through its neck before breaking the vertebrae connecting the skull to the spine. In the following days, she would excise its antlers for a new bow.

The smoky aroma, the sizzling, salty taste of meat on her tongue, did more than sate her hunger. Her brain screamed with pleasure, her muscles surged with renewal, and what little empathy she maintained for her prey felt long absent. She lamented only that she had nobody with whom to share this feast. If only she could fly home, swoop down on a pair of wings to deliver the gazelle to her starving family.

With every kill, Thelana bought another day to live, another cycle, but she wanted more than to survive. She wanted to thrive. To find the strength to leave the Wildwood and return with resources to aid her homeland.

Starved of kindling, her flame diminished to orange embers, and a great pillar of smoke climbed into the velvet blue ether as she lay herself down in the sward, her eyes carried up and up by the billowing cloud. Before leaving home, Baba had assured her that the same stars would appear above her head wherever she went. And that, when the nights were darkest, her family would gather under those same constellations to think of her, under the distant fires that spoke of other worlds—of ancient gods, monsters, and heroes—tales anyone could read, if only one cared enough to look.

DAY 74

The weather was changing. A northerly breeze rolled in from the Ukko Mountains, brushing the small hairs of her body and making the leaves in the branches shiver. She could smell the pollen from distant hills, the sour decay of fallen fruits, the grainy odor of shedding, shrinking, hibernating flora. During the high moon season, the light of day shortened as the turquoise disc became more prominent and her nightly campfires more essential for warmth.

Every day at dawn, she ate smoked gazelle and drank her fill from the stream, before deciding on a direction to venture. But with the cooler temperatures, she could explore the savannah for passings without constantly looking for shade, and trek across bare rock without burning her feet. The dominance of the Greater Moon made traveling swift, which delighted her, for she abhorred shouldering anything more than her bow.

She mapped her environment in the proceeding days, scouting for sources of water, which were plentiful, finding what plants were edible, which were scarce, and studying the migration patterns of the animals. With every outing, she widened her circle of discovery before returning to her campsite, her memory burdened by twisting trees and unusual rock formations, any marker she might use to navigate.

A day's hike along the Braid led her to the tree line at the southern edge of the savannah, and in the dirt she drew the grasslands and the plain, and a ring where the Wildwood encroached upon it. She did not like to imagine the dangers lurking in those distant woods, not knowing whether she would find prey or become prey herself, or how many days she might need to trek through it before finding the people of the Outside.

She collected flat rocks and small angled stones along the way, whatever could be worked into a sharp edge. The terrain supplied a wealth of minerals, more than could be found in the forest, but choosing the best materials took consideration, a lesson she learned after spending several frustrating nights chipping at a piece of slate only to have it shatter into fragments.

Sensing the human hunter prowling their habitat, the gazelle and the ziff migrated to safer pastures. Only the woollyhorn remained in the valley, buoying their enormous weight in the shallows of the river. As she returned north along the ravine, she came to where the giant herbivores convened, testing how closely she could approach them without their notice. And in less than a cycle, the woollyhorn became so accustomed to her odor that she could stroll within a spear's throw without scaring them away. She doubted, however, that the beasts had much to fear from her or any other predator; sheer bulk protected them from most enemies.

Rain had not fallen since her arrival, not for a cycle at least, and the craters ran dry, leaving shallow depressions rimmed by moldering sludge. The greater lakes turned murky and black with algae, shrinking to pools no deeper than her calves. With the sun directly overhead, they offered dark reflections of the surrounding, flat-topped acacia trees. Snakes sometimes poked their heads above the murky surfaces, tiny and swift and not worth catching. She might find schools of minnows in other ponds, oval fish no longer than her face, floundering desperately as their world slowly vanished from every side. She tried snatching them with her hands, given how densely they were packed, but they managed to slip away again and again, and after a passing of her thrashing about to no avail, she had to laugh at herself because her brothers and sisters were not there to laugh at her. The solution, she soon realized, was simple. She had only to aim into the water with her bow, knowing she could not miss, and by nightfall, she was pulling skewered fish from her arrows.

Fourteen days after her successful hunt, she returned to her campsite to find the remains of her gazelle infested. Its corpse had been left to bake in the sun, its ribcage splayed across a makeshift gambrel, and the blood gnats had found it. She swatted at them furiously, considered smoking them out, but the parasites were dug in too deep, and the sight of their crawling, writhing mass turned her stomach. But it was not a complete loss. Or so she tried to convince herself. Her reliance on a single kill had made her sluggish, robbed her of urgency, and the gazelle had begun to taste more like bark and less like meat. The minnows provided a welcome change of diet, but they consisted mainly of scales and cartilage, and while fishing kept her from starving, she needed more than protein to sustain her. Her joints often ached as she labored over her fires and worked on her bow, and she found herself craving sweeter fare. Figs. Plums. Lingonberries. Sesame seeds in honey, like the *pasteli* her mother made, that kept her from starving for two cycles after leaving Ilmarinen. Tastes of home.

With her carcass spoiled, she decided on a new hideout, an underground passage beneath a broad flat of granite she discovered days earlier. The ledge would protect her from the cold, help her maintain a fire, and keep her hidden from whatever animals prowled at night.

A shaft of sun illuminated the narrow
fosse as she climbed down into it, the warm
light spilling over her spear and bow and the
striped hide unfurled against the stratified
shelf. She also possessed an ivory knife, stems
to be whittled into arrows, grouse feathers to
be turned into fletching, a coconut filled with
pitch, a tangle of twine, and a short stalk of
bamboo. The concept of ownership, however,
remained a foreign concept to her. The Ilmar
did not own things. Land was lived on. Houses
were slept in. Spouses were loved. Food was
eaten. Nothing was owned. But alone in the
wild open spaces of Aenya, she had no one
with whom to share the objects she carried.

Of all the things Thelana could call her
own, the flower she kept hidden in her
bamboo stalk was the thing she most feared
losing. The ilm contained every memory of
home, all the people she ever loved. And yet,
the further she strayed from the place she
was raised, the more the petals wasted away,
until she became afraid to look at it, not
wanting to see how frail and delicate and
deathly pale the flower was becoming.

Ilms did not grow beyond Ilmarinen. She
knew this with certainty, having looked for
them in the Wildwood, in the lush groves
where the primrose, hollyhock, and blazing
star bloomed in abundance. Nor could any
flower, in her estimation, compare to its
beauty. When her father plucked the blossom
from the garden at the foot of their porch, its
fiery orange petals and violet stamens seemed

to radiate with light. Now, only a ghostly remnant remained, beset on all sides by the encroaching gray of decay. After more than seven cycles, the brittle petals had curved in on themselves, and in her clenched fist, the bulb would shatter into slivers. It brought to mind the mystics who lived in the mountains, the Keepers who, in their zeal for knowledge, ground the ilm into a powder. An elixir for their *dream journeys*, she remembered Aliaa once telling her.

A pang in her gut turned her thoughts to more urgent matters. She could endure another night of hunger, but if she hoped to see home again, she would need a regular food source. A single woollyhorn could provide her sustenance, shelter, and tools, perhaps even the means to ford the river, and if her ancestors could kill such great beasts, so could she. Only, her forefathers did not go it alone. They worked in groups to corral larger prey, and to aid one another should injury occur. A threatened giant, even a docile herbivore, could strike her dead with a single charge. Her parents thought her gifted by the Goddess, the most capable in the family after Borz. But whether she could manage it on her own, whether any single ilma could subdue such an animal, was the question that kept her awake in the dark, even when her exhausted body begged for oblivion.

Baba, tell me what to do. Please.

She could hear the ilm softly calling to her, echoing from within its casing. The bamboo stem was lined with cracks, its verdant tone faded to a pallid brown, its edges roughened where it had broken from the plant. She weighed the stalk in her hand, fingered the wax seal enclosing the delicate treasure within. The ilm grew from the cairns under which her ancestors were buried. Was watered by the blood of her people. Surely, their spirits would be watching her, protecting her, guiding her. Threading a length of twine through the stalk, she would hang the wilting remains of her homeland from her neck. Wear it as a talisman.

The day was growing long and dreary. Too late for hunting woollyhorn. Yet she went out, with stiff bones and aching muscles, climbing from her hovel to the roof of her new abode, her talisman secure about her neck.

The ledge was smooth to the touch, having eroded over the ages. She drew a knee to her chin and sat, embraced by the chill blowing from the mountains of Ilmarinen. She could feel her homeland in her pores, smell the lavender fields from afar, the oak-burning hearths, the sweat of labor and love.

The yolk of day came wheeling down to melt into the moon and the vast plane below dimmed from gold to blue, casting the acacia and baobab trees in sharp relief. And in the sky, the gods were painting. They painted with broad brush strokes from horizon to horizon in bands of yellow and orange and violet and all the colors in-between.

DAY 85

Sunlight penetrated the cracks and crevices in the limestone like dazzling gemstones, pounding her eyelids to consciousness, waking her to a stiff spine and an aching belly. Breakfast consisted of rhubarb and beechnuts mixed with chicory leaves. The roots she could not name soured her stomach, while the prickly opuntia fruit stopped up her digestive tract so that with a measure of suffering, she learned the subtle variation in the color and shape of things that should not be eaten. She relied on the ants hidden in the whistling thorn tree for protein, using a stick to fish them from their hollows. She downed what she could scavenge with little pleasure, her jaw tiring before arriving at any sense of having eaten. But always, her hunger persisted, a nagging reminder that her existence was a struggle and that tomorrow was never certain.

She was losing her battle with starvation. Her muscles shrank between her bones. Her movements felt sluggish and dreamlike, as if she were walking through water instead of air, her limbs responding like her brain and body had separated.

She fashioned her bow out of gazelle horn, joining the two ends with a peel of baobab secured with pitch and twine, after soaking it and setting it out to dry again and again. When all was ready, she took up her spear and newly made bow, her ivory knife and bamboo talisman, and set out for the hunt.

On clear mornings, she could stand atop the ledge of her home to see the edge of the Wildwood and the tips of the Ukko Mountains. The silver peaks were a constant feature in her life, as immutable as the ground beneath her feet, a way-finder for when she and Britannia ventured far from home. It reminded her of the countless steps she had taken since starting her journey, and that despite her weather-beaten soles, her homeland continued to exist. Most days, the haze in the air obscured sight of the mountains, and if she were to continue her southerly course, she would lose sight of them completely. Knowing this unnerved her. Losing sight of Ilmarinen, she might forever lose her way.

The air remained crisp with the memory of nightfall as the sun rose steadily from its cradle, a heavy orange blot in the sky. Her head felt heavy with sleep, and she negotiated the rocky terrain from the roof of her hiding place with effort, using her spear like an old woman's cane. The spiny limbs of an ocotillo shrub grew twenty feet from the base of the knoll, the red-orange bulbs splayed like fingers groping at the clouds, while the surrounding briar bushes were shriveled to little more than a bouquet of sticks. She marched westward with even strides to reserve her strength, the prickly heath tearing at the scabs of her feet.

Life in the plain was receding. The earth no longer bore traces of hoofed animals, and the minnows in the pond were dead, their silvery scales baked into the rock, their bones picked clean by carrion birds. Only the mighty woollyhorn remained, lingering in the broad waters of the Braid, proud and invincible and awaiting her contest. But the herd did not stay in the same area long. After clearing a sward in an afternoon, they migrated downriver, so that with each passing day, she was forced to hike further to encounter them. Every outing sapped her strength more and more, and if she did not return with a kill soon, she knew she would not make it back to camp by nightfall.

The violet moon crossed the face of the larger four times, until the sun reached its zenith and her lips were cracked and she could wipe the sweat from her sides to fill a cup. She searched for a way to sate her thirst, but the craters— so plentiful cycles ago— swirled with dust, giving no hint of ever having held water.

A flock of white birds blotted the sun, shifting suddenly from one direction to another, circling and twisting and turning,

forming simple angular shapes. She slid her
bow from her shoulder but doubted the
efficacy of her aim, deciding against risking
an arrow. Ibises and cranes dawdled near the
shallows, she knew, under the protection of
the woollyhorn, but she never shot at them
lest she rouse the suspicion of her prey.

She followed the flight of the birds, hoping
to be led to the herd, until they shrank to
white specks indistinguishable from wisps of
cloud. The plain climbed steadily and sloped
down again to a swale of mammoth grass and
blackthorn cacti.

She stood over the rise, listening to the
tumultuous rush of the Braid, the river
dashing against a rocky embankment where
the land bent sharply to the west. The herd
would not settle near rough waters, but here
she could sate her thirst, and if the riffle was
shallow, she might catch her next meal.

The escarpment dropped into a steep
incline, more so than she expected. She had
never come this way before, and as she
neared the bank, a sudden uneasiness came
over her.

A peculiar hill beckoned in the distance. It
resembled a natural formation, but its sides
were flat, like something manmade. The
surrounding air was stagnant, permeated with
a scent like smoke and decay. Black ash
streaked the ground, and tiny fragments
prickled her insoles like fish teeth, the
charred remnants of kindling and bones.

She knelt to examine a curved stone the color of soot, when a spider with bright blue stripes crawled from an eye socket onto her wrist. She brushed it away and watched the spider scamper under a log, before turning back to the skull in her hand. Its teeth were rotted or missing, as was the jawbone. She was familiar with the skeletons of many animals, having skinned them herself. A horned deer. A wild hog. A saurian. But the pate she held was unusually large in proportion to its nostril cavity, suggesting small, flat features, and with sudden horror she dropped the skull and recoiled.

The remains of humans and humanlike creatures were everywhere she looked, scattered and broken like twigs, femurs and craniums arranged in yellowing mounds. Her people did not burn the bodies of loved ones nor gather skeletons into piles to be mixed with that of other animals. Every Ilmarin was returned to the earth upon death, to the bosom of the Mother Goddess.

Her instinct was to flee, but she could not resist the lure of her curiosity. She needed to know the purpose of this place, to discover what kind of creatures adopted such customs.

Gooseflesh prickled her extremities as she trailed the slope of skulls, altars of bone meeting her at every turn, until reaching, at last, a solitary slab of blue at the center of a clearing. The stone stood narrow as an oak but taller than the highest trees, damasked by ragweed, stinging nettles, and sphagnum.

What she had taken for a natural formation she could now see was distinctly designed, a faceted menhir like an enormous crystal. She ran her fingers between the weave of foliage, finding its surface cold to the touch, hard as marble but smooth as bamboo. The base was couched in weeds, hiding skulls turned on their heads, their insides filled with wax and straw. A lingering scent suggested vessels for housing fires. She cleared more of the overgrowth, uncovering streaks of blood dulled brown with age, olive-black mold hardened by the centuries. The fungal coating came away in clumps to reveal rows and columns of engraved symbols.

Writing was not foreign to her. She had made notches on her cot to count the days, as Baba etched pictographs on peels of bark to track the animals grazing in the field and the crops stored in the silos. For every goat, he drew a triangle with two extending lines for horns, and for every chicken, a circle with a beak. But the inscriptions on the menhir wall were entirely alien to her. Their shape did not correspond to any animal she could think of, nor anything in nature she knew to exist. But a higher form of writing was also known to the Ilmar, to the people of the highlands, the Keepers who dwelt in the Mountains of Ukko. Only the wisest of the Ilmar could hope to become a Keeper. She had always assumed Aliaa was destined to join their company, and did not doubt whether she could have deciphered the meaning in the stone. But

Thelana, ignorant to such matters, could only stare, her imagination conjuring fantastic secrets about the place and the people who built it.

The skulls and the blood suggested the veneration of a deity, but she could not comprehend how a people so skilled in stonecutting could revel in such gruesome rituals.

The world was vast, possessing more to understand than she could ever hope to learn in a lifetime. Burdened by that thought, she resigned herself to mystery, to never knowing the reason behind the menhir's creation.

She met the woollyhorn near the southern border of the savannah, where the Braid turned broad and shallow and quiet. Having studied them for days, she could stand in their midst without masking her scent, touch their ropey hides without stirring them to violence.

She had learned their behaviors, the types of grasses they liked to chew, how the stubby-nosed youngsters enjoyed wading in the river and sidling next to their mothers, how they grouped themselves by familial bonds. The woollyhorn proved gentle to every living thing that moved, and they took care never to trample her, even as the trees swayed and pebbles hopped in their wake. They came to trust Thelana, as they trusted the birds nestled in their backs, for she did not act like the Tyrant or the Smilodon, which did not hesitate to maim and kill.

The eldest and most prominent among the woollyhorn she called Old Gray. Naming animals marked for slaughter was a mistake, and she had admonished Nicola for doing so many a time. And yet, she could not help but think of the name whenever he emerged to lead his pack. Old Gray's fur was ashen in color, his hump like the sleet gray of the mountaintop, and with his tremendous horn, he could tear any tree in the savannah straight from its roots.

The soft membrane about the sides of his skull was her only target, a direct route to his brain. She pictured it a hundred times, goring his eye to monstrous effect, only to be chased away, to return to her campsite with empty hands and pangs of hunger.

Now, when the time came to lift her spear, she lost herself to his rotund eye, her image distorted in his black, apple-sized pupil, where moisture gathered like teardrops and gnats buzzed incessantly. She could do nothing but stand amid the herd as the majestic beasts stomped about, careful never to nudge her, her eagerness for bloodshed abandoning her entirely.

Why did the gods make us so feeble? If the Great Mother is loving and kind, why then must things die so that others may live? If only she could eat grass, no creature would need suffer . . . But ilma were not herbivores and could not subsist on plants alone.

She rested her weapons against a rock and watched the herd drift away, her chest tightening with every breath, bringing pain and heaviness. She was not what her parents wanted her to be, not nearly so strong or clever. Her brothers were the true hunters, Borz chief among them. *He should be here, not me.* But her parents had sold him to the Face People, casting aside their only hope of survival, and now she was paying the price for their misplaced trust in her.

Brooding will not fill your belly, she thought. She had to constantly remind herself of this, when she most wanted to quit, and taking up her arms, she started for the riverbank.

The Braid abounded with sturgeon and eel, but fish were swift and slippery, and she did not possess the means to catch them. Her mind then turned to the tower of strange writing. If she could weave the vines together, they might make for a suitable net. It might not make for the feast she had envisioned, but a creel of fish would keep her from starving and, she hoped, provide her with the strength to leave the savannah.

The river ebbed with shades of orange, signaling the lateness of the day. Mangroves growing from its banks bowed under the wind, and silvered ripples gathered about a dark shape. She heard the braying of the woollyhorn in the distance, a sound of alarm she had never known them to make. Without thinking, she snatched her spear and sought higher ground, and there she noticed it, a dreadful, serpentine shape moving from

under the water. The herd was stampeding
now, rushing away in an amber haze. She
watched their silhouettes recede and then
suddenly change direction. Something was
driving them back, routing them toward her,
and in their panic, the docile behemoths
became a force of destruction. Acacia trees
became uprooted, mounds crumbled,
boulders flew every which way. They careened
into one another, battered by their horns, the
youth crushed under the hooves of their
elders. She started to run also, but the air was
thick, full of debris stinging her eyes, and she
could not make out their movements. Blindly,
she headed for the water as the serpentine
thing stretched from the depths, half-
slithering, half-crawling toward her.

A story flashed in her mind, told in hushed
tones, and the memory of a dreadful name.
Voorgaven. She glimpsed many scampering
legs as it came surging from the river,
winding in pursuit of the herd. The frightened
woollyhorn jostled past her like a storm, mud
spraying from their pounding hooves, their
horns grazing her forearms, threatening to
yank her braid from her skull. One wrong
step and she would be killed, crushed under
their massive weight, and yet she could not
see through the haze to know where to turn.
She was helpless but to stand and pray, and in
the rising mist, the voorgaven's long-ridged
snout reared, flaring whitely with rows upon
rows of teeth.

A trio of woollyhorn steered her way, Old Gray taking the middle, and she could not hope to evade them. They drew closer, their horns rending the air, their hooves clapping like thunder.

Nowhere to run.

Her body took over, crouching, catching the ropelike fur by the handful. The voorgaven coiled, lunging at each fleeing animal, and she found herself pulling, and finally standing atop Old Gray's hump. He was like a boat with a horn for a tiller, the muscles of his spine flexing, tossing her to and fro.

Still, the river saurian pursued, gaining upon them with every passing second, and she could only think to draw up her spear to guard against its snapping bite.

The world turned suddenly and Thelana found she was tumbling through the air, the woollyhorn beneath her feet having collapsed. Her collarbone hit the ground first, yet a searing pain shot up from her leg. She was awash in agony, on fire, even as she realized she was being dragged into the river. She tried prying herself free, only to feel her flesh tear away, the voorgaven's knife-like teeth sliding between the small bones of her ankle. Her spear was nowhere near and she could not reach the dagger at her thigh. She clutched desperately for rocks, any substitute for a weapon, anything at all. But the pain overloaded her senses. Shut down her brain. Her body grew numb, her vision cloudy, gray.

Even if she were to escape, she could not hope to survive alone—*alone*—with so severe an injury. Surrender was so much easier. To allow herself to rest. To sleep.

The world shifted into focus, and for a time she lay on her back, the reddening sun paining her eyes. Her ankle throbbed, the pain of it permeating all her senses, and yet she was alive. Somehow.

When she managed the strength to sit upright, she found the voorgaven's head still attached to her, its teeth hooked through the bottom of her left leg. But the monster was dead, its skull flattened into a round hole, its serpentine length meandering along the ground into the lapping current. The woollyhorn were gone, but the prints left by their passing were unmistakable, as were those of Old Gray. The radius of its foot formed a pit she could lay herself into.

Too hurt to move, she studied the curious pattern made by the chief of the herd. When the voorgaven attacked, the woollyhorn stampeded downriver, but Old Gray's hoofs evidenced a change in course. After falling and righting himself again, he must have pivoted back, returning to crush the river monster under his enormous forelimbs. Had he done so to protect the herd? Or had he risked his life for the small human girl?

Pain dominated her faculties, radiated from her leg with excruciating intensity. She wished she could simply shut it off, go numb and have done with it, but life pressed on, stubbornly clinging to her broken body. She could not walk. Could no longer hunt or forage. Even in Ilmarinen, those suffering from crippling injuries relied on their families for survival. She might still crawl to her campsite if only to die there. Old Gray's altruism, if that is what had happened, could only delay the inevitable.

At a whim, she decided she would rather not die in the open, where the carrion eaters might take her for their supper. But the voorgaven would not release her, even in death, from its trap-like jaws. Its draconic head measured half her length, plated in iridescent, aquamarine scales, with bony protrusions running from the horn of its chin to its fin-like ears. If she could cut it into pieces, the voorgaven could feed her for cycles, perhaps allowing her the time to heal. But she first had to lift herself up, pry its teeth from her ankle despite the searing pain.

Her screaming sounded above the din of the savannah, frightening the birds from their homes in the reeds. She willed herself against every instinct to endure, to push beyond the limits of her pain. And yet, she simply lacked the strength to free herself from the voorgaven's bite, managing but to open the wound further, allowing her blood to gush out onto the plain, to flow in crimson shades across the sediment.

Bitterly, she wept. Knowing she was helpless. Knowing she was far from home.

Human shapes were approaching her from the south. Taking them for Outsiders, she was tempted to call out to them, but then she remembered the shrine and the sudden routing of the herd, and hesitated, and as they came into view, her hope turned to dread. Like the woollyhorn and the voorgaven, she knew them by their names, by the pictographs her ancestors drew on limestone walls. They came brandishing weapons of wood and bone, walking upright but remaining hunched, so much like men in shape and stature and in the contours of their pale scowling faces. Yet their bodies were matted in fur the color of blood, their pronounced canines jutted from their mouths, and their charcoal fingernails extended like the claws of a great cat.

Halfmen.

They closed about her, making curious, guttural, threatening noises, their bone trinkets rattling from their extremities. She could but watch helplessly, her ankle spilling profusely, her life continually draining from the voorgaven's ridged mouth.

The most decorated the halfmen she took for their chief. He wore a deer's skull for a crown and a necklace of vertebrae, and with a hand that could close about her waist, he reached down, and in his dark, shimmering eyes, she could see nothing but violent intentions.

She waited, waited without protest for a death blow that did not come, until she hazily

The Feral Girl

became aware that she had been freed from
the mouth of the river monster and that her
wound was being cleansed and staunched.
But she would not be allowed to crawl away.
Drifting in and out of consciousness, she
remembered a makeshift plank, ropes
tightening about her joints, the weight of her
hanging body, and at last, the mercy of the
void.

DAY 86

Her mind drifted, sailing aimlessly from thought to thought. Islands of memory beckoned at her consciousness, but she resisted their lure, fearing what it might mean should she open herself to them. Only hunger and pain and self-pity awaited her upon the shore. Surrendering herself to the uncertain spaces between life and death, her spirit was free to forget, and in forgetting she could escape all wants. Better to dream than to live. To shake off the hurts of the world and all of its sorrows.

Still, her body stubbornly clung to existence. Time came in sudden, violent bursts, invading her with flashes of awareness. She remembered being carried by the halfmen out of the savannah, hanging like an animal from a gambrel, her joints aching in support of her weight.

They are going to kill me. Drain my blood and spill my organs and cook me. I am the gazelle now. No use fighting it.

She shut her eyes and willed herself to let go, and darkness came over her again.

DAY 88

Thelana found herself doubled over in a sort of cage, her bosom pressed into her thighs, an uneven roof grating against her curved, protruding vertebrae.

The stinging in her ankle had subsided, the surrounding tissue having gone numb. But she was too far constrained to look at it. She could scarcely move at all, confined within her oddly-shaped enclosure. She could only reach across the length of her leg to examine the injury with her fingertips. And what she found there was not what she expected. The flesh adjoining her ankle was slick and bulbous, a texture not her own, but some foreign organism compounded over the voorgaven's bite.

Leeches.

The halfmen were using leeches, a technique her mother often employed with her brothers, when Vaino bruised himself falling out of a tree, and on countless other occasions she could not recall. But to what end? Why would the halfmen minister to an animal meant for the slaughter?

DAY 90

The morning sun rose, penetrating through the openings of her enclosure. Slowly, her surroundings came into focus, until she could see out through the vertical, yellow-white beams pressed against her nose. At a dozen paces, a ruddy fence met her gaze. The tops of the logs were of chestnut, sharpened like giant spears, most likely to keep out saurians, she thought. Halfmen by the score milled to and fro, ambling from huts of mud and straw to tend to their firepits and flay their carcasses.

She recognized the hunters by their imposing size and the skeletal ornaments they wore. Her people practiced a similar custom, adorning their bodies with an animal they had killed, but never with the animal itself, as the halfmen did. Borz displayed his kills proudly across every bit of his skin, and she had always envied him for that. Women were not permitted to do the same, decorating themselves only with floral patterns.

She watched them from her cage, quarreling over food and trinkets and the attention of the females, growling and pounding their chests and baring their teeth in displays of dominance, their sinews bulging from under their glossy hides. She could tell the females by their narrower jawlines, drooping nipples, and smaller statures. Their fur was more brown than red, and the skin about their faces was less creased, closer to human in its semblance. The youth, even those with testes, exhibited a similar hue.

Her captors went about their daily routines, passing her cage without a glance. To the halfman, she supposed, she was just another oddity of the Wildwood, who moved bipedally and manipulated tools, but who was far more petite and frail than they were. A hairless animal but for the fount growing from her scalp and the patches sprouting from her underarms and crotch.

They are not so different from us. Only, I am to be the food.

It was only fitting, after she had eaten the tortoise and the gazelle. So why had they yet to kill her? Perhaps she was being preserved. By holding her alive, her flesh would keep from spoiling.

A dreadful thought occurred to her as she puzzled over her predicament, a feeling that surprised and confused and dismayed her even as it formed inside her skull. It was the fear that she might *not* be killed. And in a sudden panic, she attempted to break from her shoddy confinement, yet the position she

had been forced into made even the slightest
motion an arduous task. She was limited to
rocking forward and backward and from side
to side. When she moved to pry the bars
apart, her palms came away slashed and
bloody, and applying pressure to the upper
portion of the cell, she found herself
debilitated in her hunger and misery.

She was powerless to do anything more
than stare between the bony tines keeping her
prisoner. And after a time, she became fixated
by the world beyond her cell. She spent
passings studying the adobe hut less than two
paces from her nose despite her obstructed
view. She memorized the natural contours in
the stacks of mud and dung, counted every
stick and pebble used to fortify it, and found
amusement in the undulations of straw
dangling from its domed roof.

And in this way, she found reprieve from
her misery, shutting her mind to every other
concern but for the features of the halfman
and their dwelling, until, finally, mercifully,
sleep.

DAY 91

She awoke assaulted by sticks. Her attackers, all of them children, were jabbing her in the cheeks and chin and forehead and every spot in-between. The space around her left eye was already tender and beginning to swell shut. Could it be a game? A cruel rite of passage? She was at a loss for answers. Nothing had made sense since her imprisonment. She could not cling to reason, could not find solutions when her captors were beyond comprehension. Given the shape of their brows and the glimmer in their eyes, she knew the children were curious about her, about the strange, hairless creature living among them.

She caught the next stick passing through the bars, wrested it from the youngster's grasp, and broke it. Another boy reached his fingers inside her pen and she bit him, bloodying her teeth. He recoiled with a look of shock and consternation, as if to say, *How could you?* The older males growled and bore their teeth in protest. She met their gaze and let out a scream, the fiercest she could muster, then awaited their retaliation, braced herself for their blows.

The boy she had injured fled into his mother's arms, tears brimming from his apish, sunken face. She watched them interact, waiting for her punishment. Surely now, after what she had done, they would make her suffer. Or perhaps they would eat her and have done with it. Skewer her like livestock and end her suffering.

Her enclosure was thrown open, and she hesitated, convinced she would be killed if she moved. But again, to her surprise, she came away unharmed.

She had been cramped to the point of torment. Now the relief to her compressed spine and joints as she stretched to a seated position filled her with euphoria. But she was still numb, her long-captive muscles slowly responding to the workings of her legs. Hurried by her captors, she struggled to her feet, feeling her weight for the first time in days. And a dull ache, the memory of the voorgaven's teeth, shot up through her ankle.

Curious youngsters crowded about her, dashing any hope of escape. The shortest of them, despite his hunch, stood to her height. They parted to let her pass, muscle spasms rifling through her every sinew, but she did not have far to go. A rope slipped over her head, tightening about her throat.

She limped in slow circles about the hut, driven by a long piece of hickory, leaning onto her right side to minimize her soreness. The mother of the wounded boy glared as she walked past them, and Thelana noticed how very young he was. With his halfman-sized hands, he ate a watermelon as she would an apple. The juices dripping from his lips, and the wet crunching sounds issuing from his mouth, drove into her belly like knives.

She circled to the opposite side of the shelter, where a second female with graying features sat with a peel of bark and a pile of fish. There was no basket, only fish, scattered against the hut in the dirt. They reeked of putrescence, their eyes glazed yellow, gathering gnats, but Thelana hungered for them regardless. The elder female was carving them into sections, a familiar-looking ivory knife set between her thick, hairy fingers.

"Hey! That's my knife!"

She choked on the words as the rope yanked tight against her throat. *Stupid, Thelana. What did you expect? That they would apologize and hand it back to you?*

The huts opposite her own—for that is how she came to think of it, *her hut,* despite never having stepped inside—appeared spacious enough for families of a dozen or more. Stretched woollyhorn skins, with their distinct, ropey textures, signaled prestige. Great hunters lived under canopies of woollyhorn, in domiciles festooned with animal skulls. The grandest of these were eight-sided, supported by bones at every corner, their arched entryways framed by crossing horns.

When she was returned to her enclosure, she came upon the skull of a saurian, and given its enormity, knew it could only belong to one kind of animal. Her cell was the mouth of a dead tyrant, its jaws serving as hinges, its teeth forming the bars. As her halfmen escorts pried the skull apart, a panic seized her, her mind jolted by the realization of what was about to happen.

"No!" she screamed. *I don't want to go back there! I won't go! I won't let you!* But she did not have the strength to resist them. She could feel the weakness in her legs, which were nearing exhaustion, and the power in their hands, which closed about her forelimbs as a father might grasp an unruly toddler.

They left her with a few fish heads and the rinds from the watermelon, and as her new family departed, she came to understand the purpose of her existence with an uncanny tinge of horror. She was not livestock, as she had earlier surmised, but an animal kept for amusement. A pet.

DAY 92

The rinds settled uneasily into the pit of her stomach, odiously mixed with raw fish scales and cartilage. Night came on, subsuming the village in silhouette and shadow and the orange glow of distant fires. She willed herself to sleep, but her body protested, wracked by equal parts hunger and cold and the urge to vomit what she had so ravenously devoured.

Watermelons.

From the Ukko Mountains fading into the blue of the horizon, the Great River tumbled and broke apart into a lattice of braided channels, feeding into the base of the great oak. She hopped along the pebbled path toward the looming tree, careful not to dip her feet into the many creeks nested in its roots, pained with a yearning to look upon home as though she had been gone a great while. Her entire family—fourteen in all— could join hands in a semicircle about its trunk, leaving room for children yet to arrive. Old Man Oak had stood for more generations than anyone could count. Her mother had grown up under it, frolicked with her aunts and uncles beneath its boughs, as her grandparents and their parents before them, as the first Ilmarin ever to set foot in the valley.

West of the Oak, in a field of lavenders hemmed by stands of birches, Nicola, Laine, and Vaino played hide and seek, her younger sister concealing herself behind a slender striped bole. Looking east, she saw Anja lying in a bed of heathers, daydreaming of love, as young Baldr chased pinwheels and dandelions, their petals spinning and drifting away. It was the kind of day that only exists in memory, a day made more vivid by nostalgia.

Thelana was tempted to join her siblings, to wallow under the carefree sun of the low moon season. But childish amusements would have to wait, for she was eager to hear the latest gossip. Reaching the foot of the oak, she clambered up a hempen ladder, ran along the bough to a knotted rope, and climbed again. Britannia waited near the top, carving bird outlines into her brown thighs with her fingernail. Thelana straddled the branch without a word of greeting, facing her sister knee to knee, the land spreading far below them in a mottle of yellows and oranges. Britannia glanced up, her head a mess of chestnut hair and twigs, her soles encrusted with plant matter, soot darkening her coppery complexion. Mana would be furious, as always, demanding that she wash up before supper. But that would have to wait.

"Tell me everything!"

Britannia went straight into the story, punctuating all the relevant parts with glee. Baba sent Borz, Lodr, and Heimdl out on a hunt a cycle ago. "Make sure you come back with something, or don't return at all," he had said to them. This Thelana knew. What she did not know was what transpired while her brothers were away.

They looked for prey for two days, tracking further and further into the woods, never straying from the Braid. By the third night, the boys came back to camp with their heads bowed and empty-handed. So they broadened their search the next day, moving away from the river, and still, they caught nothing. Worse than that, they were a half-cycle from home and they'd eaten all their rations. Borz decided it was time to go home then, but they got themselves lost after a heated argument about which way they should go. Thoroughly lost. *Those idiots*, Britannia added.

When they finally found their way, their bellies were grumbling quite badly. And that's when they came to the farmstead, marching through the lowlands a day's hike from home, the Korhonen farmstead. The one with all those watermelons. You know the one.

Well, the boys, you can imagine, just couldn't help themselves. They each grabbed a melon—Borz stole two, I heard—and went running for the hills. When they were a good ways away, they started into the fruit, eating every last bit of it except for the rinds. With eclipse coming on heavy, they went to sleep under the stars. But all that watermelon filled up their bladders in the night. And boys being boys, they just couldn't let it out.

Competitive peeing was a favorite pastime of theirs, Thelana remembered, albeit a disgusting one. They usually tried for distance, but sometimes for power and accuracy. A good stream can strip the seeds off a rind, and that's just what they did with the remains of the watermelons, Britannia told her.

Thelana rolled her eyes. She could not imagine acting so wastefully. It was a gross game to play and she wanted no part in it. She would have refused them even if the Goddess had granted her the ability to compete.

Britannia went on: So the boys got up the next day with the sun in their eyes, realized they'd overslept, and panicked, not wanting to miss another meal or sleep away from their beds. But hunger hit them again. They argued over going back to the Korhonen home, but that was the opposite way, and they were already feeling guilty for stealing them. Then Lodr looked at what was left of the watermelons and suggested that maybe, just maybe, they hadn't quite peed on *all* of them. Heimdl agreed, picking out the pieces he thought were clean. And Borz, well . . . he came around eventually. By the time they were done picking out their breakfast, not a single rind remained.

The Feral Girl

Britannia could not help laughing, pointing out the obvious, explaining that her brothers had eaten their own pee. Thelana thought the story gross but could not help sharing in her sister's enthusiasm, breaking into fits of laughter—laughter that rang out across their home, across Ilmarinen and into the future, erupting from the prison of bone where she slept, in a sound of mirth betraying her loneliness and despair.

DAY 99

Each time she was escorted to her cell, she changed positions, lying either on her back or side, but always with her legs pulled against her bosom. She tensed up when she was not sleeping, squeezing her fists and balling up her feet to pump blood through her limbs. She could not allow her muscles to atrophy.

As night approached, the halfmen withdrew into their tents, and she went to work, furiously digging her fingers into the earth until her nails came away shredded. The dirt beneath her cell had the consistency of bark and did not yield easily. And even as she shoveled it from between the tyrant's teeth, she could feel the weight of the skull threatening to sink down into the earth to entomb her.

Since her capture, her body continued to mend itself, until she could no longer wile away her days in slumber. Escaping through memory came to be more and more difficult, the agony of her waking reality increasingly inescapable. And yet she held firmly to the faces she remembered, thinking mainly of Britannia and the days they shared together.

They seeded their row for tomatoes, but after cycles harrowing the soil, every other crop came up *except* for tomatoes—sunflowers, eggplants, napshins—but not one tomato. Whether the foreign seeds were carried by birds or the wind, they never learned, but the boys teased them for the rest of the season.

Farm work had been a big part of her life, but not all of it. Adventure often called to them when they felt the need to journey far from home—or what they had believed to be far—until they found themselves high in the mountains with night fast approaching.

They were frightened because they were not yet ten years old. Thelana insisted that they hike back under the moonlight, while Brit wanted to wait until sunrise. And in the heat of the exchange, they wrestled, tumbling down a slope end over end into an anthill. Mana was furious the following morning, finding her daughters covered in tiny red pustules.

Before Borz went away, prior to her crazy venture from home, that day had been the worst experience of her ten-year-old life. But she had been with her sister then. Now, she could not think of a time from her youth without bitter fondness. What would she give to have Britannia by her side, to look into her familiar, dirty face, to hear her eager, giggling voice?

DAY 115

Thelana was growing accustomed to captivity, like a beast of burden whose will had broken. She no longer made any effort to escape, even when the strength returned to her limbs and the bite about her ankle closed to a hard-knotted scar. Her captors, in turn, entrusted her with greater freedom, loosening her bonds and taking her for longer walks about the village.

The senior members of the tribe, those too old for hunting, appeared to be grayer in color and shorter in stature, their arching shoulders curving level with the ground. Elders were afforded greater respect than their crimson-hued kin despite their decrepit natures, and chief amongst them was the village shaman. The shaman lived in a twelve-sided hut on a hill. From what she had seen, the adobe domicile exhibited several skeletal remains from saurians and other large animals. It was supported on all sides by woollyhorn ivory, with the voorgaven's fanged mouth overlooking a doorway curtained with finger bones.

The Feral Girl

The hut stood near a koppie in the center of the village. A solitary slab could be seen on that mound, a smooth-worked menhir like the one she discovered on the savannah. She had gone out many times but never saw the halfman approach it; whether out of reverence or because of fear, she could only guess. But today, she sensed a change in the attitudes of her captors, a change brought on by the alignment of the moons. It formed a single blue disc in the sky. *The All Moon*, her people called it, a cause for celebration, revelry, and lovemaking. Yet she suspected the halfman custom differed from theirs.

Hundreds gathered about the monolith, beating their drums, howling and gesticulating in a manner that made her shudder. Answering their summons, the shaman emerged from his many-sided domicile, his fur yellow-white under a panoply of bones, his weather-beaten face shriveled like the roots of a desiccated stump. Atop his head, he wore a horned carapace like a crown, and about his neck a frayed stalk of bamboo, and in seeing what she was so certain was lost, she gasped. Her talisman was unmistakable.

The shaman placed a hand upon the stone, the tips of his fingernails slowly scraping the surface with an awful noise. He rounded upon the tribe with a sudden, feverish intensity, his voice low and guttural like grinding stones. She understood none of what was spoken but could feel the heavy weight of his words, the violence laced in every syllable.

All but Thelana fell prostrate before the shaman and the sacred stone. Spittle flew from his gums as his sclera-lined eyes grew wild. As if by magic, a frilled cassowary appeared, its squawking, thrashing body breaking into a feathery pulp between his powerful fists. Blood spattered against the menhir, gradually seeping into the cracks, filling the indentations to delineate the archaic runes in gleaming red. The halfmen wailed with approval, dancing to the resounding drums, their bonfires rising, filling the air with glowing embers, suffusing the village with smoke. A gourd blackened with pitch rattled in the shaman's fist, and the cacophony crescendoed into sounds of ecstasy.

What followed was the choosing of a young warrior, an orange-maned halfman. He was escorted by two elders, all-a-quiver but never resisting, and as he ascended the koppie, everything became still, caught in a moment of tension. To Thelana, the halfman looked pensive. Resolved to his fate.

The shaman raised a heavy instrument, a wooden cudgel perforated along its rim by obsidian shards, as the young halfman dropped in supplication to his hands and knees. Then, in a sudden single stroke, the white-haired chieftain removed the youth's head from the shoulder. The open cavity sprayed out, showering the gathering in gore.

Her stomach turned at the sight, but the onlookers seemed to revel in it, drinking from the rim of the koppie where the blood pooled and dripped down to the reddening soil.

She wondered what the halfman's crime had been to deserve such a fate? Or did his demise signify something other than punishment? A sacrifice to the stone and to the cruel god it represented?

The shaman retreated to his abode as the moons separated into their violet and turquoise counterparts, and the tribe, satisfied by the ordeal, disbanded. Thelana was promptly returned to her cell but could not shake what she had witnessed. The halfman was brutal, without any sense of mercy, and the hope that she might be shown some measure of kindness was extinguished. But it was to her talisman that her mind ultimately bent, and the ilm hidden in the stalk about the shaman's neck. The flower belonged to her and her alone. It was her father's parting gift. And the more she thought upon it, the greater the rage quietly built inside her.

DAY 121

The night air whistled through the cavities of her prison as ribbons of smoke curled from the firepits in the halfmen's dwellings. And all the while, she lay shivering in the dirt, worn by her body's involuntary efforts to keep warm.

Sleep continued to elude her, her own troubled thoughts, more than anything, threatening her peace. Something dangerous lurked in her mind, a notion she had long buried, a question she had feared since leaving home. Despite her efforts to shut it out, it festered like a tumor and continued to grow as she watched the hunters return with their gazelle and ziff and woollyhorn carcasses suspended from their gambrels.

Her people long abhorred the slaughter of animals. But when the cold winds rolled from the East and the land turned barren and dust covered everything, the body of the Goddess had failed to provide for them. And yet her people were not without recourse. The annals of the Keepers ran deep, and the way of her ancestors had not been forgotten. Baba knew to turn the spear and hurl the atlatl, and taught his sons the way, just as Borz had taught her.

Father had also known never to send her brothers out alone. Of all the beasts of Aenya, the ilma was the most feeble, and yet the Goddess had shared with them her most precious gifts: thought, imagination, and creativity. A successful hunt required wit, coordination, and the efforts of a group. Even the halfman, with his size and strength, relied on routing tactics between three or more of their tribe. But who did she have to rely on? Her attempt to bring down the woollyhorn failed because she had been alone. And if not for the halfmen taking her in, she would undoubtedly have succumbed to the voorgaven's bite. So why had she been sent out without a companion? With her brothers at her side, with just Britannia, she might have corralled the herd. Working together, they might have fed every house in the valley. A troupe of Ilmar, armed with cleverness and courage, might even topple the Tyrant from his throne.

You are strong, her parents had assured her. You will survive. But they must have known. Must have known better. And as the cold, dark truth surfaced to the fore of her mind, warm tears boiled up over her eyes in the cold dark of her cell.

Her parents had sent her away not to find her brother, not to survive, but to die.

DAY 132

She lay in a pool of her own sickness, the earth beneath her damp with sweat and urine and the fetid matter dredged up by her stomach days ago. Unable to eat, racked with fever, she waited for the inevitable embrace of the Taker.

Occasionally, the villagers threw shreds of bone, peelings of sinew, bile-filled organs into the cavity of her cell. She never bothered to examine what she was eating. The flesh of some animal, spoiled and diseased, too foul even for a halfman to touch. Long past hunger, she worked the morsels down, her tongue working like a dry twig between her molars, insensitive to taste. She ate out of habit, out of a desperate need for something to do. But she need not bother. Starvation was a remedy, the key to freedom, but shaking her addiction to food was not without its challenges.

Death loomed, omnipresent. Yet he remained just beyond reach, teasing her with the sweet promise of endings. An end to hunger, to nights of uncontrollable shivering, to the rank odor emanating from her cell. Why was the Taker taking so long? Why was her body stubbornly clinging to its basic functions against her wishes? It was not her intention to keep on living. She lost the fight after realizing her parents had never meant for her to survive.

When the sickness started, she spent the night vomiting on account of something she was given. And fever slipped over her like a cold membrane in the following days, she welcomed the sensation. She curled like a fetus under a cold sun and waited, her limbs aching, the world pressing hard against her tender skin.

This is how it happens. I will decay, waste away to become fauna, and my spirit will flit into the Solstice Night to the next womb, to start again.

She had only to find patience, overcome her instinct to persevere, and let the chill hands of the Taker seize her. But in the far reaches of her mind, something nagged at her like a fisherman's hook, a memory she did not wish to revisit. Yet the thought persisted the more she tried to push it away until that part of her opened to a host of tangential memories, each one a tether, holding her fast to her mortal shell.

"I want to marry you someday."

Dawn was creeping over the hills, painting the world in jade and gold, and the fingers from the trees cast deep wells of shadows across his face. Borz was tall for his age, broad-shouldered, with well-defined forearms and thighs. He was what every man was supposed to be, like the Batals of Legend, what Baba no doubt resembled before he was old enough to grow a full beard. She longed for his courage, his resolve, and his strength.

He laid his spear across her feet and stared into her, his eyes shimmering like amber in the morning sun. "You know you can't do that, little sis."

"Why not?"

"It isn't allowed."

"But why?" She was too young to understand. The particulars of the Solstice Night, the pairing of male and female, were still mysteries to her youthful mind.

"Mana never told you?" He grinned. "That's how you get bogrens."

"Bogrens!" She twisted her face into the ugliest scowl she could muster, letting her tongue loll from her mouth and twitching her ears. But she had never seen a bogren and could only imagine how hideous they must be. "You mean, bogren babies?"

"That's right."

The recollection made her cringe. She had felt so foolish at the time, and as she grew to understand the different kinds of affections between people, she took special care never to sit too closely or stare too long at his body. But he never brought it up or pretended he did not remember.

Borz never hesitated to share his adventures, often leading her into the woods to teach her the secrets of hunting. Girls aren't made for hunting, her mother told her; leave that to the boys. But she could see no difference between herself and her brothers. Or none that mattered. The extra organ between their thighs—the joke of the lesser goddess from when *Man* was first created out of *Wo*—only got in the way.

Borz never listened to Mana, and neither did she, and in time, Thelana proved more than capable. She excelled in the spear and the atlatl and moved effortlessly to the tops of the trees. Even Baba could not deny her prowess, until her siblings started joking that she was his seventh son, born into the lithe body of a daughter.

Her brother stood proudly by, watching his favorite sister achieve greater levels of skill, the sister who loved and admired him. He had been her guide, her source of strength after Baba had grown too weary of the world to offer it. Then he was taken away, stolen in the night by the Face People, and all his might amounted to nothing.

Borz is still out there.

Maybe her parents had given up hope for him, but she hadn't.

Thunder rolled and crackled from afar, and she raised herself to her knees, scraping the ceiling of her cell. Her prison offered little room to maneuver, but she had shrunk somewhat over the past few cycles, giving her the impression that her enclosure had expanded.

BOOM.

Another blow, closer this time, the hammer of Strom pounding the dome of the world, followed by the deep rumble of his chariot turning over the clouds. She peered out through the dead tyrant's eye socket as white-blue fire speared the sky.

A storm was bearing down on the village. She could feel its weight in the air, the swirling wind and quivering leaves, the thunder in her veins. Rain had not fallen in the savannah since she first arrived, and now she welcomed its raw power. It called to mind the Goddess's gift to all living things, the perpetual will to overcome, to eke out an existence despite incalculable cosmic adversities.

The world flickered again, and in the brief radiance, the village looked small, cowed by the imminent deluge, the surrounding trees writhing like a gathering of frightful onlookers.

The first few drops came down hard and heavy. She lifted her face to let the water pour over her nose and lips. She should have been quivering, reacting to the sudden drop in temperature, but the storm's power was invigorating. Another flash cast the village in sharp relief. She caught glimpses of smothered fires, curling smoke, panicked silhouettes flitting across her cage.

She tried to move, slipped to her stomach, and regained her kneeling posture. The ground was turning to mud and she was sinking into it.

A solitary shape broke from the frenzied mob, deep as a shadow under the moonless sky. She watched as he approached her cell.

What are they going to do to me?

The floor of her prison was fast disintegrating, turning to a pool of sludge, and she reconsidered escaping for the first time in days. Perhaps, she could dig her way out, claw through the mud to freedom. Too late! A grim figure awaited her by the teeth of her cell, crouching, calling out.

"Thelana?"

She yelped, daring to take him in, to behold those familiar amber eyes, the subtle stubble of his chin, afraid to look away lest he disappear. "Borz . . .?" Her voice failed as she called his name.

"Give me your hand. There isn't much time."

"But how? How can you be here?" It could not have been him. It was not possible. And yet, somehow, it was.

"No time for questions, sis. I need to get you out of here."

She brushed at her face. Her cheeks were warm to the touch. She watched him struggle, pull at the edges of the tyrant's teeth, too mesmerized by his sudden emergence to move.

"Hurry, Thelana! I think they've seen us!" He turned to confirm it. "They're coming this way."

"I can slip underneath! But you have to lift it."

He stooped down, his biceps flexing, his face straining with the weight. And in turn, she swam through the black, thick water, dirt piling over her eyes, pebbles filling her mouth. Blinded, suffocating, she pushed forward as the weight of the jawbone caught her and pressed down on her spine. She could hear him call out to her—call above the thunder. His fingers slipped into hers, warm and reassuring. She felt like a newborn being born from the earth.

She stretched to her full height, standing to let the rain wash the grime from her body. The saurian skull seemed much too small, without her rope collar, without her halfman subjugators steering her into it. She could not believe how she could have endured it.

"Thelana . . ." He was out of breath. Gasping. "The halfman are afraid of thunder! But it'll soon pass. We have to go. Now."

Hearing her name after so many days was euphoric. It reaffirmed her sense of self, the fact that she possessed a name at all, without which she feared she might not exist.

Borz led her slowly through the village as flashes of lightning illuminated the way. Her muscles had atrophied despite her efforts, failing her at times, forcing her into a hobble. Yet she pressed forward, wincing with every step, his arm firm under hers, until they finally came to a broad gap in the wall of logs.

"Wait . . ." She pressed her forefinger to her throat. Something was missing, a part of her that had been stolen, and a sudden rage made her tremble. "I have to go back."

He shouted over the din of the rain. "Are you crazy? They'll kill you!"

"I have to try," she murmured. "It's important. Don't worry. I'll be swift. You taught me how."

She did not know how Borz had managed to sneak into the village unnoticed or even how he could have known she was there. But she trusted he would be safe—knew it somehow—as she wheeled around to face the halfmen's domain.

The storm seemed to threaten her approach, but she did not heed its warning, pushing blindly through the lashing wind and rain, her forearms raised over her brows. Halfmen hurried from curtained doorways, their visages twisted, their miniscule eyes trained on the sky. It was as if they had never witnessed such weather. They chased windswept pots, wicker creels that rolled from hut to hut, taking no account of her. She would be safe so long as the storm held, and Borz would be waiting for her by the gate.

Homes flooded, footpaths became rivers, and low-lying areas turned into ponds. She kept to the high places and worked her way to the center. It was easy to find even in the chaos of the storm. Every domicile was arrayed in concentric circles about the stone altar, and after a short distance, she saw it.

The village was surprisingly no more than a brief stroll across. Being marched around by the neck, bound like an aurochs to a harrow, had given her a false sense of its scale.

The shaman's grand residence stood at the north end. She had spent enough time as a captive to find her way toward it. The prominent ivory buttressing its walls stood apart even in the dim light and falling rain.

Starved and sick, she should have been freezing, too exhausted even to contemplate her actions. Perhaps, the Goddess had taken pity on her at last. Or, what she thought more likely, there was greater sustenance to be gained in feeding the heart. Seeing Borz again, knowing he cared to seek her out, was reason enough to go on living and fighting for what was hers.

The worst of the storm was subsiding, the wind-driven rain striking her less abrasively, pouring from overhead instead of into her face. Yet time was pressing. She prowled ahead, keeping to the shadows with her head low to the ground.

Lightning flashed with instances of daylight, outpacing the speed of thunder, silently rending the air, and raising the hackles of her skin. The sound that followed was deafening, leaving a lingering tone in her ears, and as the blue-white fire receded from the stone slab, she saw that the runes were glowing with the same light, with the fire of the gods. A ghostly apparition emerged from the shrine, assuming the vague, flickering guise of a man. He resembled one of the Face People, though his outer layers were more tightly fitted to his body, defining his human shape. Halfmen gathered about the mound to gaze upon this new manifestation, but their curiosity quickly turned to dread, and they fled from the ethereal form. She understood that the menhir was not of their making, but had been stolen from the valley and delivered to the village to serve the shaman's rituals. And now, their dimwitted brains could not fathom what they were seeing.

Raindrops fell through him as he stood and smiled. He spoke in words she did not know, gesticulating like a scout offering directions. It was a greeting of sorts, a friendly welcome. Runes circled over his head and lines converged to form a map. She recognized the winding course of the Braid and the Ukko Mountains to the north. Then something big and sprawling and complex materialized in the air above him, a kind of maze, a vast region of dwellings across the entire western rim of the Wildwood. She thought to walk up to him, ask him where she might find the Outside, but the blue light surging through the stone was draining away like water through a sieve, and the man began to flicker, becoming less and less substantial until he was no longer there.

She turned to the shaman's hut with the image of the man burned in her head. A log for flaying meat lay just beyond the doorway, with a knife still embedded in the wood. The handle and blade were of ivory, made from the serrated tooth of a tyrant. She yanked it free and pushed through the curtain.

A pungent mix of sweat and smoke and burning meat filled the space. The dirt floor was festooned with animal skins, simple tools of bone, and the suspended remains of prey with bits of flesh still clinging to the ribs and vertebrae. A ring of orange-hot stones was set in the center, sending ribbons of smoke through the open roof. Females huddled at the corners, their frightened young clinging to their shaggy undersides. A younger pair, with fur the color of maple, lay draped over the shaman.

Thelana was struck by a feeling that she did not belong there, that she was intruding upon a place no human eyes were meant to see. But she had suffered too much to let it go. Her talisman was all that she had of home. Of her father. With the knife flat against her thigh, she clenched her teeth and marched across the floor to the furry mass opposite the entrance. The shaman raised his enormous head to acknowledge her, his all-black eyes glistening, his bare face deforming into a puzzled expression.

"That doesn't belong to you." She pointed to the necklace of vertebrae he wore about his neck. A dozen miniature skulls dangled from it, and a single bamboo stalk.

His eyes drifted to the space between his collarbones, his nostrils contracting from the bone running through it, his lips parting to expose his piercing, fetid, yellow teeth.

"That's mine," she said, as if this time he would understand, as if he were likely to oblige her. "My Baba gave that to me."

The humanlike, curious expression washed from his face, and he grew larger and more intimidating. His mouth expanded to reveal teeth she did not know he possessed, his tainted fur stiffening to quills, his veins coursing, reddening his aging jowls. Even the young females wrapped about him slunk away.

He was on her before she could think what to do, her arm like a twig in his powerful grasp. She could feel the small bones in her wrist constricting, threatening to snap, and then her other arm came around in a blind arc. The impact reverberated through her fingertips, hair and soft-tissue and bone parting from the ivory edge of her knife. She stumbled away, stunned by her own brutality, her killer instinct. The blade was buried to the handle in the shaman's temple, deep enough to keep the blood from spilling out, and a silent moment passed between them as he stared into her eyes and she stared back. Free of his grasp, she tore the bamboo from his neck, leaving vertebrae to clack together in the dirt. The females started to wail as she rushed off with her prize in hand. Screams of rage and agony, and the thump of heavy footfalls, followed her through the curtain door. Her only hope was to race through the village, keep hidden under the rain, for she could not fight even the smallest of them.

She ran, ran over flowing water and drifting debris, through the gate to where her brother still waited. Exhaustion set in as her panic subsided, and she was reminded of how sleep-deprived she was, how terribly malnourished. She tripped over her own feet, blackening her knees in the mud, her aching palm still clutching to the bamboo shoot. Her bones felt like iron. Too heavy to lift. She wanted nothing more than to collapse on the spot and never move again.

Borz raised her up, giving her his strength. "Thelana . . . What did . . . What did you do?"

The village was ablaze. Fire was spreading along the thatched perimeter, leaping from beam to beam. The halfmen were too preoccupied with the devastation to pursue them. Except for the chieftain, who came charging out of the gate, his bellowing voice a mix of bestial and human fury.

She wanted to answer him, to hold the shape of her brother's face a while longer, the glinting of his eyes in the light of the fire, but the shaman was almost upon them.

Borz ran ahead, leading her into the forest. She hoped to lose their pursuer in the dense flora, taking sudden turns to throw off the chase, but the halfman's frantic grunts continued to ring in their ears.

They rushed hand-in-hand through the foliage, stumbling over roots and cutting stones. Mammoth fronds battered their faces.

Barbed branches snagged at her hair. Where the shadow of the wood deepened, she navigated by way of touch, by the twigs and needles designating the path underfoot, and fleeting glimpses of her brother gesturing this way or that.

The boles of the trees, slender and gray, caught in the glow of the turquoise moon breaking through the canopy of leaves. They raced toward the light of the open sky, probing the uneven, sloping terrain, slipping and righting themselves again, the ground turned soft by the storm, slick with mud and gravel and wet with leaves. And still, their pursuer came on relentlessly.

Thelana could feel her resolve wasting away with every step. Borz could see it in the sluggish way she moved, could see the surrender in her eyes. "Come on, Thelana!" He was partly pleading, partly commanding her. "Don't give up now!"

The trees crowded in on them again, impeding their trespass, forcing them to clamber over the low-hanging limbs and duck under the tall boughs. From behind, the crackling sound of foliage filled them with dread. She could feel the heat of the halfman's breath, the wetness flying from his gums, the decaying odor of his mouth, pushing her beyond the limits of exhaustion.

"This way!"

She followed her brother's voice through a narrow passage hidden by the nettles and down an escarpment where the trees gave way to a broad swath of ferns. Their fronds were soft to the touch and dripped with rain.

Her lungs were burning. She stopped to take in air, feeling like she had been holding her breath since leaving the village. She then looked into her hand, almost surprised to see what she was holding and that she had yet to lose her bamboo talisman.

Where is the shaman? Did we finally lose him?

The momentary peace, coupled with the wide-open space, was reassuring. Here, they might stay hidden under the ferns, crawl on hands and knees if they had to, while watching for enemies.

Borz stood in the midst of the field, bathed in starlight, and in the stillness, she could hear the distant rush of water. *The river!* They could make for the river and ride the current away from halfman country.

But the hidden passage had bought them only a short reprieve, a moment's rest. The shaman burst through the trees above, his matted fur, bluish in the moonlight, stained from the blood draining from the stab wound in his skull. He gazed upon her with a confused expression, his rage blunted, his breathing coming with great deliberation. He was deflated, looking older and weaker than he had been. She lowered her hands in a gesture of goodwill. Understanding crossed his brow. He seemed to consider letting her alone so they both might rest, but something stirred in his pitch-black eyes, a sudden recollection. He caressed the side of his head, fingering the bloodied knife affixed to it, and his face contorted monstrously.

She and Borz ducked into the field with the shaman at their heels. They traced the sound of gushing water until slipping through the mud down a narrow channel. The storm was draining into the lowlands and taking them with it. They slid uncontrollably, from side to side, crashing to a halt where the channel spilled over a rocky plateau. She managed to pull herself up, her body caked in leaves, her hair heavy with twigs and pebbles and clumps of earth. The tumult of water roared in her ears, and she knew they were close. She crept over to the drop, which was almost invisible in the dim light, and peered down over the chasm. A broad current dashed from the boulders below, the froth glinting faintly under the turquoise moon.

Borz called out, somehow always ahead of her, always there to lead the way. "Over here!" he cried. "I found a way across."

She tracked his voice, just as the halfman arrived in an angry heap of bloody fur behind them. A tree had toppled over, its roots freshly seared by lightning, its length spanning the chasm. Her brother motioned to it, and she started slowly across, testing her weight, the trunk no broader around than her waist, watching her footing lest she tumble over a knob and fall into the river.

The shaman dashed across the makeshift bridge without pause, and the whole thing began to sway and twist from its precarious position in the rock. The halfman had caught up to them and she could no longer run. She watched him race toward her, his arms swinging savagely, and braced for impact as the log came undone, and they both plummeted.

The cold surge of water was numbing, the force of its pull overpowering. She kicked to stay afloat, gasping for air, too weary to feel or think, or even consider the whereabouts of her brother and the shaman. A slippery mass swam beneath her, gliding under her soles and flailing limbs. Scales. Fins. Round yellow eyes. Fish that could swallow her whole. They were spawning, swimming against the current. She groped at their slender bodies, caught hold of them where she could, losing her grip and catching another, struggling with and against their thrashing movements for what seemed like the entirety of the night.

She lay sprawled beside the river, face down in the mire, breathing hard from the corner of her mouth, her every sinew wracked with agony. She considered finding a better resting place, a more comfortable position to recline in, but lacked the will.

Perhaps she and Borz might fashion a net by morning and make spears for the bigger fish. It was a pleasant enough thought, a hope to cling to, if only he hadn't drowned . . .

Someone was approaching her. Roused by the noise, she lifted herself to see who it was. "Borz? Are you there?"

No answer came. She undoubtedly looked a mess—like a creature born from the mud—covered as she was. She called out again. Her voice carried hoarsely, a feeble murmur across the torrent.

The figure ambled toward her with its back hunched, its torso pulsing, its face bloodied. It was not Borz. His claws were already closing about her throat, the stench of his breath already scorching her nostrils. She reacted without thinking, shoveling fistfuls of mud and granules and whatever else she could grasp in his eyes. He briefly recoiled, and she slipped away, her body unexpectedly sluggish, weighed by the hardening silt. An arch of boulders, forming a dolmen, beckoned a short distance from the river. It stood tall to make a hideout. Halfmen were efficient climbers, but she had nowhere else to go.

She hobbled toward what she could only pray was sanctuary, her legs burning with every step, feeling as if someone had ripped the muscle of her thighs from the femur. But the halfman was faring no better, having lost a great deal of blood, and was slow to pursue.

She reached the dolmen, clumsy with fatigue, and collapsed. The shaman came limping up from behind, the bones adorning his body clattering, his eyes wild and his mouth frothing. She tried to regain her footing, but her limbs gave out and she dropped again.

The storm had flooded the river, spreading sludge beyond the bank. She slid over the syrupy surface like a tadpole, clawed her way across it as she searched for a stone, a stick, anything she might use to defend herself. The shaman, all the while, lurched toward her on feet and knuckles, the knife in his head gushing blood like a spring. And then, a curious droning assaulted her ears from the roof of the dolmen, a swarm of black bird wasps issuing from a huge, bulbous nest. She noticed the uncertainty in the shaman's face, the doubt clouding his pupils, if only for an instant. But he would not stop. Could not. He was a dying animal, determined to avenge his murder.

"You know what to do." Somehow, defying all reason, Borz stood there beside her, his voice unwavering, giving her strength. "Break it! It's the only way, Thelana."

With her back against the rock and the shaman still advancing, she pulled herself up with what little life remained in her, slamming her mud-caked fists up through the pockmarked shell above their heads. And a cloud of death came down upon them.

DAY 133

Borz . . .
        The steady flow of water swirled in her ears.

We made it, Borz.

She found herself awake and sat upright with slow, deliberate, aching movements. A stone roof shielded from the sun, and where the slabs joined above her head, the sticky fragments of the wasp's nest hummed with activity. The black drones were busily repairing their ravaged home, though their number had greatly diminished. If they had not attacked her already, she doubted they would.

She started from under the dolmen on her knees and elbows, deposits of sand and clay flaking from her skin as she dragged herself along the ground, her head feeling as if it might roll from her neck. She found the desiccated remains of the shaman chief not far from where she had been lying. The wasps had meted out their vengeance upon him, targeting the baldness of his brows, the bare skin about his cheeks, and the open wound she had made in his skull. She found him difficult to look at, his face unrecognizable, swollen and deformed with pustules upon pustules. Killed by a hundred tiny stabs, while she, armored in nothing but mud, had survived the night untouched.

She set foot atop the halfman's bosom and let out a scream of triumph, like a beast for all the Wildwood to hear. To hear and cower before her. She was Thelana, born of Ilmarinen. Human. Apex predator.

But she could never have done it without Borz, could not have found the courage or the strength to escape the halfmen's capture, or been clever enough to break the wasp's nest.

"Borz!" She called his name, her heart swelling with pride. "Borz, we made it!" She was eager to celebrate their success, to plan the journey they would be taking together through the woods. But no answer came to her summons. Again, she called out. Shouted his name only to hear the echo of her own voice.

Water coursed through a narrow gully, dashing between the lush flora growing from the steep walls. She craned her neck to look upon the beginnings of an archway rising over the ravine, where the sides of the cliff came together, nearly touching. It was here she had crossed in the night, where a tree had fallen over during the storm to span the divide. She measured its height and was astonished, not knowing how she could have survived such a fall. And Borz with her.

The rocks channeled the stream's flow into eddies no deeper than the length of her arm. She dipped her palms into it, dousing her face, washing the grogginess and the grime from her eyes, working the stiffness from her neck. She contemplated how long she had been out and why Borz had wandered off alone. Surely, there was greater safety in numbers.

A stone's throw from the bank, a frill protruded from the surface. She saw her talisman anchored there, hooked by its thread to a tongue of rock, bobbing like a tiny boat. Thanking the Goddess, she walked into the shallow stream, running her fingertips along the creases of the bamboo shoot where the green had peeled and was beginning to split. The cork stopper remained in place, but she did not know whether the halfmen had opened it. She could only trust that her ilm was secure, too afraid to look. Still, even if she had lost her flower, she could ask for no better reminder of home than her brother.

But where is he?

She fastened the talisman to her neck and went in search of him, shouting his name until the air in her lungs gave out. No answer returned but the indifferent sounds of tumbling, spraying water. She sidled along the crag as the ridge continually narrowed and disappeared, leaving only rushing waves and sheer walls on either side. She scraped against the glistening boulders, her feet dipping into the glittering streambed. The water was

numbingly cold but soothing to her wounds,
dissolving the layer of protective silt from her
skin, flowing over the tops of her toes, rising
to her knees and then her thighs. But she kept
on as the current gently tugged at her and the
algae below threatened her balance.

"Borz!"

She clambered over the rocks, watched the
stream grow faster and more dangerous,
before deciding to head back. *He could not
have come this way.*

Where the water deepened, silver shapes
could be seen gliding under the surface,
calling to mind her tussle from the night
before. *Gar.* The fish could expand
indefinitely in size, so long as they avoided
getting eaten. While most of them lived to
become no bigger than her forearm, many
turned into giants, their long, tapering snouts
filling with thorn-like teeth, set in a mouth
that could open to devour a man in a single
bite.

As he made her way back, she spotted
their scattered corpses along the ridge, their
sparkling scales dulling in the sun. The storm
had flooded the region, and where the
channel came together, the gar had surged in
numbers too great for the stream to sustain
them. So long as they had not yet begun to
decay, she and her brother could have them
for a feast. Eat fish until their bellies burst. If
only he could be found.

"BORZ!"

Again and again, she called for him, until she wept his name, until her voice gave out and turned hoarse, breaking to a whisper.

How could he have left her alone? Unless something horrible had happened to him. Did the shaman kill him? Did the wasps chase him off? Did he slip in the river and break his neck?

No.

A small voice spoke in her head. She could make no sense of the words, but the meaning was clear. Looking for Borz was a wasted effort, time better spent on survival. She accepted this intuitively, deeply, like realizing she had been lied to. Only, it was a lie she had told to herself, a reality she willed into being. But she could no longer pretend she did not know the truth, however much it pained her to accept it.

Hunger often made her delusional. Made her see things that were not there. Nicola appeared before her, solid as anything, but her sister had not been real. And in the same way, Borz never materialized to rescue her from her cell. She had done it all herself. She would not find him, not here, not in the Wildwood, because he was nowhere to be found. As always, if she hoped to stay alive, she would have to do it alone.

She fought the urge to sit and weep, to drown herself in longing, returning at last to the dolmen. Empty, drained of all emotion, she set mindlessly to work. The corpse of the halfman was sure to attract scavengers or, worse, others of his kind. So she rolled the body into the water, where he was swept up by the current. She then gathered up the fish that lay dead atop the rocks, throwing the smaller gar over her shoulders while leaving those her size to the carrion. When she had enough to sustain her for a cycle, she set them up on stones to bake in the sun. By midday, she found her ivory dagger, which she had used to stab the shaman, submerged in an alcove.

The ravine offered abundant resources and a clear view of her surroundings. Should any hunter, halfman or otherwise, seek her out, she had only to climb the cliff and go into hiding, or leap into the waves and swim to safety. But she could not ignore the uneasy sensation that someone was watching her, and on more than one occasion, she stopped to catch sight of the interloper, only to see the gentle swaying of the ferns in the clefts of the rock.

By nightfall, exhaustion set in. She had long to eat a proper meal, and as darkness spread over the sky, she warmed herself by her fire and awaited the stars and the blue-green glow of the Greater Moon. The chorus of the Wildwood put her mind at ease, the perpetual trickle of water, the crackling of kindling, the chirp of the crickets, the intermittent howl of unseen prowlers.

She cooked the gar over a bowl of twigs, watching their scales shrivel and turn brown, their glassy eyes lose their luster and shrink to dots. Her mouth moistened as the tangy aroma caught in her nose. *Life for life.* A small prayer, thanks given to the Goddess. She seared her fingertips in her eagerness, peeling the skin from the white flesh beneath, and whatever her fears, doubts, and sorrows at that moment, they all faded in the sating of her hunger.

DAY 135

The Braid branched across a skein of increasingly diminishing streams, tumbling into countless shallow pools, where the rocks churned the water into froth. Here she stood astride two boulders, a foot upon each, the white foaming water below teeming with silvery scales. With her makeshift spear—a whittled branch bound to her dagger—she hoisted the spawning gar onto the rock, where they twisted and leaped until leaping no more.

A ways off, she saw Mother standing in the river with Anja, the gentle flow trickling down from the rocks to pool about their shins. Her sister was tall and beautiful and could not help but admire herself in the water's reflection. She pirouetted from side to side, studying her sinuous shape from every angle, her long white thighs and broad hips, the locks of her hair laced into a single gold thread that swayed from her neck to the curve of her buttocks. Amina, crouched atop a boulder beside them, watched her younger

sibling's performance with a mix of
disapproval and amusement.

They were joined by Jarvn, the neighbor's
son from the Virtanen farmstead. An
elaborate thread of bones circled his neck,
and a shock of chestnut hair masked the left
side of his face. He knew fifteen years and
was eager to jump the fire come the Solstice
festival. Like most boys his age, Jarvn had his
eyes set on Anja. He stood in the rushes with
his spear in hand, the wicker creel at his feet
hopping with his catch, unable to hide his
growing excitement as Anja continued her
display.

Mana caught his eye and shot him an
irritated glance, forcing him to shrink away
before directing her attention to her child.
"Anja! We're here to catch fish, not boys."

"Oh, Mother . . . I'll have men to do that
for me. My husband and my sons."

Without argument, Bryseis thrust a
sharpened length of wood into her daughter's
unwilling grasp. She was not one for wasting
time, but a hard woman of few words and
lesser patience.

The sunlight ducked behind a passing
cloud, dulling the glassy surface of the Braid,
and Anja looked down past her reflection to
the schools of fish darting between her
ankles. "I can't do this!"

"You *can* and you will," her mother
insisted, leaning over her shoulder to guide
her arm.

Jarvn, looking for a reason to be there, fetched Amina a fish from his creel. She picked one out, watched it dance against the rocks until it was motionless, then turned her attention to her sister.

Anja pushed the tapered point through the roiling surface in a half-hearted attempt at skewering something. Her face contorted with disgust as a myriad of aquatic creatures slithered over her toes and across her calves. Amina cupped her mouth to hold back laughter, but eleven-year-old Thelana, watching from across the bank, failed to keep it in. Anja looked as if she might weep, yet her beauty showed through, her watering eyes a dazzling topaz blue in the midday sun.

"I don't see why you brought me here. I still don't see why the boys can't do this."

Jarvn continued to gawk at her, an awkward, absentminded smile spreading over his lips. "You can have some of my tarp, Anja. I've got plenty."

Mana rounded on him like a tiger about to pounce. Thelana had never seen her so furious. "Hurry home, Jarvn! And comb that silly hair of yours."

Torn between yearning and fright, he gathered up his catch and receded back through the rushes. Anja did not watch him go. She knew every boy in Ilmarinen was enamored with her, and admirers were easier to snare than fish.

"Amina," Mother said. "What were you doing with that boy?"

"We were only talking."

"What is there to talk about with *him*? Did he try and touch you?"

Her eldest daughter let out an exasperated sigh. "No, Mana, of course not . . ."

"Good. I don't trust *that* boy. You wouldn't want to have bogren children now, would you?"

"Mana, please!"

Without the neighbor to impress, Anja relaxed into a more natural pose, letting her shoulders drop, her spine come forward, and her ample bosom surrender to its weight. Thelana doubted anyone could think less of her this way, but her sister was adamant that she maintain the illusion of Goddess-like perfection. At least for now, with Jarvn absent, Anja might focus on the lesson while allowing herself to perspire, to sully herself in the muck of the river, to twist her pretty features in consternation.

"Listen . . ." said Bryseis, "high moon is nearly upon us and the larder is only half-stocked. If you ever bothered looking at anything but yourself, you'd notice the harvest getting smaller every year. Someday, the crops may not come in at all, and what will you do then? You must learn other ways to feed yourself, Anja, and if you intend to jump the fire, you must learn responsibility. Becoming a woman means bringing new people into this world, people you will have to provide for. Love is secondary to survival."

"By the Goddess, Mana," Anja said. "You make everything sound so miserable!"

"Life *is* miserable . . . for the unprepared."

Thelana remembered her sister squirming and squealing as her mother endeavored to teach her the proper stance, the most advantageous way to angle her spear, the perfect moment to strike. Anja was repulsed by the whole ordeal, only going through the motions to satisfy her mother's wishes. Whenever Bryseis held the shaft to demonstrate the technique, the tarp appeared to willingly impale themselves on the wood, while Anja found fortune only once, by accident, skewering a minnow no bigger than her hand. Success turned her grumbling into yelps of glee, but the moment was short-lived, expiring as her prize slipped from her grasping fingers the moment she attempted to retrieve it.

The day wore on, the sky turned to ruddy hues, and the tarp grew wise to her family's incursion, dwindling in number until they were gone. Bryseis returned home with her three daughters and a few bony slivers for a family of fourteen.

The familiar ebb and flow of the Braid brought the past into focus, conjuring images of Amina and her mother beating the day's bounty against the rocks, with Anja looking on in horror. Thelana had been innocent at the time and unaccustomed to killing things for food. Even now, there was a finality to watching fish die that never failed to unsettle her.

We struggle as they do, fighting to keep on breathing until we can't. And then it's over. And then our struggle ends.

Thelana could have spent her life in the ravine. Everything she needed was provided for. The tributary sated her thirst and her hunger, and even if her fish were to spoil, they were easy enough to catch, flopping into her palms from the crest of the falls. But the halfmen lived less than a day's hike from her camp, and she did not doubt they would eventually find her. Should she evade their capture, she could not hope to remain in hiding forever, living and dying alone in the wilderness. She had set out from home to find her brother and bring aid to her family. Whether her parents had sent her out to die or not, she would continue on as if she were meant to succeed.

She made her way back over the jagged terrain, swiftly but carefully, so as not to cut her feet or fall into the stream below, returning to the dolmen with a half-dozen impaled fish thrashing from her spear. Her fire had gone cold in the night. She would need to start again, find enough kindling before dark, but first, she would draw a map.

She knelt beside the embers, sifting for useful material. The blackened end of a twig made for a marker, and a flat piece of slate served as a canvas. She outlined the mountains in the north and the Great River

136

coursing south, then paused and backed away. She studied the sketch from different angles. There was something familiar about those lines, those shapes, and she remembered the ghost from the shrine on the night of her escape. The apparition had shown her a similar map, with a maze of sorts displayed along the southwest border.

The halfmen lived east of the Braid. West of the river, she frequently crossed paths with the Tyrant. But here? She did not know for how long she could remain safe, whether the saurian was able to enter the narrow pass or if she risked discovery by leaving. But she could not shake the memory of the map, drawn in the air by the fire of the gods. Could it signify her destination? Lead her to the land of the Outsiders? And Borz? Whatever it was, it lay west of the river, within the hunting grounds of the Tyrant.

DAY 136

Survival meant work. Baba had taught her that lesson on the farm, when he made her pull weeds, shovel and redistribute manure, milk the goats, and hoe tracks of dirt for planting.

Staying alive was a constant struggle even for the hunters in the family. But had it always been that way? Had her ancestors prospered before the rains stopped? Before the land turned brittle and parched? When she was young, standing no taller than her father's waist, she could only remember times of plenty. Days of honey and sesame seeds. Bread and olive oil. Games and laughter.

These thoughts weighed heavily upon her as she explored the ravine for provisions, everything she would need for the coming days. One moment, she was climbing, and the next, wading through frigid waters. But she always moved carefully. Alone in the Wildwood, a single faulty step, a fractured leg bone, could mean a slow death.

She passed a crevice dark with foliage on her return to camp. How far into the hillside the opening went, she could not see. But a disquieting sensation seized her whenever she crossed into that area, a feeling like she was being spied upon. She only ever managed to glimpse a rustling in the nettles, yet her mind filled the gaps, conjuring vague, humanoid shapes. Could they be real? Or were they merely symptoms of her fears?

She kept working, knowing that dwelling on the interlopers could only hinder her progress. From sunrise to moon fall, she gathered brush and clipped branches. She filleted the gar she caught, coating each piece in silt and wrapping them in leaves, and whittled reeds and withe together to fashion a creel to carry them. Borz had taught her how to soften and bend the stems so they would not break. And as she sat under the moons by her fire, her mind turned to his sacrifice and the people who had stolen him.

The Face People were far more akin to the Ilmar than the halfman. Yet, the Outsiders were more clever by far. They possessed resources her people could not replicate, tools stronger than stone, weapons keener than slate, and fine materials to decorate their bodies. When finding them, she would adopt their secrets and return home having learned new ways to survive.

She watched her dying fire as the day's toils pressed on her, lulling her toward oblivion, her bamboo talisman set firmly in her hands. She held it as if she were holding her family in miniature. The hollow stem quelled her loneliness, but she resisted the urge to inspect it. On the day she set out from home, Baba had told her that the ilm was the rarest and most beautiful of all flowers. But was it still? Did anything of her ilm remain?

DAY 137

The gourd grew from a vine near the top of the hill. She groped at the narrow handholds leading up to it, balanced over slips of rock just wide enough to support her feet, and lifted herself higher. Veins of blue and silver cut across the cliff face, strata composed of curled mollusks, horseshoe crabs, and an assortment of petrified saurian wings. At last, she stood within reach of it, her toes clinging precariously to the narrow outcropping as she poked at the plant with her spear.

The fruit plummeted down into the turbulent riffle below, and she raced down after it, catching the gourd before it could be swept away by the wider current. She then cut a hole in its shell with her ivory knife and scooped out its insides. Before leaving the pass, she would fill the gourd from the stream and strap it to a belt she would make from ivy.

She later fashioned a bow out of yew wood, careful to avoid the tree's toxic resin. But the weapon would not penetrate a saurian's hide, or any creature of that size, for she could find nothing in the ravine stronger than fish teeth to make her arrowheads. To the Tyrant, Thelana was insignificant, little more than a buzzing gnat.

The Goddess had not granted the Ilmar claws or horns or immense strength. What was given to her people was cleverness and the hands to make use of it, and to survive west of the Braid, she would need to be clever.

She looked to the arch of stones and the dark cloud rebuilding its nest. Wasps were minuscule compared to most creatures, but she had been afraid to take shelter under the dolmen where they congregated. The Goddess had also given them a gift, and they had used their talent to kill what even she could not.

She collected as many dry plants as she could, building a brush fire near the stone columns of the dolmen, then raked the flames with a mammoth frond. The smoke wafted through the archway and the swarm scattered, flying erratically until their confused, writhing shapes dotted the ground. Quickly, lest they recover and she suffer from their stings, she squatted over the wasps with her knife, cutting the deep-purple ichor from their bellies, thanking them for their gift as they squirmed out their last.

That night, she lay under the flickering faces of Alashiya and Skullgrin, thumbing the talisman about her neck, examining each new item she had made: a bow of yew, a stock of arrows, a spear, a creel of gar, a water-filled gourd, and a pod brimming with venom. And she considered then that she had been wrong after all. While her brother did not appear to rescue her from the halfmen, he had saved her nonetheless. He was saving her still.

DAY 141

Wind flowed unimpeded through the pass, helping keep the flyers away, but by morning she would be waking to a bevy of welts, and by dawn, her eyes would be feeling heavier. She wrestled with her bedding of scale leaves, turning from rash to bruise to sore spot in a desperate attempt to ease her weariness. When her body settled, she counted the stars, which shone more brightly over the ravine. But sleep remained elusive, despite the day's arduous routine. It was her mind, more than her body, keeping her from a night's peace. The intrusive memories swirling tirelessly in her head.

Life is for the young.

She could faintly remember her father uttering those words, when he thought the family was away doing chores. Mana insisted she shelter them from the harsh truths of the world. Children need not be burdened by such concerns, she would say. Her parents kept it all secret, every misfortune they knew to fear, every calamity to befall them.

Thelana watched her father's angst grow
with every passing year, when the earth failed
to produce, until the day he seemed to break—
break with the realization that a husband and
wife can labor until blood and sweat stream
in equal measures and still lose everything.

The truth could not be hidden from the
children indefinitely. Thelana caught bits and
pieces from her parents' hushed exchanges
and learned what she could from gossiping
neighbors. *Did you hear? The family across
the river buried their third child. Did you
know? The couple up the hill had to eat their
infant daughter. Cut her up and served her
with vegetables.* Nobody could ever be sure
what was real and what were the workings of
their fearful imagination. She doubted even
Baba knew the whole story. But in her youth,
Thelana had understood that such things
weren't supposed to happen, couldn't happen
in a child's world—the Goddess blessed those
who persevered and were brave. She now
believed differently. Her parents' assurances
had been a comfort to them, a way to preserve
their innocence for a time, and Thelana never
faulted them for it.

If there was ever vitality in her father, a
sense of adventure, time had beaten it out of
him. Baba was now a shell of his old self and
could never have survived the Wildwood.
Only Thelana could have gone out into the
woods. When Borz was traded for a season's
grain, no one in her family possessed her
strength, experience, or the obstinacy of her

youth. Life was, indeed, for the young, and survival for those who believe better days lay ahead.

A hazy light filled the ravine, the rising sun suffusing through the morning fog, and the world took on an otherworldly appearance. She knelt beside the stream to rinse the dryness from her mouth and wipe the crust from her eyes. At the start of day, a cold splash never failed to wake her senses. She then combed her hair of gravel, leaves, and needles, which collected during the night, before securing her braid again.

She gazed over the ever-changing stream, watched the water split over the rocks into a dozen tributaries, delivering schools of fish in a cascade of colors. A silver length suddenly emerged from a niche under the surface. The thumb-sized minnows scattered from the snapping barbs of its mouth, the gar desperately thrashing in pursuit of them, thrashing to no avail. Alone, the smaller fish were vulnerable, but their numbers had outwitted their attacker. The Goddess was trying to teach her a lesson, she could see, if only she were patient enough to hear it, to focus her mind on the present and not dawdle on the past. But was she the predator in this example or the prey?

She walked a short distance to the circle of stones marking her camp. More fish, she thought with a sigh. What she had been so grateful to receive nearly a cycle ago, she was beginning to loathe. But having a choice in what to eat, she reminded herself, was a luxury.

She ate briefly, eager to set out from camp, sucking the fat from the seared carcass she had left on the coals, praying that the strength from the gar was enough to sustain her journey. But she did not know how far she would have to travel before reaching her destination or even what her destination might look like. The Outsiders' homeland was entirely foreign. Did they live in trees like her people? Or in straw huts like the halfmen? All she knew was that she had spent too long in the ravine, her resolve softened by easy access to food and water.

When all her provisions were prepared, she returned to the silt deposits gathering along the riverbank. She slathered herself in greens and browns until her body turned invisible against the backdrop of the forest. When the viscous layer hardened to clay against her skin, she carved patterns into her thighs and hips and along her ribcage, abstracts of every creature felled by her hands: the chobo, the turtle, the gazelle, the shaman, even the voorgaven. Every encounter had tempered her in some way, had made her stronger, like a piece of slate hammered to the fine point of a spear.

What Thelana most feared was not the Tyrant, but a life without consequence, surviving to an infirm age as a solitary denizen of the wild, never to set eyes upon a familiar face. But the King of the Wildwood made her hesitate, doubt what was possible, as did the unseen humanoids leering at her from the trees.

Who were they?

She could only draw from her people's stories, from the record of their history in the Painted Caves, and the myths they shared on Solstice Night. *Alashiya's firstborn was the giantess, Wizzeria,* the High Priest recited, *who represents trickery, who can be seen by the light of the lesser, violet moon. When the Goddess brought new children into the world, Wo and Man, Wizzeria became jealous, and in her jealousy, she mocked the Goddess's creation, joining brother and sister together in the flesh to make bogren.*

She remembered Aliaa telling her how humans were cousins to many species. But which of them was stalking her from the trees? Could they be bogren, the progeny of Wizzeria? Or vengeful halfmen eager to ambush her?

Enough.

Her imagination was like a poison crippling her mind. Escaping the halfmen had been a gift of the Goddess. She could not waste that freedom by cowering. If she were not determined to move on, to seek the place from the map branded to her memory, she would live out the remainder of her days in hiding.

Mustering her courage, she gathered up her supplies and made for the narrow opening leading out from the ravine. The break was narrow, hidden behind a veil of ferns and bracken. She pushed through it, drawing her arms close to her sides, as morning dew shook from the mammoth fronds, dripping from her scalp to her backside. She hated tight spaces, the feeling of being confined, dreading what might happen should a snake or spider appear where she was unable to maneuver. But if an opening awaited her at the opposite end of the crag, she was determined to find it.

She turned sideways to squeeze through the defile as stratified limestone pressed on her, scraping her knees and shoulder blades, caking her brows with dust. The jagged edges caught in the twine holding her equipment, nearly tearing her quiver and gourd from her body. She extended her arm, her questing fingers probing the rock face, groping blindly as she sidled through the pass. And still, the walls narrowed, until she doubted whether she would even fit or be forced to turn back around.

Something was drawing her onward. She could hear it now. The deep woods with its calling birds, croaking frogs, and chirping crickets. She could feel the change in her skin, the breath of life in the air.

At last, she emerged from the hillside and into another world. Or so that is how it seemed. This part of the Wildwood was unlike anywhere she knew, more a well-tended garden than a forest. A canopy of leaves obscured the sky, leaving great sunlight shafts to penetrate down through the verdant expanse like great golden columns. Many of the plants were strange to her, the browns and greens so common to her experience supplanted by bright oranges, vivid blues, and rich shades of purple. Her camouflage was less effective here than in other parts of the woods, but there was greenery enough to take advantage of it.

She stepped lightly, the haft of her spear tight in her hands, the rich soil sinking under her feet. Leafy shadows patterned the uneven terrain of nettles, beard moss, and clovers. She recognized the kinds of fauna that thrived under heavy rainfall: towering palms, veiny banyans, and giant kapoks with their smooth curving trunks. But there were just as many oddities to be discovered: mushrooms taller than herself and flowers the size of trees. She proceeded from one marvel to the next, intoxicated by their strange forms, beautiful colors, and pungent smells. A white-violet hibiscus stretched wide enough to cover her head. A yellow tongue stood twice her height, wrapped in a single, twirling, indigo petal. A broad-faced flower with red-orange spots gaped open, its mouth sprouting tendril-like stamens, reeking like a decomposing carcass. She might have used it for a bed if not for the smell.

The ravine was far behind her now. Turning back, she would never find her way. She was lost, lured by the variety and abundance of living forms, her doubts and the weight of her past receding from her mind.

Butterflies the size of eagles drifted overhead. Colonies of ladybugs as fat as her fists hopped from a giant caterpillar—long as an ox—as it scurried past her. A trickle of water, smaller than a brook, seeped up from a subterranean reservoir. She bent down to drink, her knees turning cold and wet, but hesitated. The liquid had a silvery tinge to it she did not like. This is what's feeding the plants, she thought, which must be affecting the animals that eat them.

The sun grew heavier in the sky, and the turquoise light of the Greater Moon was beginning to filter down through the trees. How had the day passed so quickly? Did time itself act differently here? Or merely her perception of it? Either way, night was fast descending, and she did not wish to go looking for a campsite in the dark.

But she was unnerved by what she did not know and could not see. She could hide in the hills in the ravine, while the low-lying gully provided ample viewing of her surroundings. Here, the garden's lushness blinded her to everything beyond arm's reach. She had found safety in the tallest trees in the north. But the banyans offered little sanctuary, sagging to the ground with their ropey limbs. She could walk their manifold boughs, easily reach the tops of their branches, and any predator could find her. For all she knew, she might unwittingly camp beside a nest of carnivores and be devoured in her sleep. The garden appeared innocuous, yet she did not trust it. Killers lurked in every habitat, and if she did not see them, it meant only that they were better at hiding.

She sat under the iridescent blue-red petals of an enormous flower. It sprouted from a yellow-spotted mound of emerald sphagnum and long-stemmed mushrooms. There, she removed her quiver and creel, and set her bow and spear and gourd to the ground. It was a tremendous relief. The weight of her supplies made the muscles in her neck and shoulders sore, and the twine used to carry them drew lines into her flesh.

As the Greater Moon filled the gaps in the treetops, the air turned clammy, and she could not keep from shuddering. She needed a good fire, but every branch she tested proved damp. Nothing she could find would burn, and the temperature continued to drop. She then looked to the giant flower under which she had taken shelter. The petals were firm and silky to the touch, and if she were to wrap herself in them, she might make a kind of cocoon for herself, a protective layer like the Face People used. Before setting out from home, Mother had given her something similar to wear, a frock made from a goat. But she had hated the constant way it grated against her. She never understood the need for an extra skin when she was not an Outsider, and thirty days into the Wildwood, her mother's frock turned moldy and fell apart, and she was only too happy to abandon it. Still, absent proper shelter, she preferred the flower's touch to shivering in the night.

One by one, the golden columns of the sun diminished as green-blue moonlight washed softly over every leaf and clover. She drew a knee to her chin, taking occasional swigs from her gourd, her senses keen to every stirring leaf. A wall of hedges, an ideal hiding place for small predators, germinated a stone's throw from where she lay. She kept watch as the night bore on, fondling her talisman, a hand ready at the spear across her thighs. But her many sleepless nights, all those restless passings thinking about her father, were beginning to take their toll, and her pupils drifted, losing their focus.

No!

She shook herself awake. Falling unconscious posed too significant a risk. Something lived in those trees; she could sense them on the back of her neck. When she squinted hard enough, she could almost make them out. Their silhouettes in the green.

"I see you," she muttered to herself. "But you're not going to kill me. Not if I kill you first."

When her eyes fluttered open again, she found herself in a far more alien and wondrous environment. In the dark of eclipse, the garden blazed with its own light, the blue fungi giving off a faint azure glow, the enormous petals radiating purple, the tips of the leaves emitting jade. The spots on the frogs, and the diamond shapes on the tails of the lizards, shone just as brilliantly, as did the flyers with the golden fires in their bellies that swarmed from tree to tree like living embers.

She was too awestruck to be afraid and could think of nothing but to run about like a giddy toddler. And for a time, she did just that, abandoning her equipment to snatch up glowing plants and catch fireflies in her palms. She roamed without care, ever deeper into the garden, not once considering where she might end up or how she might return. Her perpetual dread of the Wildwood, and the responsibility she carried for herself and her family, were too cumbersome to endure without some respite. At least for now, she would cast it all aside. Rid herself of every trapping and let fate come as it may.

She woke with a start, dropping sharply into a pool of rainwater. It lapped against her knees, murky and numbingly cold in the damp night air. How had she been so reckless, so blind, not to notice it? She pulled herself free and stepped away. The surrounding glow lit upon the dark shape of the trench. And as her mind settled on what she was seeing, she came to the slow, awful realization that she had seen that shape before.

"No . . ." she murmured. "Not here. Not here!"

She reached for her spear, only to discover she was without it. She then hurried back from whence she came, as swiftly as she was able, the earth sodden under her feet, the slick maple leaves turning against her toes, offering little traction. A rumbling followed in her ears. Tremors rattled the bones of her legs. A dark shape was in pursuit of her, tall enough to blot out the stars and moons. She could not hope to outpace it, for each of its strides counted for several of hers. Seized with terror, she stumbled, and her face sank into the damp soil. The creature lumbered over her. She gathered herself awkwardly, her knees buckling with nervous energy, catching sight of teeth, serrated teeth like curving knives—the meat-threshing knives of the Tyrant. She wheeled on her heels and made for its tail, slipping between its thighs as those teeth came down to snap her in half.

To survive this, she would need to hide, not run. She dashed for the hedgerow not three paces away as the Tyrant circled, its sweeping tail tearing flowers from their roots and toadstools from their bases. But the wall of foliage was denser than she had hoped—an impenetrable mass of tangled stems and branches. If only she had not been so reckless in leaving her spear and bow behind, she might have cut through it or given herself a chance to fight. Without tools, ilma were powerless, and without a weapon, she was helpless. She twirled around, desperately searching for a means of escape, but was forced into the shrubs. Thorns dug into her spine as she retreated against the hedgerow, the Tyrant advancing upon her, fully emerging under the moonlight. The mere sight of the saurian, its enormity, its gaping maw, was enough to make her heart fail. Without anywhere to run or hide, she could do nothing but wait, wait for its teeth to dip into her flesh.

She wondered if it would be quick. How badly it would hurt. And she lamented that she would never find her brother.

A strange thing happened then that she did not fully comprehend. The plants impeding her passage opened to receive her, drawing her in until she was enveloped. She stared out through an aperture of twigs, like a hare hiding from a cat, as the Tyrant lumbered about in confusion.

Her breathing came in hard, painful gasps. She was sure the Tyrant could hear it, if not the erratic drumming of heart, and that at any moment, the reptilian-bird mouth would burst through the thin wall separating them. But its minuscule mind did not linger on things unseen, and after a short while and with little fanfare, the saurian wandered off.

She waited for a time, like a terror-stricken bird in its nest, fearing the Tyrant's return. Waited until her heart quieted and her wheezing became a steady drone, before finally daring to step out from the wall of plants, which allowed for her egress just as it opened to receive her.

For a long while, she stood dumbfounded by what had transpired. She was certain the hedge was too dense for her to pass. Even now, at her touch, it seemed in every way impregnable. Yet, the garden had protected her.

Yes, it was the garden itself.

Too weary to think, she decided not to question it further. She was too tired for mysteries, wanting nothing more than to return to her supplies, perhaps rest a while, if she could calm her heart enough to do so.

Before starting back, she absently moved her fingers across the bare spot of her throat, where her collarbones met, and was shocked by the emptiness there. Her talisman, her bamboo casing, was missing. In her erratic flight from the Tyrant, it had come loose, was perhaps snagged by a branch.

The garden was luminous, brighter than the moons on a clear night, yet finding her talisman would be difficult, if not impossible. Deep wells of shadow permeated her surroundings, abutting the faint glow of the fungi. Still, she could not hope for daybreak. Her ilm was all she had of home. She retraced her steps, scouring every speck of dirt, and would continue her search until sunrise if need be. Search until she collapsed.

She discovered only fragments, a broken shell from a bamboo shoot, stomped into the ground by the saurian's feet. What remained of the rest was nearly unrecognizable, plant matter mired in black, damp, and wilted. She bent over an olive sliver, a hint of orange, a smear of violet.

". . . the most rare and beautiful of flowers," Baba said, plucking the ilm from the porch. Delicately placing it in her hand. Closing her fingers over the soft colors as tears streamed from her cheeks. "Beautiful like my daughters."

She collapsed, pinching the remains between her thumb and forefinger. "Everything . . ." she sobbed. "I've lost everything now. I have nothing left . . ."

Sorrow swelled in her bosom, overwhelmed her senses. How could such a little thing mean so much to her? What value did it have, truly, other than the value she had given it? The ilm was a reminder of her slowly dying homeland, a reminder of aging and death. She was a fool to have wanted it, to have kept it, knowing what it would become, knowing how its colors could only wash away with the coming days, wilt to nothing as all things must. Yet she could find no solace in the inevitable. She had clung to what she had been given to cling to, an imaginary bit of home, a magic totem. But she had nothing to hold to now, and at that moment, she thought only to seek out the Tyrant. Throw herself before its merciful teeth and be done with her struggles.

A humanlike shadow passed over the moonlight, and she knew she was not alone in her sorrow. Someone, or something, stood beside her. A tingling in her pores, coupled with the flowery scent of gardenias, hinted at its presence. But what she saw when she raised her eyes was impossibly thin, a creature with a spine for a waist—a tree branch for a spine—leaving no volume for intestinal organs. He was all lungs—if the thing she was looking at was a *he*—with skin the texture of leaves, a scalp and chin speckled with moss, and lichen hanging down from his loins as a man might have hair.

She gazed long at him, at a face devoid of a mouth, at his long tapering nostrils, into the still black pools of his eyes, and she was curiously unafraid. The green man lowered his unusually elongated arms, and his stick-like forefinger stretched, like a rapidly growing shoot, to soak the tears from her cheeks, which he seemed to drink like a plant.

Others of his kind emerged from the lush places of the garden. They had been there, perfectly camouflaged, studying her. Dozens gathered about her now, staggering like infants unaccustomed to bipedal motion, their limbs creaking like old trees in the wind. And the one who stood nearest her reached into her palm, where she kept what little remained of her home. Then slowly, ever so slowly, she watched the fragments of her ilm coalesce, shiver into life, and sprout again.

DAY 142

She remembered the tale of the *Stillfolk*, whom her people also called the *Green People*, and *the gardeners*.

When an infant is born in silence, never wailing when she exits the womb, never taking its first breath of Life, the still form is wrapped in the tendrils of a specific kind of root. The High Priestess buries the bundle in rich soil like a seedling in the ground. After nine cycles, the pod takes shape, reaching up from the earth with a shoot-like arm until the entire body emerges, neither plant nor animal, but as one of the Stillfolk.

While Thelana had never heard of any such thing happening to anyone she knew, she could not deny the evidence of her eyes. The myth proved true, fanciful as it seemed. Stillfolk had saved her from the Tyrant and restored her ilm to bloom.

She spent the following morning learning everything she could of her new companions and most of the afternoon trying, often with frustration, to communicate with them.

"What is your name?"

He or she made no sound, gave no hint of understanding, yet she could feel them contemplating her. She sensed a deep welling of intelligence behind those eyes, a wisdom borne of decades or multiple centuries, for all she knew. They reminded her of the Keepers. The Ilmarin elders possessed the same look on their wizened faces when reciting an old ballad or passing sage words from generations gone.

"I am Thelana," she tried again, her fingers pressed into her breastbone. "*Thelana.*"

The plant-animal hybrid simply stared. They all did. She could feel their curiosity and suspected—hoped, really—they wished to know more about her. Or was she confusing her emotions for theirs?

"You . . .?" She gestured from her bosom to his. "What do I call *you?*" She over-enunciated every word in a slow, deliberate tone, as if she were conversing with a two-year-old. But even a small child would have responded to her in some way. He gave her nothing. Perhaps, she had asked the wrong question.

Do they even have identities? A sense of self? Does the tree ever think to itself, "I am," or is that a human idea?

Lids gradually extended over its eyes, like moth wings camouflaged to look like leaves, and its head tilted ever so slightly in what she took for a nod. But no names were offered.

And she started to wonder then about her own place in the world.

Am I still Thelana if nobody calls me that?

The *gardeners*, as she preferred to call them, were sexless, speechless, and exuded a strong scent like sap mixed with bark. They were composed of arms and legs and a torso with a solitary head. But despite their humanlike configuration, they were sometimes difficult to separate them from their surroundings. Their appendages were long and sinuous, and she sometimes mistook a thigh for a trunk, a forearm for a bough, fingers for branches.

A stemlike abdomen, no broader around than her leg, suggested they were without a digestive system of any kind, without stomachs or intestines or kidneys or bladders. Not a single organ for the processing of food. Basking under the sky, they fed directly from the sun's warmth while absorbing other nutrients through the roots of their feet. She thought of all the work she put in to stay alive—acquiring food, preserving food, and digesting food—and was tempted to trade her humanity to become a plant. But the Stillfolk's way of existing was not without its drawbacks. Proving true to their namesake, they moved imperceptibly slow, like the bud of a flower that turns to drink in the light. Yet the gardeners were not incapable of sudden motion when the need called for it. Their upper bodies were shaped much like her own, possessing the mammalian furnaces necessary for power, drawing air into their robust lungs through the oversized nostrils in their faces.

Even as she grew accustomed to their presence, the gardeners remained reclusive, lingering at the edges of her perception like the imagined shapes she and her siblings might see in a cloud or a patch of bark. Often, when she thought herself alone with one, many more came to her notice, their subtle outlines becoming more distinct as they materialized from the bushes. But the unease she had felt in the ravine when she suspected they were observing her, was replaced by a sense of security, a comfort she had not known since leaving home. The gardeners were gentle, timid beings, as incapable of cruelty as a fig tree. They knew only curiosity and community, and she longed to commune with them however she could.

Having no mouths and no ears, the gardeners communicated using body language and sometimes symbols. Likewise, she scrawled images into the dirt, forming lines for the river, arrowhead shapes for the mountains, and simple contours for the animals. Answers to her most basic questions came after passings. The waiting made her storm about in circles and stomp her feet, as if the Stillfolk could be hurried. But she eventually came around to their methods, relearning what to expect when interacting with other intelligent beings.

Nick Alimonos

She thanked the Goddess for their
company, despite her frustration, for
creatures whose faces she could almost
mistake for human in the dim light, whom
she could be confident existed in reality, for
her imagination did not lend itself to such
creativity.

When symbols and gestures failed them,
she continued tirelessly into the night,
craving companionship, needing to speak and
be heard, even as they stood about like lifeless
effigies, showing no sign of empathy. She
described fleeting fragments of home,
precious moments she held to: the Braid
streaming like white webbing from the hills
of Ukko; the lavender fields where her
siblings liked to hide in; her Baba, drenched in
sweat, tugging at the harrow with his muscled
arms as their ox lay beside their silo with a
twisted hoof. She told them of her foray into
the Wildwood, how the Tyrant stole her
chobo, how the halfmen kept her for a pet,
and how she escaped from their village. The
gardeners remained rooted, never blinking,
their eyes shimmering like pools of tar. They
nodded whenever she emphasized one part or
another, responding solely to the emotions in
her voice. And she pretended they were
longtime friends. Because she needed them to
be so.

165

DAY 143

The voorgaven snaked from the water, lunging at her hungrily, clamping down on her in a spray of blood. Pain overwhelmed her senses as the small bones of her ankle were nearly shorn from the leg.

Her flight from the Tyrant had been taxing, bringing old wounds to the fore of her mind. It was heartbreaking to discover that it still hurt, that what she thought fully mended would never be the same. But the river snake had also given her a gift. She sat on a mammoth leaf with her back against the curving bole of a kapok tree, tenderly probing the hard knot over her foot, the scar crossing from the base of her fibula to the bundle of nerves above the heel. Her brothers—Borz most of all—would have envied such a mark. It would make for a great story, or better yet, a song for the ages. One for her children and theirs. Her body was like the inside of the caves, her unhealed flesh the paint that told her story, reminding her of what she had suffered and overcome. Those marks would never fade, but beauty was of no consequence in the Wildwood, she reminded herself.

Her flighty sisters came laughing into her consciousness, the way they fussed over the coming Solstice, gossiping over who might be pairing with whom. She remembered Anja, who fussed endlessly over her braid, and primped herself with garlands and beads of lapis lazuli. A scar like the one Thelana bore would have devastated her.

She slowly lifted from her seat as an intense burning sensation coursed through the nerves of her ankle. The pain would force her to move differently, shift her weight to her opposite foot, which could only slow her down. A step taken too late or too early, she mused, the length of her foot, could get her eaten.

The language of pain, how her body responded to it, was evident to the gardeners. Proving sensitive to her needs, they bound her ankle with twine and brought her bulbs of yarrow to dull the worst of the burning.

That night, her attempt at making fire was met with disapproval. The Stillfolk rearranged their faces into disapproving masks at the first sign of smoke, their shoulders going slack to evoke sadness, and after a quarter-passing, they raised their arms in a show of anger. Ultimately, she was forced to eat her smoked gar cold and seek warmth by other methods, under silky layers of frond-sized petals. Snuggly wrapped like a caterpillar in its cocoon.

DAY 150

Days passed strangely in the garden. The vivid, otherworldly colors, the sweet yet pungent gardenia-fragrance of the flowers, the way the sunlight filtered down through the pink and purple canopy of petals, all combined to make her feel lightheaded. It was like walking through an airy dream, and her feet, going about their motions, went nowhere, circling and circling even as the sights and sounds enveloping her continually shifted and morphed.

The gardeners acted as her guides and protectors, working with the efficiency of bees, trading her from one individual to the next, relaying information invisibly through smells, through the pheromones they excreted. When confronted with anything that might cause her harm, they demonstrated a strength of purpose she had not suspected in them.

Many fungi proved edible, while others responded to her approach in volatile ways. The *shriekers*, as she later called them, stood tall as a stump. They were pink and purple and emitted an ear-splitting wail from the cavities in their domed caps. The cacophony forced her to run in the opposite direction while covering her ears. Even Baldr's infant tantrums could not have prepared her for such a noise. The *belcher* toadstool, all the while, released noxious fumes, causing her to sneeze and choke, and her eyes to burn. Still, many more mushrooms, that clumped like parasitic growths from the cavities of the trees, glowed with a faint azure hue when the sun dipped below the treetops. The taste of them made her giddy and forgetful.

An innocuous-looking bush growing from the top of an escarpment was the greatest danger in the garden, she learned, and if not for her guides, she would never have known to fear it. The plant's heart-shaped leaves molted with needle-like crystals too small to see. Should she have brushed her hand over the leaf, the crystals would have embedded themselves under her skin, inducing a lifetime of agony. She did not appreciate the severity of the warning until seeing the carcasses, the young fawns who had flung themselves over the rise to end their misery. It forced her to reassess her beliefs, to reconsider the Goddess's benevolence. *How can such a plant exist?*

If Alashiya had given birth to all living things, why would she allow for such cruelty? Or was this plant, like the Tyrant, a mistake the Great Mother had yet to rectify? Perhaps that task—pacifying the worst of Nature's brood—was given to the ilma.

Aliaa would have loved to explore the garden. She was always going on about the different kinds of wild plants and creatures she found, excitedly describing them to anyone who would listen. Her search for new lifeforms sent her to the far reaches of Ilmarinen, knowing the further she traveled from home, the more foreign the discovery. Her sister could identify things even Baba did not recognize. But Thelana doubted she would have been able to name the garden's more exotic denizens, the giant flowers or the luminescent mushrooms. Rather than fear the *agony bush*, as Thelana dubbed it, she imagined her sister would have been fascinated, carefully sampling its poisonous leaves to add to her collection. And a yearning to share these discoveries with her sibling welled up in the pit of her being, knowing that Aliaa would never see them.

Having finished what was left in her creel, Thelana feasted on berries, nuts, apricots, and mangoes. Juices ran from the corners of her lips, her tongue quivering with every bite, the unexpected sweetness drowning her with delight. The gardeners introduced other forms of vegetation to her diet, fruits she had no names for, like the long yellow berry with its thick peel and mushy insides. And when she had had her fill, they brought her a honeycomb dripping with golden nectar, with a dozen or more confused bees still clinging to it.

The Stillfolk were aware of human digestion, but their offerings felt more and more lacking after her first night in the garden. Protein abounded in the form of giant dragonflies and centipedes she could sit on if she were in a daring mood, but insects left a bitter taste in her mouth, and the texture of their exoskeletons on her tongue filled her throat with bile.

The yellow pistil of the *titan flower* towered over her like a pair of thighs pointing to the sky, the purple, pleated petals curving about its central stalk serving to fend against dragon mosquitoes and other flyers. Now, as darkness deepened over the garden and biters came out to nibble at her flesh, she thought of the goatskin her mother had given her. The petals of her bed, while less durable than her mother's frock, were much softer to the touch and would make for suitable *clothes. Yes, I think that was the word*... Still, the idea of a secondary skin was abhorrent to her, and as she climbed into her sleeping position, wrapped tightly in the confines of the titan flower, she promised herself she would never become like the Outsiders. Never become so frail that she could not count herself among her people.

DAY 151

I n the long, idle stretches of the day, she sat with legs crossed under a bodhi tree. The Stillfolk liked to gather here, sometimes for cycles, without moving, wasting no energy. Despite her restless, mammalian heart, she learned to quiet the ramblings of her mind, to still the voices of doubt troubling her sleep.

The Wildwood abounded with ballads of woe and wonder, with the love songs of nesting birds and the chattering of crickets, with termites scratching out their homes in the wood, with ants marching on saplings pushing up through the soil. An unseen world flourished beyond her and within her. So long as she lived in the present, so long as she cared enough to listen, the whole of existence was open to her.

There was no separation between herself and Aenya. Only one breath. One entity. The Goddess in all her myriad manifestations.

DAY 153

She sat in a luminous grove, a cloud of living embers dancing over her head as Stillfolk thronged about her, their gnarled limbs swaying with urgency.

Her hybrid friends were not as selfless as they first appeared. This became more apparent as the days passed, as she further explored the garden. They needed her to embark upon some quest, to do what they could not with their botanical limitations. Only, she could not decipher their gestures.

She carved the Tyrant into the bodhi tree, and the one she thought of as their chieftain—the gardener who had revived her flower—responded with his own sign, a broken circle enclosing her sketch. What did the ring signify? Did they intend to trap the saurian? Build a wall to keep it out?

Daylight spilled in bright golden patches across her shoulders as she made her way to the garden's edge. She stood looking northeast. The ground was spongy with fallen flora, crackling and slimy beneath her feet. Layers of leaves, petals, and stems were decomposing one atop the other, giving off a faint rotting smell like very old eggs. She climbed the gradual incline, her heels growing sodden, the remains of a dying garden still clinging to her, patterning her skin.

The giant fungi and titanic flowers native to the region were nowhere to be seen from the peak of the embankment, shying from the advancing plain. Stillfolk stood in verdant recesses like sentinels, invisible to eyes not trained in seeing them. They were waiting for something. Watching as they perpetually did.

A sphagnum-caked banyan peered over the edge of the garden. Thickly braided vines cascaded from it, allowing her to swing up and up, the branches thinning to little more than rustling stems at the top. She squatted in the boughs high above, the truncheon of her spear ready in her hand, her breath rising fiercely, her every pore tightening. A dragon mosquito drifted to her neck and she squashed it, bloodying the fingers of her free hand, never turning her gaze from the sprawling vista below.

Lumbering giants shook the ground, stomped saplings into pulp, snatched antelopes in their jaws like crickets in a rooster's beak. A roving pair of tyrants, a male and a female—*there are two of them!*—wandered too closely for her liking but took no notice of her. Yet the carnivores were not alone. Reptilian creatures snaked and stalked and pounced across the rugged terrain. She saw feathery chobos, and frilled herbivores she did not know existed, and saurian-bird hybrids with arrowhead-beaks that glided through the air on leathery wings.

It occurred to her that the Tyrant she had met a cycle ago was not native to the area but an invader from outside the garden. "There is a *balance* to all living things," Father told her. "Everything has its place, its role to play, in the grand scheme of the Goddess." She had stood no taller than his waist at the time. "Should every Smilodon be killed off, the deer would grow too plentiful, and then what would they eat? And yet, without the leaf-eaters, the carnivores would also perish." She had only seen tigers in the Painted Caves, but understood Baba's lesson well enough. The balance of nature had to be preserved. Only, the land of the Stillfolk was devoid of large animals of any kind, save for the insects, who subsisted on the dead and decomposing. The Tyrant posed no threat to the garden, but prey fleeing from a predator could remain there in hiding to ruin the delicate balance.

Aenya was transforming, slowly but inevitably, toward greater hardship. What drove her people into hunger—colder winds, longer suns, shorter rainfalls—affected the outside world as well. The garden was like her ilm, a beautiful but rare oddity, an exotic niche in the enormity of the Wildwood. She did not doubt that, in ages past, the garden spread over a much greater area. Now, the Stillfolk dwelling within it were dying off, dwindling into myth, and a great sadness stirred in her at the thought. Could her own people fade into myth the same way? Would strangers from a far-flung future wonder if the Ilmar had ever lived?

Thelana was certain she could do nothing to help the gardeners defend their home from invasive species. She had barely escaped with her life after her last encounter with the saurian. How could she consider facing another? The Tyrant was more than an apex predator. It was a relentless killer, the embodiment of voracious hunger. Whatever she intended back at the ravine, however she planned to combat the King of the Wildwood, it all fell apart when confronted with the reality of its power, its size, and its teeth.

DAY 155

The day was vivid and clear, and a southerly wind carried long-familiar scents down from the ghostly peaks on the horizon. Her braid came alive in the sudden rush, coiling and snapping like a wild serpent. Woven into her auburn locks, the gardeners had set her ilm.

She could not permit herself to rest, to be made complacent by the company of her silent friends and the sweet delights of the garden. Her brother was out there, waiting for her, perhaps in dire need.

With the Greater Moon rising in the east and the map clear in her mind, she oriented north, knowing she would need to trek through saurian country if she were to ever reach the settlement of the Face People. But she was also driven by the need to ingest more substantive fare than plant offerings, and to that end, she took up her weapons and a bundle of arrows and her container of wasp venom, and set out from the garden.

A trickle of silver-tinted water fed into the lush grove from a long shallow basin, but she

did not trust it, and made for higher ground.
She walked along the ridge, sighting a pair of
gliders, her name for the saurians with the
leathery wings. They were riding the gale,
moving too swiftly for her to arm her bow, so
she ran at them, blindly hurling her spear.
The shaft flew up in a long arc and came
down again. But the gliders continued on,
oblivious to her presence. She scrambled
down the ridge, watching their shapes
diminish into the clouds, as she looked for the
weapon she had thrown away.

The turquoise moon dominated the clear
cobalt sky in the east as she ascended to the
top of the grassy slope, where she hoped to
survey the lay of the land. But what she saw
there, crowning the peak of the hill, nearly
stole her breath.

A white elk stood before her, wearing the
most elaborate headdress she had ever seen.
She resisted the impulse to draw her bow,
startled by so strange and unexpected a sight.
The beast was majestic beyond measure, its
fur gleaming, immaculate, white as the foam
of a crashing wave. Its antlers branched six
feet apart or more, radiating like stars under a
velvet sky, like the limbs of a tree silvered by
the moon. She climbed with delicate steps,
her weapon slack against her thigh, near
enough to touch the animal. The elk did not
flinch from her touch, almost as if he had
been expecting her. She was awestruck, like a
young girl who looks upon Creation with

fresh eyes, driven by the irresistible urge to touch and know.

"Goddess."

She murmured it aloud, her voice hoarse, sounding foreign to her ears. He offered no reply but gazed hard upon her, his eyes scintillating like the constellations.

The elk was like something escaped from her dreams, a primordial memory long forgotten, like her own birth. This was no mere animal, she knew, but a divine being. An avatar of the Goddess.

There were times when Alashiya took physical form. She appeared in the guise of a unicorn, a phoenix, or sometimes even a man or woman. These were her sacred animals, which the Ilmar were forbidden to hunt. Before Thelana stood another of her guises, chief among deer kind, the *archenelk*.

After all these days? After so much toil and torment? Why visit me now? What good can you do me now?

She could feel the anger rising in her throat, yet she forced it down, swallowed it. Alashiya's ways were strange beyond mortal comprehension, and Thelana was not one to question them.

The archenelk nuzzled her palm with a moist snout that fogged the air between them. His pelt felt soft and silky, and the warmth emanating from his throbbing frame soothed her scabrous fingers. She was seized by a sudden urge to embrace him, aching with the longing to be held by someone or something, to wallow in the smooth fibers of his bosom with her face pressed against it. Yet she sensed no enchantment. No divine power. Nothing to signify the elk was anything but an animal. Only the uncanny way he reacted to her presence, her caresses, suggested he was anything more.

He turned north, his sweeping horns nearly knocking her over, and she followed. The woods dropped into a broad sward of short sloping hills and low-hanging trees. They traveled exposed under a cloudless sky, the sun hard against her scalp and shoulders. She sidled as near to him as she could, matching his graceful strides. Not since the Woollyhorn Savannah had she had to endure such heat, and by midday, she felt her strength begin to wane and the dull aching of her ankle intensify with every step.

Angular hills silhouetted the horizon, like tall manmade shapes in the distance, and her heart fluttered with hope, with the thought that she may soon reach the Outside and find the people who had stolen her brother. But she was growing weary and no longer able to keep pace with the elk.

Seeing she was lagging behind, the beast paused to lower his neck. The tuft of his fur poked up like a cirrus cloud from between his ears and shoulder blades. She wanted to run her hands through it, not understanding the gesture, until she remembered the pictures in the caves. Her people did not ride animals. So when she first saw depictions of riders, she

mistook them for a single creature, an
amalgamated monstrosity, with the torso of a
man and the lower body of an aurochs. Baba
had had to explain the scene. Before the age
of agriculture, her ancestors hunted from the
backs of four-legged beasts. It had seemed
cruel to her at the time. But now, this avatar
of the Goddess—if that was his true nature—
was inviting her to do the same. Accepting
the offer felt wrong, blasphemous. Thelana
could go on. Her legs were not so weary that
she needed to burden the elk with her weight.
But the sun continued to draw every bit of
moisture from her flesh. She would soon need
water and shelter to rest in.

She gripped his horns timidly, setting her
foot awkwardly atop his bent foreleg. The
archenelk showed no signs of protest, so she
threw her leg over the base of his neck,
sinking into his spine, his thick pelt soothing
her cheeks, easing the soreness in her
tailbone. He regained his hoofing with a
sudden jerk, and she felt herself transformed
into a towering, solitary figure. They raced
across the plain as one, the surrounding trees
blurring past them, the elk's muscles flexing
powerfully beneath her.

The smaller moon danced across the
turquoise disc for many passings before the
woods grew dense again, and willows closed
about them, and a lake of ferns tickled the
bottoms of her feet. Hidden in the
overgrowth, they came to a place of hewn
stone, conjuring memories of the altar she

had found in the savannah and the menhir the shaman had used in the halfman village. They crossed over sections of flooring being slowly reclaimed by the centuries, carefully winding between towering facades and crumbling foundations, lianas and creepers entangling every beam.

They reached a circular monument set in the midst of a shaded grove. She sat gaping from the seat of her mount, her mind abuzz. The broken ring loomed taller than the tallest trees. It was what the gardeners had wanted to show her.

Who could have built such a thing? And for what purpose?

The white elk lowered his crown, allowing her to dismount, and as she set her foot down, he made as if to leave. But she did not want him to go. She gripped him by the horns, more forcefully than she intended, turning his eyes to face her own.

"Don't leave me," she said. "I need you."

She gazed at her reflection, seeing the smudges over her brows, the knobs jutting from her sallow cheeks, her tattered lips. The ravages of the Wildwood had yet to rob her of her youth, yet the child she saw in the animal's eyes looked lost. Too young to be roaming the world alone.

"Please . . ."

The archenelk made no sound, offered her no answer. She watched him saunter off, indifferent to her pleas, his hooves lightly tapping the earth, the light wavering,

shimmering around him until she could see
him no more.

She made camp in the deepening light of
the Greater Moon, the looming monuments
casting unnatural shadows around her. The
ruins were older than the memory of the
Ilmar, beyond any of the songs she knew, and
she could not imagine the people who built
them. Halfmen were not nearly so clever.
Only the Face People, she supposed, would
dare to erect such things, what she saw as an
affront to the Goddess. But if this was the
land she had set out to find, where were its
people?

Thunderclouds crept slowly over the sky,
quickening the coming of darkness. Unseen
life forms echoed distantly, turning her
imagination to dread. Could the Tyrant pick
up her scent? Was she listening to its guttural
braying even now, amid the tangle of honks
and croaks and every other creature prowling
the night?

She took account of her surroundings. The
trees were too short to hide in, and the bushes
offered no protection. She was exposed,
powerless to protect herself should the
Tyrant, or some abominable relative, seek to
eat her in her sleep. But it was too late in the
day to retreat to the garden.

She did what she could, gathering kindling
and small stones, hoping to warm herself by a
fire while keeping interlopers at a distance.
But amongst the natural deposits of earth and
rock, what she at first took for stones, she

recognized were artifacts. Remnants of the people who had lived here.

They lay hidden under the soil like a turtle's eggs, as hard as obsidian and translucent as amber. She wormed her fingers into the dirt, finding many more, all of them identical except for the ones that were cracked or broken into a crescent shape. The slivers cut her fingers, and she sat sucking at the oozing blood, trying to imagine what the orbs could have been used for. They were too dull to be decorative and too brittle for tools. But the more she dwelled on these mysteries, the more troubled she became. The menhirs, the ghost in the storm, the broken monument, and now these glassy stones . . . none of it made sense, yet they filled her with a sense of foreboding. Perhaps her people were never meant to journey so far, or dig so deeply, or know so much.

DAY 156

My neck!
 She woke to stiff joints and soreness, with her back propped against a truncated column. A nerve had gone astray in the night, bunching up to form a tight knot between her collarbone and shoulder.

It had been a long, tiresome eclipse. The uncertain noises in the darkness—prowling, slavering, hungering noises—conjured the worst of her fears. While not so different than other nights she spent in the Wildwood, the open plain invited attack. She could only hide behind the collapsed architecture and hope the scattered ruins was discouraging to predators. She had slept with her bow across her thigh and a shock of arrows ready to be plucked from the ground like spindles from a shrub. Her weapons completed the illusion of security, without which she could not hope to rest. Not here, where tyrants roamed unabated. She doubted, however, that her bow would have been up to the task, even if she were to wake in time, even if she were to trust her aim in the midst of panic. But it was still better than holding onto nothing, a weapon to defend against nightmares.

Nightmares. I had a nightmare . . .

She got to her feet, working the tenderness from her neck. Much of her legs and arms were blistered and red. *Damn parasites.* The burning, itching sensation was something she could never grow accustomed to. She drew streaks of blood across her puffy, pimply skin with her fingernails and cursed herself for wandering too far from her fire.

This was not a good day for confronting the Tyrant or anything else unpleasant. The last stretch of her journey, her final hurdle, awaited her. She needed the best version of herself, not a miserable wretch scratching uncontrollably, unable to properly turn her head, with a belly growling for breakfast. At least she was not cramping, nor shedding her divine blood. She wanted—needed, rather—to feel strong. But instead she felt lost and overwhelmed. Where was the apex predator who stood face-to-face with the shaman? That girl had run away scared, it seemed.

Baba knew how best to advise her in the worst of situations. And Borz, his words never failed to inspire, to give her courage when she most needed it. Where were they at this very moment? Did they feel as embattled as she did? Did hope still live on in them? Were they even alive?

No, it does no good to dwell on what can't be changed.

Ready or not, the last remnants of childhood had to be left behind. Womanhood meant she could not rely on anyone but herself.

That's what Baba would say if he were here.

She pushed these musings aside, standing her bow upright to test its strength. The weapon was fashioned from the limbs of a yew tree back at the ravine. But the wood remained green on the inside, having yet to harden. While the softer material allowed for a more pliable bow, the string held less firmly, which made for a weaker draw. She compensated for this with size. The limb could fit between her chin and toes from tip to tip. An increase in height equated to faster and more far reaching arrows, and enough force, she hoped, to penetrate the Tyrant's scales. But it was a cumbersome device, difficult to run with, and her arms could not manage the bow at full draw. She would need to pull with her weight, lean away from the string as she took aim.

But the woods often had a way of ruining her plans. Sometime between entering the garden and arriving in the valley, the humidity had made the twine go slack. It would need replacing.

She examined each of her arrows individually, placing them level to her line of sight. The Stillfolk had watched her straighten the stems into missiles, and helped her make more by imitating her movements.

But here, too, the damp air skewed the wood ever so slightly. A crooked arrow would veer from its target and strike with less impact. But there was no time for perfection. She would have to make do with what she had.

She was scouring the area, seeking either to fill her stomach or find raw materials for her bow, when she walked into the shadow of the broken ring. The ancient monument loomed high above the ruins, giving her a sense of foreboding. And what she saw in her sleep the night before lurched with unwelcome clarity to the fore of her mind.

In her dream, she slept on a mound of bone, over skulls piled by the hundreds, and she was driven by an inexplicable urge to break them open, to peer inside their upper cavities. But where she knew the brain to reside, she found only stones made of glass. She shattered the cranial shells one after another, and the same strange stones spilled out. And in a moment of morbid curiosity, she fingered the side of her own head, feeling the ridged bone beneath the veil of her hair, and wondered. *Is there one inside me too? Will someone find it when I am dead and heaped upon this mound?*

She stood to face the dull orange void of the sky as daylight crept lazily from the horizon. But the greater and smaller moons were nowhere to be seen. The constants of her existence were entirely missing, and the sun would never rise again, she realized, as spasms of fear erupted through her body.

Turning away, the unbroken monument met her wondering gaze, the great ring as it appeared aeons ago. Through its circular frame, she saw an impossible vista, a world peering from beyond the façade of her own, columns of black billowing from mountains of fire, embers raining down from another sky painted in the somber colors of eternal dusk. The ring was a window and a doorway to a distant land. Creatures not of Aenya, spawned by other goddesses, wandered in that faraway place. She watched them now as a sickening feeling wrung her insides, those anomalies of nature slowly stumbling over the rim of the ancient gate to contaminate her native home.

Dreams were not separate from reality, she believed, but existed in their own right, parallel to the waking world. Meaning could be mined from journeys of the spirit, serving as guideposts, reflecting where she was and where she might go. But the nightmare would have to go unanswered, for there was still much preparation to be done.

She navigated her way through the ruin, carefully stepping over crumbling debris, fractured walls rising from the tall grass like enormous teeth. She found the broken section of the ring lying in a tussock, surrounded by waist-high dandelion stems, their brittle heads stooped like haggard widows. It was enormous. More extensive than a room in her house. A winged creature with the hindquarters of a feline and the bosom of a woman emerged in relief from the stone, with eyes of lapis lazuli staring from a human face. She circled the carving, branding its meticulous features to memory, its musculature, the detail of its feathers. It was identical to what she had seen in her dream, only the ring had been intact then, the human-feline hybrid crowning the monument's pinnacle. She could not guess how long ago the piece had fallen, but the grimy strata suggested more years than she could count.

She approached the towering structure, the bottom rung rising like a wall above her head. The material was smooth, hard, and unmistakable, resonating with a tinny sound as she rapped her knuckles against it. Whoever built the ring had made the menhir in the savannah and the altar in the halfman's village. She strolled along its base, measuring its length with her steps, discovering what she feared. A three-tined depression, broad enough for her to stand in, the distinct markings of a footprint.

So the tyrants came from here, from that other place . . .

She made her way to the far side of the curve, counting as she walked, when a tremor crackled up through her soles. At first, it was subtle, increasing in intensity the further she went, a creaking noise like thin branches straining under her weight. She knelt and started to dig. The earth was shallow here, no deeper than her elbows. A trellis of crossing beams ran just under her feet. She scraped at it with her fingers, removing decades, likely centuries, of grime and dirt. Red-orange flakes came off it like breadcrumbs, or like dried-up blood when she picked at her scabs.

Iron. This entire thing is made of iron!

Years ago, the mountain folk came down from the peaks of Ukko with the gift of iron, and the lowlanders received it, making tools stronger than stone. Gods forged iron in the heart of dying stars, and when those stars exploded, the iron in their hearts spewed out across the universe. As a Keeper-in-training, Aliaa had been made privy to these secrets— secrets she shared in confidence with Thelana.

"Tell no one. Not even Mana. Not even Baba."

"Why?" Thelana asked her. "What is the harm?"

In telling her the reason, Aliaa unwittingly revealed yet another secret, something far more profound than the story of iron. "Because," she flatly recited, "'knowledge untempered by wisdom sows destruction.' It is why they have been testing me. I must prove my capacity for wisdom. The Ancients knew everything there is to know, everything about everything, but they lacked wisdom, you see, and they doomed themselves." She muttered this last part, adding, with the gravest of intonations, "They destroyed the whole world."

Thelana had not wanted to know this. The very idea that the world could not only *be*

destroyed but that it *had* been destroyed was
greatly distressing, especially for someone so
young. After that day, she had done her best
to distance the troubling thought from her
mind.

Thelana moved away from the trellised
foundation with sudden apprehension,
fearing it might collapse under her and that
she might be thrown down into some
cavernous recess far removed from the
Goddess, into some otherworldly, unnatural
space.

She pulled at the hanging liana stems,
casually weaving the threads into strings as
she planned out her journey. The village was
a day or two on foot, and the plain offered
little shelter. If she did not wish to succumb
to the heat, she would need to travel lightly.
She detached the sharpened slate from her
spear and fastened it to her waist, hanging
her pod of wasp venom from the other hip.
Her arrows she would keep strapped to her
back, bundled with her newly strung longbow.
The rest she would carry.

She set out early to race the midday sun,
drawn by the flat-sided silhouettes etched
across the face of the Greater Moon. The
impossibly tall structures beckoning from the
north, built in the fashion of the ruins, could
only be one thing. A place of habitation. A
village. Sanctuary. She was convinced of it
now. *That's where I'll find them, and Borz
too, and my journey will finally be at an end.*
The mere thought made her heart flutter. She

could already see the surprise and delight on her brother's face.

"What are you doing here?" he will say, "how did you find me?" before lifting her in his arms and holding her tight. She'll weep with long-forgotten joy, and after a tearful reunion, speak long into the night about her adventures and hardships, until talk turns to old times, to family and home. Then everything she will have endured, the rashes and the injuries, the sleepless nights and the hunger, all the times she was scared or just lonely, it all will have been worth it.

That's how it'll go, she thought, brushing the wetness from the corners of her eyes. *Just a little more, Thelana, a little farther still, and that's how it'll go*, she promised.

The featureless, uneven terrain tore the calluses from her soles. What few trees dotted the landscape looked sickly and emaciated and clinging to life. She scanned her surroundings with every step, expecting sudden movement, the sides of the hills to stand and grow scales and open to reveal slavering teeth. The flatness of the plain offered one advantage, at least; should the Tyrant appear, she would spot him from afar. *But what then?* Running, that was all. On an open field, you outpaced whatever was chasing you, or you died.

Boulders and thorny brambles promised a measure of concealment, but they were far and in-between, and she found herself moving like a frightened hare from one to the other. But she did not stray from the silvery liquid trickling down from the north. It served her as a guide, directing her to the village, but she would not go there to drink. The water gave off a metallic odor like rotting iron, or the scent that lingers after a thunderstorm, burning her eyes and nostrils.

Breakfast came at random intervals, mainly consisting of berries and the occasional nut, whatever she could manage to gather given the sterile terrain. She scarfed these down with hesitation, never knowing what might cripple her digestive tract. But out here, exposed and vulnerable, overt caution was a luxury she could not afford. The gods of fortune were smiling upon her, yet she did not trust them.

Where are all the monsters hiding?

She marched tirelessly on, her longbow hanging loosely from her shoulders to scrape the ground, her arrows slick in her sweating palms. An attack could come at any moment, but the world stood still, appearing tranquil in every way. Unnervingly so. And the anticipation, waiting for the worst to happen, was becoming exhausting.

A juniper twisted from a grike between the ground and a series of flagstones. They led her to the remains of an arched entrance holding up the sky. She took shade beneath the portico, setting her bow across her lap and planting her arrows in the dirt.

She stilled her mind as the gardeners had taught her to do and listened for the

Goddess's voice. Gray birds twittered from the nests in the hollows above, but she could not interpret what they were saying. She then broke into nervous laughter, realizing she had been foolish to worry. The Tyrant was just a stupid animal, mindlessly driven by its stomach, and would not go scouring a barren environment where there was no prey.

She sat against the pitted masonry, her knees drawn up to her face. The henna she had applied in the ravine was fading. *Hunting magic*, Borz called it, stealing power from the animals you have killed. But she would not need the swiftness of the gazelle or the brute savagery of the halfman now. She was nearly at the village, and could already make out the individual houses, the windows and doors in the distance.

The day was half over. Clouds gathered over the sky, casting the plain in violet hues. Perhaps, the gods were pitying her at last, blessing her with cooler weather. *Unless . . .*

A rush of cold brushed along the follicles of her body. Leaves carried by the wind smacked against her cheeks. Molted plumage drifted over her eyes from passing birds. The clouds were now rolling over the sun like a thick sheepskin, blotting out the moons, extinguishing the last pillars of daylight. She could feel the storm like a rumbling drum in her bones, the fire of the gods charging through her skin, combing through her hair and braid. Raindrops thumped against the flagstones, fat and heavy, hissing to wisps of steam. The plain *had* been cooked. How had she not noticed it? She examined the bottoms of her feet and found the answer. Her soles were like bleached clay, weathered and callused. She was not the same girl who had left the savannah.

A low braying reverberated in her ears, echoing from afar. She had never heard such a noise but knew the source was alive and in pain. *The rain.* She sat upright, abruptly testing her bow. The cord snapped with a violent swish. *Good, still tight.* Again, that miserable cacophony rent the air, a guttural, gasping voice, like an ox on the slaughtering stump breathing out its last.

Without warning, the dome of the sky burst open, and the rain spilled down from above like a glittering silver curtain. Mist boiled up from the baked surface of the plain, blinding her to everything beyond the reach of her arms. The deluge pounded her shoulders, cold and hard, streaming in runnels from her braid to the small of her back. She stood there, wishing for better shelter, gathering herself up to keep the heat from escaping her body, when a simple truth came barging into her mind. Saurians could not endure the heat. They were cold-blooded animals and did not do well under the scorching sun. She had spent many sleepless passings listening to them prowling in the cool night air, and now they were out hunting again, which meant she had to be swift, reach sanctuary under cover of the storm while it lasted.

The wind whipped against her, shoving her back toward the arched ruin. She pushed ahead, her feet slipping clumsily from the flagstones, past clods of mud and vegetation, occasionally losing her ankle to freshly forming puddles. Her hair was drenched to the roots, her body to the skeleton, her rain-soaked braid swinging like a weighted pendulum from her neck.

Shielding her brows with her forearms, she searched for signs of asylum. *Nothing.* The weather did not abate. All the water seemed to be emptying from the storm gates of the world, pelting her from every direction. It came down relentlessly, angrily, jabbing her with countless toddler-sized fingers, the sudden drop in temperature fusing with the wind to make her shiver uncontrollably. Perhaps her decision to vacate from the ruin had been a mistake.

Maybe there are no monsters after all.

The sky flickered, adding color and dimension to the gloom, and for a brief instant, her surroundings took form, the stands of trees gathering at the ridges and what she mistook for a mound sloping from the middle of the plain. She peered through the rain, her breathing coming fast, the wind and the water whistling through the gaps of her parted lips. An enormous shape lifted into the air, a round snaking shape, and flopped down again with an ear-shuddering crash.

The impact made the air tremble. Sludge dashed against her cheeks and dribbled down in cold globs from her sides. Thunder rumbled overhead like wheels made from mountains, and tendrils of lightning illuminated the world like the eye of the sun winking open and closing again. *Oh, goddess. What did I just see?* Flashing, fleeting images—scales and blood and teeth—and as her mind slowly pieced it together, her heart flailed unsteadily in its cage, reacting to what her eyes were unwilling to accept.

The storm was easing up now, the white noise of falling water growing quiet. But she could no longer hear the agonizing peals of the dying animal, only the distinctive *crunch* of gnawing teeth and the awful, wet, tearing sound that followed. She knew *that* sound, unmistakable to anyone who has heard it. But despite the dread rattling her insides, turning her tendons to sap, she stepped through the mist, driven by an uncanny need to see and know.

The Titan.

The largest animal to exist, dwarfing even the woollyhorn, lay on its side as if sleeping. Its neck and tail were like the trunks of cedar trees, and its organs now gushed loose and slimy from its bulbous hill of a belly, expanding into a fetid pool of blood and bile. The Tyrant leaned over the carcass, its glimmering red snout pecking down, shearing long strips of meat from the vaulted cavern of exposed ribs.

Thelana stepped slowly away, knowing she should escape, yet unable to tear her eyes from the grisly scene, watching with perverse fascination as the monster fed and fed. She could make out the Titan's pink stomach slowly deflating over the potholed earth, gray lungs lolling like two enormous fish, the scarlet fruit of its heart still clinging to the membranous threads of its ribcage. Here was food enough to sustain her family for a lifetime. But she could never carry so much meat, nor hope to preserve it, and the smell of rotting flesh would attract every predator in the Wildwood.

At least she could get away. The rain masked her odor, and even if the Tyrant could detect her presence, it would never turn from its kill. What was she to it? A morsel. A bite. Less than the scraps hanging from its maw. Yet with a will not entirely her own, she abandoned her spear—it would only slow her down—and fumbled at the pod tethered to her hip, her thumb prying the cork stopper loose.

Thelana, what are you doing? Get away! Go! Now! While you still can . . .

But she wasn't. Her other hand worked her arrow into the container with a nervous twitch, glazing the gar-toothed tip in the deep violet ichor of wasp venom.

The Tyrant had been a perpetual part of her life in the Wildwood, as certain as the rising sun, and she was tired of it. Tired of running away. Of hiding and feeling afraid. No matter how she tried to escape, the chief of the saurians had a way of finding her, pursuing her even in her sleep. There would be no end to her nightmares until she stopped running.

She shuffled forward with a primal scream—a scream she had been holding for what felt like a year—and the Tyrant noticed, raising its enormous head from the body it fed upon. Nostrils flared, chunks of meat dangled from its incisors, blood dripped from the leathery rims of its mouth. A pair of eyes trained on her from the deep cavities of its skull, soulless and glittering like obsidian, yet drawn too close together, which gave the animal a confused look. The way it stood there, too stupid to fully grasp what was happening, almost made her laugh. If she had not been so frightened, she might have.

"Hey!" she cried. "This is my world. You don't belong in it."

The last sliver of Titan flesh slid down its gullet, the Tyrant tilting its head like a bird gobbling a worm. It then seemed to focus on her, its pigeon-toed feet digging into the mud, its tail slicing the air with a swoosh. Despite her wheezing breath and palpitating heartbeat, she did not flinch, nocking her greenwood bow with a venom-tipped arrow, her leg stretched back to lean into the draw. The Tyrant grew near, and the rain turned into a drizzle. An opening broke in the clouds, and the threat became ever so magnified in the clear light of day. The sheer enormity of the animal rushing towards her, with its smooth reptilian gait and the methodical way it worked its jaw, was *all too real*, and her mind recoiled. But she could not permit herself to run. Running now could only mean death. Her only choice was to dam up her courage and stand, knowing that the closer it came, the better her aim would be and the deeper her bow would penetrate.

Just one more step. Come on, you can do it . . .

The Tyrant pivoted on its haunches, bringing its snout and tail parallel to the ground. Its nostrils flared, sucking in the scent of fresh blood. Its mouth fell agape, exposing rows of yellow-white knives and a grasping, pustule-riddled tongue. A deafening, honking, croaking cacophony erupted from the base of its throat, and the sound shook her with palpable force, threatening to overwhelm her resolve. Yet she did not waver. Even when her every instinct cried: *you should not be here!* She would only end up in its mouth, turning her back to it, and she had spent enough time caged behind the teeth of a Tyrant.

Its jagged maw expanded to consume her. She added her weight to the bow, her arms and abdomen breaking into spasms, her entire frame shuddering to maintain position until the perfect moment. When she could hold it no longer, the pregnant twine snapped, burning a red mark across her wrist and elbow. The arrow crossed between herself and impending death, flying in a wild, wobbling arc into the tender flesh of the saurian's belly. The Tyrant did not seem to notice, lumbering ever closer, its slavering mouth looming so closely she could smell the stink of its gums. She could not hope to retreat, nor did she wish to. Prey retreated, but she was not prey. She could feel the hot air expanding from its nostrils, her knees turning muddy as she slipped between its thighs, its tail whipping from side to side over the knot of her braid.

The Titan's half-eaten carcass loomed before her. She slid off her feet as she veered away, her soles losing traction over the mix of rain and blood and bile. A baleful roar hammered her eardrums, but she did not—could not—turn to see whether her pursuer was gaining. Hand over foot, she clambered up the slope of saurian flesh and dropped to the other side. The Titan's body acted as a barrier, allowing her the time to breathe, to think. But it would not last, and she knew it.

She caught hold of a protruding bone to spy over the carcass wall. The Tyrant was sniffing her out, growing ever nearer, the fletching of her arrow tottering from the scales of its underbelly. She had barely managed to penetrate its skin. A chobo would not have gone down after such a shot. Her only hope now rested in the potency of the wasp's venom, but the saurian showed no signs of having been affected.

She counted four arrows. *Four more chances to kill that—that affront to the Goddess.* Ripping the pod from her hip, she coated each tip in poison and tossed the rest away. The Tyrant stumbled over the fallen Titan's tail as she watched, her heart painfully protesting, until she could no longer keep still. She drew her longbow to her cheek and released. Her aim had been true, she was sure of it, but a twist in the greenwood and a bit of torn fletching sent the missile astray. It ricocheted off the Tyrant's bony neck and spun into the dirt.

No! I can't be losing arrows like this!

Too stupid to circle around, the Tyrant started gnawing through the remains of its kill, tunneling through tissue and tendon. She crept along the Titan's length, seeing that the saurian was preoccupied, snatching her lost arrow from within reach of its bite.

The cordon of vertebrae separating her from her attacker broke away like a curtain of bones, and suddenly she was exposed. Her ears filled with imminent doom, with sounds of sloshing mud and chattering gravel and the pounding echo of its weight. All her power, every nerve and stitch in her body, she directed it into her legs. Nothing else existed at that moment. Running meant life, and when faced with being chewed apart, the desire for life vastly intensified.

By the time she was fourteen, her brothers had trouble catching her. They had a chance in a short footrace, but she consistently outpaced them over great distances. Crossing the mark before Borz had been a cause for celebration. They hoisted her onto their shoulders and paraded her around the Oak, her eldest sibling looking on without a modicum of envy. Only pride showed in his eyes that day. Laine and Vaino had been very young at the time, arguing that girls were not built for sport, which might have been true for Amina, whose bosom had ripened to give milk and who, not surprisingly, was never in any hurry to go anywhere. But Thelana had been made for speed. While her chest could sometimes be mistaken for a boy's, she never had to deal with the pesky male anatomy that sometimes slapped her brothers' bellies when they sprinted. She was all bone and muscle and rabbit-quick for a human. But could she win against the apex of all predators? Could anyone?

The Tyrant was gaining with every passing second. Its muggy breath clouded the air, tickling her neck and spine. The rot of its gums and teeth, suffused with death and decay, turned her nostrils. She pushed forward with every bit of the strength she could muster, a fire surging through her lungs in great searing bursts over her cracked lips, the bones of her knees and calves and heels cutting like knives under the skin. She was nearing exhaustion, fighting through the pain, yet the Tyrant continued to close the distance, its teeth snapping at her braid, pulling loose hairs from her scalp.

I can't do this! I can't outrun him!

She had to think, not like a frightened animal, but a human. The saurian's senses were dull, making it slow to react. If she moved erratically, unpredictably, she might confuse it enough to escape. She lifted her head to the plain, peering through the boiling sweat stinging her eyes.

A boulder!

She vaulted over it, and the saurian rushing up from behind tumbled onto its face. The maneuver bought her time. Distance. She searched her surroundings for a direction, not knowing north from south. A glimmer of white stood beside a line of trees. She recognized the avatar immediately, instinctively. The archenelk, the Goddess, was beckoning to her from afar. Turning to the Tyrant, she fired a third arrow that went nowhere, and made for the thick of the woods.

The Tyrant did not dawdle. But she had hurt it—she could see the red blister swelling from her first arrow. The wasps were proving their mettle. If the venom did not outright kill the saurian, perhaps the poison could at least slow it down.

She threaded through the trees, backing into a mesh of nettles, and disappeared from view. The Tyrant did not waste energy searching, plowing straight through the copse, tearing roots and snapping branches. Holding her breath, crouched in the trees like an egg in its nest, she slid her fourth arrow against the greenwood shaft of her bow and waited.

The Tyrant ducked through the brush, moving slowly past her, sniffing her out. Every scrape and bruise bickered in her mind, the old wound in her ankle throbbing, flaring, piercing. She no doubt reeked of terror and perspiration. Its nostrils flared in her direction, drawing in her scent. She could almost touch the ridge of its mouth, its curving, drooling, dagger-like teeth. The saurian's ridged eye socket poked through the branches where she lay hidden. She watched its pupil shrink, glistening and angry, and loosed her arrow.

The bowstring whipped her face, almost blinding her, and with her arrows spent, she retreated into the depths of the wood. Rage and torment followed in her ears, overwhelming her senses, deafening her.

The white elk emerged again, crowning a slight rise dotted with slender saplings. She followed after him for some time, hoping to be led to safety, coming to a place beyond the veil of trees. And what met her gaze there stunned her into inaction.

But the Tyrant was not far behind. She could hear its approach through the ringing in her ears, feel the rumbling under her feet, and yet she could only stare wonderingly at the colossal structures rising before her, towering so high they seemed to vanish in the clouds. She had reached the Outside at last. But something was amiss. How could anyone be living here? In a land populated by saurians? She wanted to cry out, call for aid, but no answer would come, and she knew it.

Glancing back over her shoulder, she could see the marred visage of her would-be killer. Blood trickled slowly from its eye, down from the arrow she had planted, and she fled again despite her exhaustion.

She hobbled into the shade of the village, the hanging rooftops casting long shadows across a cobbled trail. Her mind was split between her terror and her curiosity, between the need to hide and a desire to explore. Walls met her at every turn, cracked and yellowed with lichen, creepers cascading over them like strands of sticky wet hair. Even in her haste, she could not help but wonder at every new sight she came across, the shards of pottery tucked into the alcoves, shutters swinging from their hinges, weather-beaten doors that may have been blue.

The Tyrant's attention was also being drawn away, confused by this strange new environment. It gave her time to plan her actions. She considered losing the saurian between the towers, yet they stood taller than any tree, and were too broad around to encircle, with sides too flat and smooth to perch in. Her only recourse was to keep on moving, and praying.

Yet her body was shutting down. She could feel the surrender in her limbs, the fire in her muscles, the sharpness in her ankle forcing her into a limp. The Tyrant trailed behind her, sluggishly in pursuit. Doubtless, it was also tiring and in pain, possibly succumbing to the deadly alchemy of the wasps. But something more than hunger drove the carnivore on, some instinct for vengeance. It would never surrender the chase, not while she lived to further its misery.

She arrived upon an open garden where a familiar feeling, a subtle vibration, stirred in her soles. The ground here was shallow, like the trellised flooring she discovered beside the broken ring. She had to walk carefully, lightly, lest she break through it. She could not imagine escaping the Tyrant only to fall to her death. Unless . . .

Trying to hunt the apex of all predators had been a foolish game. A way to tease Death. She did not have the strength to kill the Tyrant. No human could. But the Goddess had given her people other gifts. The gift of cleverness, and it was by time she used it.

She turned abruptly to face her assailant, spreading her arms wide, crying out. "Come get me! I am here!" Her weight might not break the trellised floor, but a larger animal might.

The Tyrant hesitated, as if sensing the trap, then slowly, its pigeon-toed foot came forward, and the ground rippled beneath them. She could not give it time to retreat or think, if such a creature possessed the capacity for thought. With renewed vigor, she bolted away, luring the saurian closer to the center of the unsteady plane. It followed.

She sensed the change reverberating from below, connections coming undone, twisting and grinding out of place, then her surroundings began to fail. Towers tilted. Walls came down in clouds of dust. Then the ground started to disappear piece by piece. She reached for a vine and caught it. The bewildered creature at her shoulder kicked desperately to maintain its footing as the surface below turned to rubble. But even now, even as it fought to keep from falling, its enormous mouth reached for her. She shimmied further up the vine, the Tyrant directly below her, leaping like a fish to snatch her in its jaws. The dangling creeper caught in its teeth, pulling her down, tearing the vegetation from its moorings. She had nowhere left to run or climb. The vine went slack, threatening to break away, and she let go, dropping atop its bony cranium. The Tyrant twisted and turned, its teeth opening and shutting like a door. She scampered over the ridged features of its head like a mouse, pulling her foot away just as its mouth clamped over it. She was in a blind panic, powerless to think, acting on instinct. Her arrow jutted from its eye still. She plucked it out and brought it down, stabbing in a murderous frenzy. The Tyrant reeled, and at that moment, she could sense a change in the way it saw her. Her triumph. The saurian was no longer trying to devour her. It was trying to escape her.

The Feral Girl

She wanted to shout something profound, something for the ages, but only two words floated out. "I am!" she cried. "I am—"

The ground opened and everything fell away. Her stomach lurched up into her bosom and she was plummeting, she and the Tyrant together, into the dark recess below.

DAY 160

The Greater Moon percolated through the crevices, washing everything in turquoise, spilling out over girders and columns, illuminating narrow walls and heaps of rubble. Ash drifted onto her face, sticking against her eyeballs and forcing her to squint. She wanted to rub the burning away, but her arm felt detached, removed from her body. The best she could manage was a cough—yet the sudden expulsion of breath ruptured her insides and made her head wobble.

For a time, she sat, unable to think. Ignorance could be a blessing. But simply knowing she was not dead came as a surprise. The gods were either very kind or very cruel. She could not decide which.

Her lower legs were paralyzed. She had only the strength to steer her pupils away to take stock of her surroundings. A mound of reptilian flesh weighed heavily upon her, staunching her blood from below the knee. The Tyrant was dead. A viscous substance spilled from the cavity of its eye socket to the rim of its mouth. Its tongue lolled from its serrated smile like a diseased, pock-ridden eel. She was close enough—if she were to reach out—to pry a tooth loose from the saurian's jaw. It would make for a nice trophy to wear about her neck, something to show the other hunters, something to boast about, to display with pride.

I killed it. It was me. Thelana.

But at the moment, she felt neither pride nor worthiness. She craved only peace, the comfort of knowing that the nightmare was dead, to close her eyes with the certainty that *it was dead.*

DAY 161

How long has it been? Passings? Days? Cycles?

A fine powder built up over her, turning her body ashen like a bleached corpse. The bone of her left cheek was swollen and throbbing. Her fall, and everything that had fallen with her, had left her battered and bruised. Had maybe broken her.

She swallowed, and her saliva tumbled into her throat like bits of gravel. The ground under her cheeks, once damp from the rain, was as parched as her lips. *Days*, she realized, such thirst can only come after days.

The Tyrant's head was disintegrating from the inside out. Maggots crawled from the pits of its eyes and nostrils and enveloped its tongue, leaving only a writhing, squirming mass. Doubtless, the same bugs were crawling in her hair and in the warm spaces between her thighs. She shuddered and struggled to kick herself away, worm against her stomach if need be, but her body was unresponsive. Parts of her were broken, pinned under the carcass of her kill and the mountain of rock piled atop it.

She wiggled the fingers on her left side with the dead Tyrant in a twisted heap on her right. Her arm felt fossilized, heavy as stone, her biceps scarcely managing its weight. But the limb came up gradually, slowly, hovering like a stick that did not belong to her body, and her ligaments screamed in protest. She clawed at the air, working blood into her fingers, then looped her arm to her opposite flank. The maggots went squish under her thumb. She counted them as they died. For lack of anything better to do, she made a game of it.

She might have considered the creeping carrion-eaters for a meal some other night, but the thought of eating anything, particularly *maggots*, made her want to retch. What she needed now was water. Water and sleep.

Yes, sleep. Sleep was salvation.

DAY 162

She jerked her leg loose as she opened her eyes. The carrion had eaten enough of the carcass to free her. Larvae were now busily burrowing through the remains of the Tyrant's head. Pink flesh and white bone showed cleanly from under its scales. She had provided them with a feast but was not about to let them dine on her. Forcing herself into an upright position, she plucked the squirming critters from the open wound in her ankle, and revulsion turned her insides. *Goddess's blood!* She wanted to curse, but clearing her throat brought pain. She could only manage a dry, rasping sound, the mechanics of her tongue and throat working like a winch and bucket descending into a desiccated well.

She crawled over the tiles in the path, feeling every bump and pebble in her knees and elbows, squeezing herself under piles of rubble framed by the fallen beams. A pot of hammered metal beckoned from beneath an arch. She reached for it blindly, eagerly bringing her lips to its rim, but it was empty of all but dust.

Containers stood everywhere she looked, tall and short and deep and shallow, some of simple make, a great many others finely worked. They were either of baked clay or a thin iron-like material. The pots fashioned from metal had an orange hue like the setting sun and made clanging noises when she knocked them over. Yet she preferred the more fragile ceramics, like the kinds her people made, because they were painted and pretty to look at. But appearances did not matter at the moment. She would have been satisfied with a pig's trough if it contained a drop to drink. Surely, somewhere in this forsaken land, she would find a barrel for catching rain or some type of retainer for water. The stone pavers were still wet to the touch from the storm but not enough to satisfy her thirst, even if she were to lick the ground.

A violet whorl spiraled over the towering walls. She saw no stars, only the vibrant sliver of the Greater Moon hanging like the arch of a bow she could pull down from the sky.

When Infinity waned into its crescent phase, she knew the Solstice was upon them. She remembered the budding excitement, all of the festivities surrounding the coming holiday, the body painting, the singing, and the silly dance where you hopped in circles slapping your rear with the bottoms of your feet. Mothers from one end of the country to another shared recipes, unwed girls primped themselves and gossiped over potential lovers, and young men strutted about like peacocks unable to hide their enthusiasm.

She looked to the heavens once more, observing the celestial bodies—the great markers of Time above—and wondered if the season of love had begun. *Has it really been a year already?* A year without a family? Without another face to look upon or speak to? Was Amina finding her mate at last? Was her destined lover pining by the sacred fire for a girl who would never arrive?

She slowly made her way on hands and knees, coming to an alcove in the walls where she would shelter for the night. The Goddess was reclaiming the land, she could see. Even in this subterranean place, grass and clover poked defiantly through the mortar and leaves flourished from the cracks in the walls. It gave her comfort, knowing that life persisted in the most remote places.

She expected the humid air to gather into dew by morning, providing her with something to drink.

DAY 163

Morning arrived like an intruder, its light creeping through passageways to break against her weary eyelids. A pall of gray swept across the sky, turning the sun distant and forlorn, like a ghostly apparition watching from above. She brought her hands together vigorously, huffing into her palms. The meager warmth of dawn—the heat she had been relying on—went unnoticed. Too little to keep her from shivering.

The urge to sleep, to waste the day in oblivion, was overwhelming. But if she did not keep moving, she would undoubtedly meet the Taker. A primal survival instinct kept her going and the need to release tension from her body. Her muscles had grown stiff and were aching to be used after exploring the garden, hiking across the plain, and running from the Tyrant. But she was hesitant to do anything more than lifting into a seated position, fearing what she might discover about herself. She did not want to know that her legs were broken—that she was bound to end up dessert for the maggots.

She quenched her thirst from the dew clinging to the leaves and went in search of supplies. Everything she had brought with her, what she labored with such effort to build, was either lost or crushed under falling debris. She would need to start again. But setting her weight to her feet was like standing on the point of a spear. The stabbing sensation ran straight through her spine and neck and would make walking impossible. She no doubt suffered from multiple fractures, yet she convinced herself otherwise.

A length of wood, the broken side of a window frame, leaned against an iron railing. The wood would make for a sturdy crutch, she thought, allowing her a measure of mobility. She tucked it under her armpit, thanking the Goddess that at least she was no longer being pursued by a predator. The pain was just bearable enough for her to limp.

She continued at the pace of an old woman, chuckling despite her agony. *If only my sisters could see me now! They would call me Yaya!*

Sheer walls met her at every turn, heaps of collapsed masonry blocked every opening, and workings of iron protruded through piles of rubble like the ribs of a Titan. She sorted through the smaller pieces, attempting to dig her way out, but the heavier blocks fit too neatly for her to pass through them. She tried hoisting them away, but the blocks refused to budge, and the agonizing pinch in her spine quickly dissuaded her of the notion. Her only other option was to climb—that was her talent, after all—but even in her injured condition, there were too few handholds to reach the top of the wall, and the little vegetation growing from the cracks would not support her weight.

She continued searching, hobbling through archways into vacant rooms without any discernible exits, and when the pain became too great to endure, she slumped into a corner, and wept.

Frustration turned to boredom and boredom to curiosity. She wondered what the village had been like when humans occupied it. How they could hew minerals to build such massive homes. Her bower in Ilmarinen had been cut into the trunk of Old Man Oak and was just big enough for her to stand in and lay across when she slept. But here, she imagined a single chamber housing an entire family. They could also have been used as silos, she thought, or barricades to protect from saurians. If that were so, did tyrants eat all of the inhabitants?

A deep-seated desire for answers drove her deeper into the labyrinth. She crossed slowly from one space to another, angular shapes and flat surfaces pressing from every direction, until she was lost and disorientated, not knowing how long or far she had wandered. Hidden from the movements of the sun and moons, day and night became indistinguishable.

She meandered narrow passageways, moving from doorway to doorway, dreading that at any moment, an opening might shut from behind to leave her trapped. Everything she looked at was dim and cold and lifeless. She could feel nothing beneath her soles but dry, dusty flagstones, the touch of the Goddess having yet to penetrate the winding depths of the village.

Dwellings in Ilmarinen were alive, accentuated by swirls of wood grain and climbing flora. Insects skittered along the beams, birds nested in the ceilings, and tiny mammals scurried in and out of the walls. Even in the Painted Caves, fish swam, lizards crawled, and bats slumbered. She could not imagine growing up in such a sterile world as this. The deathly vacancy of the rooms, the eerie stillness in the halls, settled on her like a cold weave of cobwebs. Did children once play here? Did they know laughter? A parent's embrace? She could almost hear their whimsical voices like a faint echo in the air.

Living spaces in her homeland were partitioned by curtains of bead and coral. Only when the land began to turn, and predators from the outer woods started to encroach upon their farmstead, did she become accustomed to solid barriers. She could never hope to wipe from her mind the day she was forced to leave home, when the door Baba had built with his own hands separated her from her loved ones. Mana had pleaded for him to let their daughter in, and he had refused. She hated barriers like she hated the Face People's coverings, but turning the corner, she could see only closed doors.

Rich hues greeted her gaze, mosaics of beryl and jade and lapis lazuli patterning the hallways and arches, lanterns of hammered metal fitted to alcoves in the wall. She continued down a broad flight of steps, her sense of wonder masking much of her pain, finally coming to a splintered door. The symbol drawn under the lintel was eroded and nearly indistinguishable, yet an uncanny feeling came over her when she stopped to look at it. She was intimately familiar with its shape, but her dulled mind could not conjure the when or the where. She rubbed at the planks with the heel of her palm to clear away the grime but only managed to obscure the pattern. She stepped back into the passage again, feeling foolish, finally recognizing the repeated mosaic. The same abstract flower could be seen on almost every wall.

She needed only her crutch to force her way through the doorway. Thin rays of daylight seeped into the room, delineating drifting dust motes. And as her eyes adjusted to the gloom, she found that she did not possess the words to describe what she was seeing. Nothing in her experience could make sense of the artifacts adjoining the walls, cluttering the shelves, and filling every available space in-between. The furnishings were all oddly shaped, rectangular and rounded, symmetrical and uniform, and impossibly smooth to the touch. Their metallic makeup suggested various tools, yet their purposes eluded her. Nothing made by an Ilmarin potter or woodworker could match the precision of the pieces, yet she did not find them beautiful. She felt something lacking in their perfection, a fallibility that gives an object its soul.

Soulless creations for a soulless world.

A large table inlaid with floral scrollwork dominated the center of the room. She recognized the grain in the mahogany despite its unnatural sheen. But the table stood unusually high, elevated to her waist, and sets of smaller tables crowded around it—possibly, she thought—places for sitting. Tiny knives, with edges too blunt even for paring, were neatly positioned in rows along its length, and accompanying every knife lay a three-tined metal comb. She briefly pictured a family of giants, kneeling at their supper over the tall table, working the delicate instruments with their fingertips, but she just as quickly dismissed the thought from her head. *No, the villagers were human.*

She surveyed the area for anything that might be of use. But the more time she spent there, the more she became distressed. The overabundance of *things*, the sheer excess of it all, was repugnant to her sensibilities. How could any race function with so much to distract them? It was no wonder they cared so little for the Goddess.

Among the countless oddities she could not name, she also found ceramic dishes, soft-cushioned niches for sitting, and a simple doll of woven felt. *Children. They did have children.* Toys were known to her people, though Baba never had the talent or the patience for making them. A thumb-sized woollyhorn, a ziff, and a Titan lay in a small box. The miniature basswood animals made her smile. *Baldr would have loved these.*

An object the size and shape of a honeydew sat on a pedestal in one corner. She studied the colorful, enigmatic contours, running the tip of her forefinger along its ridged surface. This was no tool, she determined, but a kind of map. *A map shaped like a melon?* Nonsensical. The wide swaths of blue reminded her of water, but if the bumpy parts were mountains, how *could* it be water? So much water did not exist in the world.

Thelana's people were known as River Folk. Her family rarely used the term, except when they met with other families for trading, or during the Solstice holiday. Among her countrymen, there was also Hill Folk, Mountain Folk, Bush Folk, and Lake Folk—distinctions she became aware of the day she learned to swim.

Baba roused her and her siblings at daybreak. She had been overly excited for the trip, sleeping too little the night before. They would take the northerly route over the hills into lake country. She recalled the scent of the highland grasses as they hiked the escarpment, the chicories and coneflowers and rare ilms growing through the grikes demarcating the limestone. Above the tree line, the high mountain air gusted fiercely over her pores and the tiny hairs of her body. She was overly accustomed to the sensation, yet it never failed to sharpen her sense of being alive. The Goddess moved through the wind, continually breathing life into every creature.

Standing at the cliff's edge, the whole of creation seemed to spread before her feet, and she looked upon her homeland as she never had before. Thelana could make out the rising and falling curves of the sleeping Goddess, the contours of her hips and bosom in the hills, the sun-gilded tributaries forming her Braid. She had been blind to the beauty of Ilmarinen that day, for she was only a child, and overly accustomed to beauty.

By midday, the family descended from the slate gray peaks of Ukko, gazing out over an expanse of water. The lake was richer and deeper than the sky on a clear day. It pooled at the base of the sloping woods like a jewel in a bowl. The Lake Folk called it the *Eye of Alashiya*. Judging by the surrounding trees— which looked to her like blades of grass from the hilltops—they would need passings to walk around it.

They formed a line as they started down the hill. The narrow path had been beaten into existence after centuries of passing feet. Baldr raced eagerly ahead, hopping from stone to stone, occasionally turning to urge his family on. Amina called for him to be careful, in her best imitation of Mother's voice, but he did not listen because he never listened to anyone. The zigzagging line of bodies comprised of her brothers and sisters and a gathering of migrant children from across the land. When Nicola grew tired, Baba carried her on his shoulders, and when Thelana grew tired, Borz lifted her onto his.

The Lake Folk lived in the spruce and poplar trees huddled about the water's edge. They carved canoes out of white cedar and used nets for catching fish instead of spears. Baba traded the vegetables from their garden for trout, but she and Britannia could not help dashing away. Thelana had never before seen so much water, not in one place, yet she had no time to marvel at it. Borz was already tossing her in. She remembered the sudden shock of cold, her legs frantically kicking into the depths.

Thelana had been so furious with him that day, had even screamed at him. But the more time she spent away from home, the more trivial her old grievances seemed, until the whole of her childhood transformed into a blissful dream.

She replaced the round map and turned to
an ornamented box perched on a small table.
The box produced a leather pouch bound in
string, and she hoped that here, finally, she
might find something useful. It weighed
considerably in her palm for an item so small
and chimed when she shook it. She turned
the pouch over, spilling its contents over the
table. They were perfectly flat and round and
rattled like pebbles. A few rolled off the table
and across the floor. She picked up one of the
pieces, closely inspecting the tiny facial
impression stamped into the bright yellow
metal. A phoenix with its wings spread apart
appeared on the opposite side.

"*Guld*," she murmured to herself.

Captain Aola and her soldiers were the
only Outsiders to treat her family with
kindness. When Thelana showed an aptitude
for their language, Aola became especially
interested in her. But the captain was not
without her biases. Like every other foreigner,
she infantilized her people, believing the
Ilmar did not know how to fight or make
weapons. She had not understood that in
Ilmarinen they relied on the bounty of the
Goddess, in the harvesting of the earth, and
had yet the need for killing instruments.

"I know you don't trust us. And I don't
really blame you." Aola marched into the
woods, wiping the sweat from her brow while
hacking at the branches with a metal blade.

Thelana kept the pace, skipping atop the boughs above the captain's side.

They reached a clearing enclosed by great leafy boughs of oak and camphor, the limbs reaching down with forked, knobby fingers to the ground. The swirls in the bark were like familiar faces, old friends, but in Aola, she sensed apprehension, as if there was something to fear from the forest.

"Your father has been a great service to us," she said. "Our wounded would likely have perished without his hospitality."

Thelana's household did not have much to offer by way of food, but Baba could not turn the strangers away. Custom demanded that anyone seeking shelter be treated like family. "Yes," Thelana admitted.

"We are friends, then?"

"Friends," she mimicked, smiling.

"I know you have questions for me," the captain went on, "that you are curious about us. I want to answer the best I can, so our two peoples will learn to trust one another."

Thelana sat down, straddling the maple bough with her hands tucked between her thighs and her feet dangling playfully over the leafy ground. "*Naked.* The others, your men, say this to us." She spoke carefully, forming each syllable with consideration. The speech of the Outsiders was still quite foreign to her ears. "What is it, *naked?*"

Blood rushed to Aola's cheeks, turning her shades of pink, and Thelana noted the remarkable whiteness of her teeth. She was pretty in her own way, at least the parts of her that showed. Her dull blue eyes were sometimes the color of jet, and her hair spilled in yellow curls over her shoulders, free from the customary braid Ilmarin girls always wore. Aola would have made a fine bride, but whether the Face People knew anything of brides or mothers, Thelana did not know.

"M-Maybe you shouldn't sit like that," she said, urging her down from the tree.

Thelana was confused by the disapproval in her voice. All of her sisters sat in trees, even her mother, on occasion. Perhaps, they did not have trees to sit in where the captain lived. But she did not argue, leaping to the ground to face the strange woman in her strange trappings. "Tell me! What is naked? Is it . . . we're *ugly*?"

"No! Nothing like that! To be naked means . . . Well, it means that you're not, that you . . ." She struggled to find an answer, until her posture changed, and she lowered to meet Thelana's steady gaze. "It really doesn't mean anything, to be honest."

"So, why say it?"

"Damn that Brutus! He thinks himself so high and mighty, thinks we're all so . . . superior." She stared at the weapon in her hand for a long while, a dark cloud growing over her eyes. "If only he knew how wrong he was."

A nearby stream cut its way across a stony, moss-caked embankment, feeding into a shallow pond framed by the fallen leaves. She and her sisters often came here to bathe. Aola knelt beside the still water, wetting her face and the back of her neck. "It sure gets hot here. Much too hot, if you ask me." With a sigh, she turned to Thelana. "Alright then, I'll show you."

"Show?"

"That we're not so different. You and I." She peered uncertainly through the branches, and Thelana could sense her unease, the nervousness creeping over the captain. Taking a rock for a seat, she tugged at the rigid fittings of her feet, revealing her toes. The rest of her coverings came off in layers, like the rind of a fruit, first the shiny metallic shells of her torso, followed by a leather hide. Lastly, she peeled away the soft material wrapped about her bosom and waist, leaving it in a heap about her ankles. Seeing everything strewn about the ground like that made it seem all the more excessive, cumbersome, and wasteful.

Thelana saw Aola as she truly was, human and female. Only, the Outsider's skin looked as pale as bone, while her breasts were the color of sour milk, a sickly, deathly hue starkly contrasting Thelana's coppery skin. Aola reminded her of an elder, despite a youthful face, the venerable grandmothers and grandfathers who kept to their beds awaiting the Taker.

"See?" She spread her arms wide, with her palms turned out in a display of openness. "We are the same."

Thelana gave no reply, instead pressing her fingertips into the small space between the woman's bosom, feeling the steady rhythm of Aola's heartbeat.

"Where I come from, it is not so blasted hot. I wear these for protection. For comfort."

The captain often spoke to them as if they were breast-feeding children. But Thelana had long grasped the utility of body coverings, even before the first Face People came to Ilmarinen. Turtles had their shells and wolves their pelts. Yet ilma were different from the other animals; humans could make shelter and build fires. Her people were not confined by what they wore, never suffering needlessly under the sun as the Outsiders did. Thelana wanted to explain all this to the woman, to show that her people were not entirely ignorant, but could only manage, "Is it not hot, now?"

"Well . . ." Aola trailed off. "I suppose it isn't that simple. At least now, I can wash up. I must smell like an old boot. Been cycles since I've had any real privacy."

Thelana tried piecing together the words, but her mind was still reeling from the discovery that they could reveal more than their forearms and faces should they choose to do so.

"Would you mind watching out for me?"

"Watching? For?"

"See if anyone's coming. Please. The men would lose all respect for me . . . if they were to catch me like this."

Again, she failed to understand the captain's apprehension and would likely never understand it, yet she rounded the clearing nonetheless, ready to warn her of trespassers. Aola was her friend, and Thelana could never wish her harm, however unfamiliar a form that harm might take.

She and Aola grew close that day, but Brutus continued to leer at them, to stare hungrily at her sisters like the foxes that liked to encroach upon their goat pen. He seemed to favor Anja most, like all boys his age who had yet to be joined, though Thelana could not imagine what he could have wanted from her. Brutus did not belong to her people and held no respect for their ways, nor could any of his ilk think to partake of the Solstice ritual.

One day, Thelana returned from fetching water to find him with Baba. Anja stood between the two men, captive in Brutus's grasp. Like a confused animal brought to the slaughtering stump, she twisted and turned in a feeble attempt to escape him, but he never so much as acknowledged her. A kind of madness drove him, Thelana could see, and the fear Aola had expressed by the secluded pond started to make sense. Brutus produced a bag in his free hand, and her father's cheeks flared. His eyes grew round and bloody, and Baba shouted some slur she had never before heard. He then raised up his arm to strike Brutus in the face, but held back, only to slap the offending offer away. The bag flew skyward and *guld* spilled out of it.

Whatever it was that had Baba so incensed, Thelana wanted no part of it. So she set the guld aside and took only the bag.

She left through the doorway to explore the other houses but came across only vacant chambers, stubborn barricades, and passageways sealed with debris. Finding no ramp, stairway, or vine to reach up to the forest level, she could only trace her steps and go back the way she came, thoughts of the village and its denizens weighing her every step.

The Outsiders were not so different from the Ilmar. They ate, slept, made love, and birthed children. They were curious and inventive. And yet their customs, their way of living, could not have been more foreign. They lived like rabbits in warrens below ground, but in the towers above, they nested like birds. Everywhere she looked, nature's gifts had been reworked, exploited, often defiled. How many households did she have yet to discover? The village inhabitants—if *village* was even the right word—were beyond counting, more numerous than all the children in every family in Ilmarinen. *No, not rabbits.* The Face People were more like termites, gathered together in one giant colony. But without farms, where did they procure their food? Could starvation explain their disappearance? Or was it thirst? *Thirst!*

The mere thought made her choke on the air. What of the Outsiders' remains? Did the last surviving members bury the bones of the deceased? Or did the villagers abandon the ruin to migrate to other places like a great gaggle of geese? She supposed such mysteries were not meant to be unraveled. History keeps silent where the dead leave no traces.

Sunlight cascaded in slim folds through the trellised rooftops, forming radiant pools against the adjoining walls. In the cold gloom where day failed to reach the avenue, she was led by touch, until pavers warmed her soles again, and she could see the weeds poking up from the grout. Her surroundings gradually came alive with creepers and lichen and climbing liana. Still, she did not fail to notice the repeated mosaic, the semiprecious stones glittering through the layers of time. The abstract flower pattern appeared at regular intervals, as did the etchings of the round stone.

Thanking the Goddess for her guidance, she returned to the place she left, a short stroll from the rotting saurian. Her nostrils burned with the decaying odor, and she would have preferred keeping at a greater distance, but did not wish to stray from the lights of the sky, from the only remnants of the world she still recognized.

She set her crutch down atop the flagstones and squatted, absentmindedly searching the shards of pottery littering the hall. Lines drawn into their ceramic surfaces intersected to produce the familiar flower pattern, reminding her of the henna her sisters used to adorn themselves. Other pieces depicted life in the village. She saw no plowing, no fishing, no hunting, only the same scene over and over—human figures holding the round stone in their outstretched palms. They seemed to carry the stones everywhere they went, their delicately painted eyes perpetually trained on them, transfixed. And the longer she studied the impressions, the more she was convinced that the stones floated beside their possessors like moths. She strained to understand their significance, what they could have been used for and how they related to the flower, but her skull throbbed whenever she tried to think.

She went slack against the corner, feeling drained and defeated, her head aching as if someone was trying to break open her skull. She brought up her palm slowly across her eyes, nose, and mouth and came away with bloody fingertips. Her lips were split, splintering like the seams in the walls. The morning dew had not been hardly enough to sustain her. She forced herself to swallow, to draw out some measure of moisture, but her throat felt full of pottery shards and sand.

The sun perched dully and indifferently in the sky, framed by the rising walls of the ruin. Gray clouds swept feverishly overhead, teasing her with rain, but after passings of waiting, no rain came. She begged the gods for mercy, for a single wet drop to soften her

tongue, but the gods that day proved
merciless.

DAY 164

S he slept fitfully in the cold recesses of
the ruin, occasionally waking to the chill
wind whistling through the streets, the
unyielding masonry pressing into her spine
and neck, and a whirling circle of nightmares.

Orbs and flower patterns assaulted her in
her dreams, ghosts of the dead, laughing
children. They came at her swiftly and
violently, threatening to tear down her sense
of self, push her beyond the edge of no return.
She was standing at a threshold,
remembering everything she had lost. Baldr
and his toys. Borz by the lake. Anja and her
raging, protective father. And she moved a
hand to her eye to catch a tear that would not
form.

*Bryseis, my beloved mother. Borz and
Baldr, Heimdl and Lodr, Amina, Anja,
Britannia. Nicola. Oh, Goddess . . . Who else?*
She hammered her skull with her fists,
angered by her own stupidity and hating
herself, as if by forgetting her family, she was
leaving them to die. *Oh yes! Aliaa, Vaino,*

Laine . . . And, Father. Baba! What was your name?

She balled into herself, agonizing over her father's name, wondering if she had even ever heard it. When his name did not materialize, she felt her heart shatter, and from some secret reservoir within herself, the tears began to flow.

She had failed them. Failed to survive. Failed to bring help to her family. Failed to save Borz. She continued rocking against the hard bedding of debris, her sobs echoing through the dark, forsaken, cavernous space. And in a small, whimpering voice, she spoke the words she never thought she would.

"I want to go home. I want to go home."

DAY 165

The Solstice was two nights away and
their mother's sister, their chachi, Leep,
had come to visit. Thelana knew this
because Britannia was tugging on her forearm
and screaming with delight.

"Let go, Brit. You're hurting me."

"Goddess's blood, Thelana, you're acting
like a crybaby. You'd never survive it in the
Wildwood."

She pried her arm loose, turning to race
her sister up the path. "Why would I end up
in the woods? I'm not the one losing my way
home every day."

The sun recessed into the arms of the
Greater Moon, its glow washing across the
sky, casting shades of purple over every leaf.
Shadows followed, spilling across the valley
like pitch into the low lying-places, rolling
over steep boulders and slopes of heather,
seeping under the girthy boles of the great
oak and camphor trees. Even in the waning
light, Thelana and her sister rushed ahead,
keen to every stone and log bridging the

snaking brook since they were old enough to walk.

They arrived at the foot of the hill as dusk turned to eclipse. Old Man Oak waited at the peak to invite them home, scaffolding crossing its arms, ropes swaying from their bowers in the branches, firelight glowing in the windows.

Britannia bent over double, her breathing coming in short, sharp gasps. "Beat you here."

"No, you didn't! I wasn't even racing."

"Oh? Then why were you running?"

Thelana returned her sister's smirk with her own before taking off again, dashing up the foot-beaten path as swiftly as her legs could carry her, not bothering to check whether Britannia was on her heels. As she neared the curtained doorway, Baldr came waddling out of the house. He was making strange trumpeting noises, mimicking the bird he met that day, his upper lip frothing with spit. She managed to twist away in time, but Britannia, sprinting from behind, failed to notice him. The impact knocked them both to the ground, and the boy tumbled into a seated position, where he started to wail. Such accidents were not uncommon, and more often than not, they involved Britannia. As usual, Mana rushed to the scene, her face flushed and furious.

"It wasn't her fault," Thelana tried to explain. "I challenged her to the top, and—"

"Never mind that!" She scooped her youngest into her arms, where he continued to plead for attention. "What happened to your feet?"

Thelana checked her soles, but her mother's eyes, glinting with rage, were directed at her sister.

A brownish substance caked Britannia's heel. She only now appeared to notice, scraping at the underside of her foot with a stick. "Eww!" She always feigned disgust for Mana's sake, but Thelana knew better because nothing ever seemed to gross out her sister. The offending mass glommed onto the piece of wood, swirling into a brown-black whorl, deepening the stain in the cracks of her skin. Thelana leaned in to catch a whiff and recoiled. She knew immediately what it was and could only hope her mother didn't.

"Where in Aenya have you been walking? Please, *please* don't tell me you've been in the goat pen again!"

"Well . . ." Britannia turned crimson, curling up like a pill bug and hiding the stain with her hands. "I only wanted to help with the milking."

"And *now* you're touching it!"

Thelana thought Mana might erupt like a thundercloud. "Get out! Get out and don't return until you've washed up. I won't have you tracking excrement through our house."

Baldr hopped from her arms, having long stopped crying, a mischievous grin spreading across his little round face. He seemed to enjoy these spats, watching the contest of wills between parent and child play out. "And that's why she'll never find a husband. Isn't that right, Mana?"

Her mother glowered at him. "Baldr, be quiet."

Thelana wiped her feet and stepped into the room. Amina, Anja, and Aliaa were warming themselves by the crackling chiminea, as was her aunt, Leep, and her son.

She almost did not recognize her eldest sister. Amina was particularly done up this year, covered from scalp to heel in ochre, being the most eager to wed. Her body resembled a garden adopting a woman's shape. Leep had used the reverse technique, caking her sister up completely before scraping the dye away, leaving swirling, blossoming lines where the skin showed through.

Anja needed only her blonde locks and curvy hips to enthrall the boys. So she adorned herself for her own sake, donning garlands of lilies, roses, and tulips about her head, neck, wrists, and ankles.

The two girls sat on a pull-down bench, chatting away as they busied their hands mixing sesame seeds and honey. Laine and Vaino were no doubt soaking their stings in a salted tub. The image never failed to make her laugh. Every year around Solstice time, the boys agreed to raid the beehive despite the trouble it caused them. *Pasteli* was Thelana's favorite part of the holiday, and her mouth started watering just watching Amina and Anja knead the sticky mixture into shape.

It made for a delectable treat, and the leftover honey helped satisfy their hunger when food became scarce.

Aunt Leep's only unwed son, And, sat opposite the fire strumming the olol in his lap and humming a tune. The music board resembled a drum with strings, was made from a single curved sheath of bark, and played with the flat part of the palm. And often came to mind whenever Thelana pictured the male of her species. She loved the soft blue of his eyes, the cut of his jaw, his squared shoulders, and his well-defined torso. But his presence made her nether regions tickle, and that frightened her. While she was beginning to show hair about the loins, Thelana had no intention of jumping the sacred fire with him or any other boy. She dreaded the thought of pregnancy, the agony every woman is tasked to endure to bring ilma into the world. When her younger siblings were born, she could not tolerate standing in the same room with Mana. Yet she feared the responsibility that came with motherhood more than the delivery, the thought of leaving her family and childhood behind for a life she did not ask for.

Ignoring the boy and his olol, Thelana turned to Leep and Aliaa, who could not have been more different in shape or size. Her sister stood to her aunt's chin with a slight build and a figure as curvaceous as a stick. Leep, by contrast, had a body like a bowl of fruit. Thelana thought her the most beautiful woman in the world, the iconic representation of the Goddess. She was round in all the right places, with a silvery mane cascading across her rotund areolas to her noumena. If Mother could be believed, their chachi had given birth thirty times in so many years, with nineteen of her children surviving to start their own families. All except for And.

Aunt Leep now occupied their home, working a mortar and pestle to make the ochre *koiob* and olive-hued *talaog* needed for the henna. Nobody mixed henna like her chachi did. Nor could anyone apply such intricate patterns. She watched her uncomely sister's transformation as her aunt went about accentuating curves Thelana did not know her sister possessed. Aliaa rarely ever bothered to adorn herself, yet she was now radiating with pride, motioning from side to side to show everyone in the room the fresh design winding from her collarbones to her shins.

But Leep was not done, holding her back with a firm hand. "Sit still, my dear. I'm nearly finished."

Mana strolled in to address her, the calm having returned to her face. "Well, aren't you going to greet our guests?"

Thelana offered the boy a timid nod before falling into her chachi's waiting arms. Leep held on as though her life depended on it. Her aunt's enfolding body felt safe and warm, like a second mother, and she could not have loved her any less.

"Will you do me next?" Thelana asked her. She did not care much for beauty, hoping to avoid attention over the Solstice. During the pairing ritual, she always made certain to sit away from families with sons or any boy who might fancy her. Yet she still wanted to belong, to participate in the fun everyone was having.

Aunt Leep looked over her body like a potter preparing a vase to be painted. "Of course, my dear."

Britannia poked her head back through the doorway, hesitating to return to the house. "What about me?"

Mother shooed her away. "Wait right there! Let me see those feet!"

She made an exasperated sound as she retreated to the safety of the porch. "Aw, don't you trust me, Mana?"

"I said out!"

Leep started on Thelana's hands, applying line after line until a familiar pattern emerged over the tender bridge between her knuckles and wrist. All her sisters would be given the same design as every other girl in Ilmarinen. The ilm was more than a decoration. It represented their people, their most cherished traditions; they were the *People of the Flower*, after all. But as Thelana watched the flower take form, an uneasy feeling came over her, a sense that she had relived this exact moment before, but in another place, a strange place, though she could not remember the where or the when.

Without lifting from her work, Leep said to her, "Do you know how the ilm came into being?" She asked the same question every year, and shared the same story before every Solstice, and always Thelana pretended to forget so she might hear it again.

Amina and Anja paused from their pasteli making as And continued to strum his olol. Aliaa threw herself beside the hearth with her chin in her hands, rapt by the soft color of his eyes and the cords resonating from his fingertips. Perhaps she would become his bride, Thelana thought, though Aliaa never showed any interest in boys. Never one to miss out, Britannia stood with her ear in the doorway, listening to the music fill the carved room. The melody was as old as the making of the first drum and accompanied the telling of any story, with some variation to match the speaker's rhythm.

"It all began with Solos, God of the Sun, who sat on his chair of kindling in his abode of fire, brooding over his sister, Aenya, whom we call Alashiya, who is the Goddess that is in All. Solos had become despondent—"

"What does despondent mean?" Aliaa was quick to inquire.

"*Sad*, dear, it means he was sad. Now, please don't interrupt." Leep had told the story dozens of times but never in the same exact way. Each year, she altered the words to make them sound newer, or fancied up the language to emphasize the poetry. "Anyway, where was I?"

"Solos was sad," Thelana chimed in.

"Yes. Right. Solos sat in the sun for aeons upon aeons, and even after all that time, he noticed that his sister remained utterly barren, without a single child to call her own. And so, taking pity upon her, he devised a solution. For you see, Solos is cleverest amongst all the gods and wise in the ways of invention, and he set himself about the task of aiding his sister give birth to *Life*.

"Deep in his workshop, where the sun burns hottest, Mighty Solos took up his cudgel, which he called *Gravity*, and in his other hand, he gathered up the lightest wisps of air that he could find, which he called *aether*. And for many more years, more years than can be counted, more years than all the pebbles in all the riverbanks of the world, he hammered the aether, pressing it down and down with Gravity until . . . Do you know what it was he made?"

"*Light?*"

"That's right, my dear!" Leep always sounded surprised that Thelana remembered the conclusion, though they both knew the roles they were playing, the storyteller and the audience. "Solos made light! And he sent the gift of light down to his sister, Aenya, whom we call Alashiya, and with this seed, she became heavy with child. And the first of her many, many children became the first of all flora. The *ilm*."

Dreams existed in a peculiar way. She was brought often to places of terror, her mind manifesting the worst of her waking fears. Yet, on rare occasions, she found herself reliving instances of joy. How many years before leaving home had she spent the night warmed by the hearth with her mother, sisters, and aunt beside her, listening to that familiar tale? And why had the vessel of her mind delivered her to that moment precisely? It could not be mere happenstance. The dream held some meaning for her, a message for the future hidden in the carefree jollies of the past.

Another when and where, another day plucked from the stream of her childhood. It was after the irrigation channels ringing Old Man Oak's roots had stopped flowing. The water draining into the mountain aquifer was cleaner and better for drinking, so Baba sent her out, with Britannia and Aliaa, with pots dragging at their heels.

The chore made them miserable, for they had to spend a good passing reaching the aquifer and another two getting home. Coming back was far more of a pain, with the weight of the water precariously balanced atop their heads. They grumbled all the way, their necks and spines strained, their arms aching for relief, except for Aliaa. She accepted her responsibility with quiet resolve.

"I really don't see why the boys get to go hunting, and we have to do this," Britannia said, crooking her shoulder for a better grip. She had mentioned this several times already, in as many different ways, losing a trickle from her ewer every time.

"If you don't stop complaining, you'll have nothing left when we get home," Thelana remarked.

Aliaa was continually changing her posture. She first stood the pot on her head, then cradled it like an infant when her neck became sore. Now her arms were giving out, forcing her to shift the weight from one elbow to the other.

"Hey, um . . . maybe we should take a break? I don't think I can go on like this."

They agreed to stop for her sake. Had Aliaa not been with them, Britannia would have challenged Thelana to a test of endurance to see who would tire first. Or it might have been a game of dexterity, the girl arriving home with the least amount of water spilled winning. All of life was a game for Britannia, every ordeal a means to prove oneself.

The midday sun claimed the sky as they each found a shady spot away from the heat. Thelana and Britannia sat facing the path, the rocky slope poking their shoulder blades. Aliaa crossed her ankles opposite them, picking spurs from her feet, her back against the gnarled bark of the giant willow overlooking the drop.

Sparing a quarter-passing to regain their strength, Britannia eyed the twittering birds above their heads and signaled to her younger sister. "Hey, think you could guess the number of finches up in that tree?"

"I'm not so sure those are finches," Aliaa said. "You see, finches have clipped wingtips, and their beaks are quite short, and—"

"You're really no fun, you know that?"

Thelana peered under the canopy abutting the cliff, focusing on the chirping sounds, trying to distinguish one voice from another. "I'd say there are about . . . a dozen? Not counting hatchlings."

Aliaa rolled her eyes. "How would you even prove she's right?"

"Well . . ." Britannia started, a mischievous grin splitting her face. "I know a way." She then hurled a palm-sized stone into the branches, and the startled denizens fluttered away in a flash of feathers. "See? There aren't any finches in the tree. Not anymore."

Aliaa rocked to her heels, looking perturbed. "Oh, you think you're so very clever, Brit! I bet you, for a fact, there are still a few up there." She ducked under the low hanging strands, examining the willow from every angle, circling around it until disappearing.

"At least now you're playing," Britannia called after her.

Thelana waited, but when Aliaa failed to reappear, she knew something besides the game had caught her sister's attention. Aliaa was prone to forgetting herself, her curiosity constantly sweeping her up.

Britannia moved ahead to investigate.
"Are you all right, Ali? Did you find a weird
bug or something?"

"There's something here." She answered
matter-of-factly but with a hint of urgency in
her voice also. They gathered by her side,
surprised by the dirt path cutting into the hill,
having walked the same route to the aquifer
on countless occasions without ever having
noticed it. From either end, the track was
undetectable, hidden by scattered rocks and
briar shrubs and the strands of the willow.

"Where do you think it goes?" Britannia
murmured.

"Probably nowhere," Thelana said. "I
mean, we've never seen anyone come down
this way, and we come here all the time."

"No." Aliaa let out an exasperated breath
as if she were about to teach Baldr a difficult
lesson. "This tree doesn't belong here. Giant
willows don't normally grow on slopes like
this. They don't have such deep roots, you see,
and they rely on steady access to water."

Thelana felt blind to the obvious, noticing
the scarcity of woodlands for the first time.
Undoubtedly, her sister was right; the willow
could only be an anomaly. "What are you
getting at, Ali?"

"I think someone put this here."

Britannia spread her arms about its
fibrous bark, emphasizing its girth. "Who'd
plant it way out here? And how long ago was
this? This tree must be a hundred years old!"

"I'd say several hundred by the looks of it," she said.

Thelana could see her sister clearly now, Aliaa's wide forehead, flat cheeks, and maple-colored eyes. She would never be bonded to another nor be honored with children, for she was too clever for this simple life, and she loved knowledge more than anyone or anything.

"So, wait, you're saying someone put a tree here hundreds of years ago to hide the way?"

Aliaa nodded. "I think so. And, by the looks of it . . ." she peered ahead just to be sure, ". . . it's been seeing quite a bit of use."

Britannia started up the slope, not bothering to ask any more questions. She preferred action over thinking, always worrying about the consequences later. It's what drove their mother into a violent mood. "Well, what are we waiting for? Let's go."

"Are you sure it's a good idea?" Aliaa said. "I mean, someone didn't want us going up there for a reason, and if we don't get back by supper with the water, Mana will beat our butts red."

Thelana tugged at her arm. "Aren't you always going on about the Keepers and the great mysteries of the universe? Well, here's a mystery for you. Don't worry. We'll make it back before anyone notices."

The three of them marched up the narrow row of dirt without further discussion, their fatigue absent from their minds. The way forward was steep and narrow, bordered by jagged rocks and barbed brushes, and they were forced to walk single file, with Britannia eager to prove her courage at the fore, Thelana following from behind, and Aliaa lagging at the rear. They kicked up dust as they wended their way upwards, their feet scattering bits of gravel where the hill cut away sharply and pebbles danced down and down with a clickety-clack below. The span of dirt switched to and fro until vanishing under the choking weeds. There they wavered, doubting whether the trail was anything more than a track where shepherds came to graze their goats, something made significant by their imaginations and a craving for adventure.

Solos stared low from his seat on the horizon, his fire-orange fingers dipping into the faint ring of the moon, heralding the coming of dusk. But the afternoon heat still clung to the air, wet and oppressive. Thelana wiped her brow to clear her eyes, helping Aliaa over the rise with her other hand, their wrists entwined like strands of rope.

The climb leveled off until the three girls stood elbow to elbow atop a broad plateau overlooking the valley. Mottled greens and veins of indigo spread beyond the reach of their eyes. Thelana could not remember having ever ascended to such a height and wondered if she could spot their treehouse from here or if she was even facing the right direction.

Opposite the precipice, a crevasse in the slate wall opened to a cave, broad as two doorways across. A stone slab stood adjacent to the entrance, made from the same smooth mineral, but was unusually angular in shape. It looked as if someone had cut away a piece of the hill and set it aside, like a woodsman splitting a plank of wood from a log.

Britannia was the first to speak. "What do you think it is?"

Aliaa ran ahead, invigorated by the discovery, then hesitated. "This place . . . I think I know what this is . . . I think this is sacred ground. *The Omphalos*. Sanctuary."

Thelana stood near the mouth of the cave. A yellowish glow danced along the uneven periphery as a flicker of light issued from its depths. Burning hickory stirred in her nostrils, mixing with an intoxicating incense that set her mind abuzz. The scent kindled memories of the Solstice, of the High Priestess prancing into the late passings of eclipse before the great bonfire, pirouetting with the flaming Hoop of Eternity over her head.

Aliaa's voice came low and measured, as if she were in a trance, carrying an air of authority exceeding her years.

"Aeons ago, long before the record of song, Alashiya's name became lost to memory. Never was it spoken by the tongues of her children, nor ever was it heard in their ears. Thus, ilma became greedy and wasteful and spread like a sickness throughout all the lands of Aenya, devouring everything born of the Great Mother. Then Solos, watching from his dominion above the clouds, burned with love and vengeance for his sister. So great was his wrath that he scorched the sky, tore down the trees, and drained all of the rivers. From the mountaintops, where the people lay cowering, the men wailed and the women wept, and in one voice, they shouted to the heavens, saying, 'Oh gods, how shall we eat? How shall we drink?' And the Great Mother, hearing the lamentations of her offspring, took pity upon them, for no mother can abandon the fruits of her womb even when she has been forgotten. So Alashiya called upon Kjus, who remained faithful and wise in the ways of the world, and to him, she imparted the secrets of the universe, and thus Kjus became the first of the Keepers. Burdened with knowledge, Kjus gathered together the whole host of humanity, all of whom had yet to forget the name of the Goddess, and he led them to a place hidden in the hills of Ukko, to a place of sanctuary, which was called, *Omphalos*. Down and down into the dark of the earth they went, into the very womb of Aenya herself, where the Great Mother sheltered her children from her brother's fury.

"Seven ages would pass and another seven again before Solos's fury abated and ilma could walk safely under the light of day. And it was in that time, that the Greater Moon, brother of Alashiya, stood tall in the sky to remind mankind of his hubris and to protect

the new world she had brought into being.
For in her eternal mercy, the Great Mother
protects us all.

"Omphalos," Aliaa murmured. "The name
means, 'navel.' It's Alashiya's bellybutton."

Britannia shot her an incredulous look.
"How did you memorize all that?"

"The High Priestess sings it every year. It's
my favorite part, actually. Don't you ever
listen?"

"Sorry. I'm too busy dancing."

"And wrestling with all the boys?" Aliaa
was the most timid person in the family, or so
everyone thought, but now she had caught
her sister speechless. Britannia could only
fold her arms and stick out her tongue
defiantly.

Thelana sensed an argument brewing
between them and cut in. "Do you think the
songs are true?"

Aliaa's maple eyes darted to the gray
ribbon wafting out of the cave. It seemed as if
the answers were written in the smoke. "Why
wouldn't they be?"

"I don't know," Thelana said. "I just
assumed they were . . . you know . . . fancy
made-up stories, like when the boys come
back from hunting, saying they've seen a
Tyrant or a Titan or some ridiculous thing."

"I'd like to see a Tyrant . . ." Britannia
interjected, eager to jump back into the
conversation.

"No, you wouldn't!" Aliaa shot back. She
acted like her sister was readying to search

for a saurian that very moment. "He'd eat you! Gobble you up in a single bite."

They continued to squabble as the glimmer emanating from the cave drew Thelana's attention. She felt its call like a presence, like a secret whispered in her ears. But while her curiosity often led her into trouble, she was not one to ignore the frightful warnings of her heart. It was Britannia who never thought of danger, who balked at the Taker as if she were too nimble for his grasp, not her.

"So, if this is the same Sanctuary from the story, why is smoke coming out of it?" Thelana inquired. "I think someone is still living here."

Britannia shrugged. "Maybe nobody gave them the message? That it was safe to come out?"

"After thousands of years? No, someone's camped in there," she said, adding, after an uncomfortable silence, "someone should check it out."

Aliaa tugged at the frayed ends of her braid. She did this whenever she felt nervous. "I don't think that's such a good idea. What if there are bogrens?"

"Want to play *smacks*?" Britannia said. "Loser has to go in." She would have done it on a dare, Thelana knew. Her crazy sister was just looking for a chance to compete at something.

"Fine. You win, I go. I win, you go. Deal?" Everyone knew the game, though the fun of it seemed to wane as they got older. Even now, Thelana felt it was a silly pastime. The rules were simple enough for a child of five to learn. She and Britannia had to mimic one another's movements, slapping their own body parts, the arrangement becoming more complex as the game progressed, until someone made a mistake. They started with their elbow, moved on to the knees, then their palms touched together, and back to the elbows again, the rump, palms touching once more, and so on. Thelana had spent passings with her sisters, smacking herself silly until her flesh turned raw, though she never regretted those moments. They never failed to produce aching belly laughs, feelings of giddiness, and sisterly love. But now, with the stakes set so high, the game took on a somber dimension, and after a tense exchange lasting a quarter-passing, Thelana mixed up her ankle with her wrist, and Britannia stood with her arms crossed, smirking and triumphant.

Aliaa looked on, annoyed, fondling her braid and rolling her eyes. "How old are you two again?"

"It's all right," Thelana said. "I'm not afraid to go in." And, to prove the point, she darted into the cave without another word, ignoring the oddly shaped slab set by the entrance.

The air was cold and damp, its clammy touch enveloping her in an instant, prickling her shoulders and forearms as she moved further from the warmth of day. Step after brittle step, she navigated the cavern's rugged terrain, its surface rippling like the whitecaps of a stream frozen in time. Rocks the color of curdled milk glittered underfoot, scraping her sides, as the roof spiraled down like melting teeth to poke and prod at her scalp, forcing her to crouch and then crawl. Here she remembered how she hated tight spaces, how she preferred sleeping under the open stars. Yet the manmade fire beckoned from the depths, dazzling her senses, promising something worth discovering.

She could feel her growing hesitation, her pace slowing with her unease. The flickering light could not be much farther, yet the distance seemed to be increasing. She glanced nervously over her shoulder. The sun looked small and frightfully remote, diminishing through the gold-rimmed mouth of the cave, and she held herself tightly, shivering against the chill, wet air. How quickly could she get out of the cave at a full sprint? What if the ceiling suddenly collapsed, burying her body forever so that even her parents could never find her? What if she were intruding on a bogrens' lair? Or could some other unimagined creature call this place home? Not seeing her sisters, Thelana was tempted to shout their names, wanting to hear their voices, if only to be assured they had not wandered off. But how could they think to abandon her? No. She was being foolish, yet she could not help wishing Britannia and Aliaa had gone along with her, and that she had never agreed to play that stupid game. Thelana hated being alone when she was far from home. Alone, anything could befall you, and no one would know to lend a hand.

She found her courage again and forced another step, moving deeper into that shadowy vacancy, edging ever closer toward that orange prick of light penetrating the gloom.

Crawling over a lip of rock, she came to an expanse of swirling limestone columns, the dimensions of which were beyond her reckoning. Stalactites hung a hundred feet or more above her head, their bases receding, vanishing where the light failed to touch them. At the far reaches of the chamber, ominous structures loomed vast and unnatural, teasing out the worst facets of her imagination.

The blaze occupied the center of the space like a miniature sun, drawing long shadows on the ground and casting her shape across every surface. She hurried toward the fire with equal measures of excitement and apprehension. Pebbles skipped from her shuffling feet, the chattering echo disturbing the deathly silence. The light grew tenfold as she advanced upon it, its brilliance magnified by a shimmering pond of fiery yellows and oranges.

A woman sat within reach of the flame, so composed and still, Thelana could have mistaken her for a natural formation, a slip of rock and a trick of the mind. Shadows huddled about her like smoky apparitions. An array of concentric chalk figures—drawings of hares and ziff and gazelle and other animals Thelana did not recognize—emanated from the spot where the meditating figure was rooted.

Thelana waded quietly into the shallows, the water lapping over the bridges of her feet, rippling outwardly into rings of gold. She could see the woman clearly now, a priestess and an elder coated in white ash, her hands turned up in her lap, her nipples pointing into her swollen belly, her hair bundled into a mesh of earth and twigs and bird bones. The priestess showed no signs of life. Ribbons of smoke diffused across her eyelids, rising from the pit of her crossed legs, from the embers she held in a clay vessel—a bowl painted with hilly landscapes and starry skies. Yet her stony countenance remained unchanging. Thelana was eager to accost the stranger, to learn what she could of this place and the ritual being performed, but the smoke was far more potent than she had ever known it, and her feet grew heavier with every step, and the ground pitched and rolled beneath her like a canoe in tumultuous waters. She lurched forward, forgetting where she was going or why, tripping over her own limbs, reaching to catch herself from smacking into the rocks. But her hands had swollen to the size of melons and her skull was inflating with air. She felt her head might pop from her neck at any moment and go floating off. But then a tranquil feeling washed into her, saturating her senses, and her every concern melted away.

A hand fell heavily atop her shoulder, and Thelana nearly screamed. The man at her back put a finger over his lips, the intensity in his eyes urging silence. He led her away, tearing her eyes from the scene. The man was powerful despite his wiry frame, and she stumbled as he dragged her back through the cave, scraping her knees and elbows and the tops of her feet, leaving pebbles to poke at the tender cups of her soles as she stomped through the twisting wynd of rock.

Thelana stood in a daze, the sun paining her eyes, unable to believe how quickly she had been brought out. The priestess and her fire sat a few short strides from the entrance.

Britannia and Aliaa were huddled by the cave mouth under a reddening sky, their postures slacking, their eyes full of remorse. The strange man released her, and she turned to face him. She could now make out his hairless scalp, a head too heavy for his neck, the lines stratifying his nose and mouth, the wisps of hair fringing the bones of his sallow skin. What little showed of his manhood was couched in patches of gray that sprayed from his body like wild urchin weed. Decaying vines engulfed him to his knees so that he took on the appearance of a solitary boulder consumed by vegetation, and he carried a staff made from a single tall branch. Thelana could only stare at him agape, never having met such a decrepit-looking human being.

"Do you know what you could have done?"

She did not answer, too startled to speak. All of them were.

"Well then," he said, his voice like a mouth full of dirt. "I will tell you. That woman in there, you nearly touched her. But she is not presently in her body. Do you understand? She has taken the dream journey. Her spirit roams beyond this world, outside of Time and Space. If you were to have moved her, she might never have been able to find her way again. Lost forever! Can you imagine? Even in death, the spirit finds its way to the womb. Not so, when one's body is moved and their spirit is off wandering the outer planes of existence."

Thelana did not know what the man was talking about, but she understood his anger, sensing the gravity of what she had almost done. "I . . . I'm sorry . . . I didn't know."

Despite their trouble, Aliaa could not contain her excitement, her eagerness to speak. "Wait. Are you a Keeper?"

His haggard eyes focused on hers, and his frightening demeanor changed somewhat, becoming more paternal. "Indeed, I am, young lady. The name is Quasil. But if you know who the Keepers are, you must know there is knowledge in this world that must be kept hidden from the uninitiated."

"*Knowledge untempered by wisdom sows destruction*," she recited.

"That's right!" His face eased into a knowing smile. "Perhaps, someday . . ." He combed his fingers through the scraggly hairs of his chin, trying to remember what he had wanted to say. He then turned back to his cave. "I go out for one passing!" he exclaimed, "one passing, and you see what happens?" after which he did something Thelana would never have expected. Looking back on that day, it always made her feel foolish that she had not noticed it, not before the ancient Keeper pressed his hands against the unnatural-looking stone to seal up the mouth of the cave, hollering, "Go on now, girls! And watch before you go wandering in places uninvited!"

A door! The Omphalos Sanctuary was secured by an enormous stone door, that became invisible when shut, marked only by the faint outline of an all too familiar pattern. Thelana knew she was dreaming when she lifted her hand to her eyes. The floral design between her knuckles and wrist, the ochre shape so delicately penned by her aunt, was identical to the one on the door.

The warmth of day turned cold as the voices of her sisters became distant echoes. Endless walls pressed on her, colorless and indistinct, the wind soughing through the caverns of the past to the doorways of the present. She tugged at the fraying ends of her childhood memories, held to it with every bit of her strength. Still, wakefulness came hurtling at her like a rolling boulder—

unstoppable—and she found herself crouched against the merciless corner of the derelict village aching and alone and yearning for the youth she would never know again. She continued to gaze at her outstretched hand, numb to her thirst and the stiffness in her spine, still holding to the fading pattern of her dream.

Like the priestess in the cave, she had also taken a journey. And what she had witnessed there had not been by chance. The deep parts of her mind were trying to reveal some truth hidden in her past. Her recollection became hazy, as dreams tended to become upon waking, fragmenting with every passing second. Yet the essential details lingered. *The stone door with the ilm on it.* She had seen it somewhere in the village only yesterday.

She took up her walking stick and hurried down the passage, wiping the grime from the mosaic tiles along the walls to study the repeating pattern, fingering the lines forming the petals in the masonry. The markings were not identical. She would have recognized it immediately if they had been. But the flower was distinct enough, a simpler variant of the one she saw etched on the cave door, similar to what her chachi had drawn on her hand. Removing the stems, stamens, and leaves, the unique arrangement of heart-shaped petals could not be mistaken. The ilm flower decorated every corner of the abandoned settlement, was a recurring motif in all of the Outsider's art. Alone, this would have been no cause for excitement. It was her discovery the day before, rather—what she had not bothered to notice—that had her brain buzzing.

She hobbled into a run, ignoring the sprain in her foot, hoping against fear she was not deluding herself. Rounding a flight of steps, she came to a wall that was not a wall, but a door riven by deep time. She scraped at the once smooth surface, removing ages of lichen until the skin of her palms started to peel away. She then stood to examine her handiwork, seeing what had only been hinted at before. The pattern of the ilm on the door.

What does this mean?

She wished her sister could have been there to provide an answer. Aliaa would have known. Aliaa knew everything. But her parents had sent her away instead, the simple one, the stupid one.

Stupid Thelana.

She forced herself to think, strained her mind against the constant throbbing of her thirst-addled brain. *Wait. What would Aliaa say? If it's the same door, that must mean it was built by the same people. The old man had been a Keeper. But the Outsiders couldn't be Keepers, could they?*

Whatever it meant, the door itself would not budge. Not with the strength of ten men. She knew this intuitively, by the dull sound the stone surface made against her rapping knuckles.

An earthenware bowl, no bigger than the cup of her palms, lay flipped on its face amid the corridor. It was a plain cream in color, without hills or stars, and a hairline crack ran down its side. But it would have to do.

If she had been more lucid, she would never have followed through with the idea, would not have thought to tug at the bands securing her braid. But she felt only loosely tethered to reason.

Her hair cascaded over her shoulders, leaving the petals carefully folded into the strands by the Stillfolk to drift lightly into her palms. *Baba's gift*, she mused. What remained of her ilm lay shriveled and brittle and colorless, but its potency magnified as it reduced with age.

The ilm reminded her of home, of family, and she could not bear to destroy it. But the breaking of a sacred taboo troubled her just as much. The Ilmar were forbidden three things: the bonding of the flesh before the Solstice, the hunting of other ilma, and embarking upon the dream journey when one has not been initiated. The risks far exceeded death, she knew. She could lose her soul forever, to never be reborn into a physical body, and even if she were to find her way back to the waking world, her identity could be wiped clean. The ilm destroyed memories, erased personhood. It was the high price paid for greater truth and the attainment of higher realities.

She wavered, considering this last point. What did she have left but her remembrances of home? And yet she refused to surrender to

the whims of circumstance. To wait for lack
of water to sap away her life. Any risk was
worth taking for Borz, for her family, however
significant the consequences.

The Keepers transcended time and space
to unravel the secrets of the universe. But
Thelana only wanted to know how to escape
the village, if not through the door with the
ilm on it.

She assumed the posture of the priestess,
and in the parched air, the twigs she gathered
caught with little effort, and the bowl in her
lap grew bright and orange and warm. Then,
she opened her palms with some trepidation,
dropping half of the petals into the flame,
keeping what little remained for a memento.

Deep breaths. Closed eyelids. Smoke filled
her nostrils, rolling over and into her lips and
mouth. She let herself go, consumed by the
curling, encompassing, intoxicating scent of
the burning ilm.

The world shifted on its axis, tilted slowly
away like the sides of a canoe, making her
want to vomit. Her reality was coming
undone, the muted greens and blues of the
hallway turning more vivid and less distinct.
Shapes contorted into myriad facets she could
not process. Her sense of occupying space
ceased to exist, leaving her with only a
lingering impression of self, until this too
broke apart. The burden of existence lifted
from her mind, every hurtful sensation, every
woeful thought to cross her ravaged brain—it
all went rising up from the tether of her

memory. Who she had been, the totality of her story, was now no more substantive than the flap of a butterfly's wings. It all became terribly obvious, the illusory façade of reality and the inherent flaw of meaning. She peered through the Veil, witnessing with eyes not her own the underlying, hidden Nature of all things. And she realized she was gone. Gone from the shackles of identity.

DAY ...

*N*othing is anywhere.
It was her first thought, and she did not quite know what it meant. She felt only an inexorable forward motion, but knew she could not be walking, because the throbbing in her ankle had entirely ceased. Instead, she drifted like a leaf in a current.

She found herself in the blank spaces between thought and substance. Whether up or down, she could not say, and why she could not say, she did not know. Direction here was meaningless. Vertigo consumed her, a perpetual spinning sensation as she groped blinding at foundations that were not there, while that same enigmatic force tugged at her being, pulling her inexorably . . . somewhere.

Passings, days, aeons meant nothing. She occupied a space outside of Time, though she held fast to the concept. A sea of emptiness threatened to drown her, to erase her from existence, and measures of time and place were her only moorings.

*Am I dead? I must be. This must be what
it feels like, this losing oneself, this slipping
away from everything, and everyone . . .*

Like everything else, her fear died away,
for emotion could not endure against the
eroding tide of eternity. And for an uncertain
dimension, she waited to join that emptiness,
finding soft solace in the loss of pain and
sorrow, knowing she would never again have
to live as she had lived, waking day after day
after torturous day.

Nothing lasts forever was a comforting
thought.

The Cycle turned as it always must, and
out of that emptiness, a spark gave shape to
the darkness. She saw the campfire in the
cave again, luring her toward it with the
promise of knowledge, the way an infant
seeks to know. The white-gold light was
omnipresent, stretching like sunlight across
an infinite expanse, but its brightness did not
hurt her eyes because she did not have eyes.
Its radiance became a part of her, had been a
part of her since her birth, and her movement
through it formed a luminous *tunnel*. In
Ilmarinen, tunnels did not exist, only
passageways formed by openings in the rocks,
footpaths covered by overarching branches,
but never anything so uniform. Yet somehow,
she knew the word, *tunnel*. And the force
tugging at her was the undammable *River of
Time*, the course of her life making up an
infinitesimal part of its flow.

The uncontrollable spinning, the sense of vertigo, began to slow. Locality reasserted itself piece by piece, and her feelings of disorientation and disembodiment—that she existed outside of herself—became a memory. She felt alive again, solid, in possession of weight.

She gazed out into the luminous void, searching for any semblance of place, any recognizable thing to hold to. That she was anywhere at all was a welcome notion. But where could she be?

She watched the light gradually gather into shapes, vague and blurry shapes. Colors and lines swam about her head, intersecting and coalescing into images she could scarcely discern. It was like her vision returning after staring directly into the sun.

After what seemed a lifetime of waiting, an alien landscape emerged, but what she saw made little sense, and she again felt the need for new words, for the vocabulary to describe her surroundings. Towers climbed skyward in numbers beyond counting, rising from every slope and valley, a sprawling, unnatural forest of worked stone and iron reaching the horizon. They stood taller than redwoods, their silhouettes cutting darkly against the smoky, amber atmosphere, the highest among them breaking up through the cirrus clouds above like the prow of a canoe diverting the flow of a whitewater stream. Window panes covered every wall, reflecting the sun like gilded pools of still water. Delicate webs of brick and iron crossed impossible divides, bridging high and low, arches overlapping arches.

The land bustled with activity. It should not have surprised her to see them, but it did, humans everywhere, no bigger than mites from her vantage point, scurrying anxiously, urgently. She could not make out what they were doing, yet they reminded her of herd animals, penned between the walls of their making, beneath the shadows of their monuments.

Plants were bound to particular regions, their roots confined by ribs of iron and stonework, the limbs of the trees kept short, never allowed to flourish to their fullest. Grasses were cut into perfectly rectangular fields, courting walls, and hanging loosely from terraces, while no other vegetation was permitted to grow. Every wild thing was stripped away, culled from the stem, and what little diversity remained had become tame and lifeless. For the sake of orderliness, she could nowhere see the strokes of henna adorning the world.

She could have marveled at these mysteries the entire day, spent passings observing the endless throng of people and the eclectic features of that great city until the fall of eclipse. *City.* That was the word she had been searching for, the word she needed to describe the Outsiders' settlement.

This is a city.

Other words filtered into her brain like scales sinking to the bottom of a water-filled tub. *Colonnades, domes, minarets, stadia.* How did she know these terms, and from whence did they come? The cerebral onslaught was disquieting, frightening, as if another person, another mind with her own thoughts and memories, had taken residence inside her skull.

Stadia were built for games and celebrations and could seat tens of thousands. But such numbers did not exist in Ilmarinen. Baba and her brothers cut notches into posts to mark chickens and sheep and stores of grain, but nothing worth counting amounted to more than a thousand. *One-hundred* was the biggest number known to the Ilmar. She doubted ten-thousand people lived in the whole of her country, yet everyone she had ever met could fit comfortably in a single stadia.

A sound like rolling thunder pealed across the sky, and her eyes were drawn to a winged shape ascending to the clouds. It resembled a bird in every way, complete with feathers, talons, and a beak. *It has to be a bird.* But the feathers were individually sculpted like a toy whittled out of wood, and its surface shone like brass, with the tip of its beak and the dome of its eyes gleaming a metallic orange hue.

Goddess! Even the birds are manmade!

The spectacle filled her with awe, but also with a sense that what she was witnessing was an affront to the Goddess. The cleverness of her species exceeded the scope of her imagination. But if the ilma of the city were so very clever, how then did they perish? Surely, if they could fashion a bird of iron and make it fly, they could produce food and draw up water.

The flying contraption screamed higher and higher into the ether, above the gold and pink clouds, diminishing from sight until she could no longer make out its arrowhead shape. She considered where it might be going, when a sudden sinking feeling came over her, and she had to tear her eyes from the sky lest she toss up the remains of her stomach. When she dared to look up again, she became disorientated, unable to find her bearings. The Greater Moon, the familiar curve that followed in her steps no matter how far she trekked from home, was not distant, not faded, but gone. Entirely gone.

The sky was the wrong color, absent the turquoise glow of Infinity, nor could she find the smaller, violet moon. Even the sun looked strange. It appeared slightly larger, now that she really looked at it, and a lot more yellow. The atmosphere was also different, more hazy and gray than she had ever seen it. The air smelled of charcoal, and enclosed spaces, like pockets of air trapped under the rotting muck of the earth, and she suddenly found it more difficult to breathe.

The uncanny feeling of otherworldliness, of being where she was not meant to be, churned in her insides. Gooseflesh broke out across her skin. It was an eerie feeling, an alien form of dread, an emotion she could not describe, bringing to mind a fish in a net experiencing dry land for the first and only time.

Before the Greater Moon . . .

Yes. She remembered the stories, what her sister, the plain-looking one—*what was her name?*—had said to her. She was in the time *before*, before the moons guarded the land, when Solos ruled alone in the sky.

I have to get back! That was her immediate thought. A solitary, pressing thought. She could not remember how she came here or why, only that she had to go. But as she turned to find her way, she realized that she could no longer feel the textures under her soles. *Shoes*—another new word—encased her feet in rubber, lacing in a crisscross fashion to her calves. Her arms were also covered in long hanging sleeves. The same jade color continued to conceal her midsection, noumena, and thighs. Feeling trapped and suffocated, she wanted to tear the fabric from her skin. She then brought her hands to her scalp, fondling the dark follicles draping neatly over the top of her spine, discovering with a twinge of horror that her braid was also missing.

I am not me! I am—!

She felt faint, seized with vertigo, and nearing collapse. The body she inhabited did not belong to her. It was the wrong shape, softer and more supple and less slender than the one she used to occupy. But if she was not herself, who was she? And would this person wish to rid herself of all her clothes? *Clothing*, another pivotal word, was the defining characteristic of civilized society, that she knew to be both customary and mandatory. She remembered Aola's apprehension when she bared herself to bathe in the woods. How might the Outsiders judge her if she were to do away with her outer layers? Might she be cast out? Imprisoned? Killed?

She needed to return to her own body, to be free of this fish-out-of-water sensation, but she had come here for a reason. At least, she thought she had.

She spotted a door opposite the ledge. It shone with a brilliant hue, clean of the centuries of built-up grime, the standard of the ilm displayed prominently across its face. The two halves of the door parted at her approach, recessing into the wall with a subtle swish to reveal a small rectangular room. *Down.* If she were to step into it, the four-man room would carry her down to the city's lower levels, where the body she inhabited took up residence. But she did not want to go that way. She dreaded meeting with the natives of this age. Keeping to the parapet, she could remain safely out of reach, protect her mind from the madness of the masses below.

A peculiar artifact caught her eye, an oddity set into the wall adjacent to the elevating room, and a confluence of disparate thoughts hit her at once. What she saw was both familiar and unfamiliar. Part of her recognized the runes from the savannah and the halfman village. The shaman had used the decaying menhir as a sacrificial altar. But during the storm, the altar had come alive, waking with the fire of the gods, with *electrical* fire, to reveal its true function. The device was all too common to the woman whose body she occupied, a critical component of everyday life, as essential as a pottery wheel. Without thinking, her fingers moved over its face—its *panel*—and a tiny door unfolded like the ripening bud of a flower. The pupil in the metallic iris popped out with a whizzing sound and circled about her head. She watched it go, and that doubling sensation came over her again, the feeling that what she was seeing was somehow both magical and mundane. Her two sides saw the object differently, but the primitive naked girl recognized the glass ball from the pile of broken artifacts she found buried in the city's outskirts.

The sphere paused beside her face, defying the pull of gravity like a hummingbird, but without the distinct flurry of wings—or wings of any kind.

"Are you in need of assistance?" a feminine voice sounded from within the glass.

"I . . . Um." The language of the period
dripped from her tongue, increasing her sense
of duality. But she did not wish to give sway
to the other person inside of her. The woman
she inhabited would not know what to ask,
unaware of the dream journey or the plight of
the starving girl from the future.

"It looks like you have not activated your
memory module. Would you like me to
activate it for you?"

She instinctively slipped her hand into an
opening in her clothes, her *pocket*, closing her
fingers about a smooth round object. *I have
one too . . .*

Sensing her hesitation, the orb triggered
with a flash. A faint blue glow expanded from
the point of light, shaping itself into limbs, a
navel, a curtain of dark, shoulder-length hair,
and a young woman's face with luminous
skin.

"Your heart rate appears elevated, and
your pupils have dilated. Would you like me
to contact medical services?"

She stared through the flickering female
pattern, into the simple mound emulating her
bosom, past the abstract features of her nose
and eyes, to the door set in the wall behind
her. It was like looking through a human-
shaped mist. "No, no . . . I'm fine. I think."

"Based on my records, your name is Tel'na
Oren. Would you like me to contact a
member of your family?"

The ghostly woman appeared to be
imitating speech, like a marionette, her lips

infrequently aligning to the syllables, sometimes missing words altogether. The Ilmarin inside of Tel'na thought the apparition as bewildering as it was mesmerizing, stirring within her a bevy of questions. *What exactly is this thing?* Did she have her own thoughts? Was she alive or just the reflection of a person? And how would she go about contacting members of Tel'na's family? She did not see anyone around, no one within earshot, anyway.

"I would like some answers, please . . ."

The face mimicked a smile, while her eyes remained hollow, displaying no emotion, translucent as ewers of water. "I am delighted to be of assistance."

"What—Who are you?"

"My name is Simqua. I am your personal information assistant." The woman composed of light conveyed a welcoming, friendly disposition. But it was all false, her smile no more genuine than a rock resembling a human head.

"Do you know when, I mean, where I am?"

"You are located in the 23rd district of the South Main Tower—"

"No, stop . . . what I meant to ask is, what land is this, exactly?"

"This is the Urba Province," Simqua said plainly. "Would you like to know more?"

"Yes, please."

"In 7801, the Urba Province was established in the southeast continent along the Quebla River Basin. After less than a century, Urba became a central hub for commerce, with a focus on graphene production, antimatter production, and other high value exports. Approximately forty million people live and work in Urba today. These populations are concentrated within Urba's major metropolises, the largest of which include Tennia and Zenttyr. Tennia serves as Urba's administrative capital and is an information research and development center. In 9760, Kjus K'lon was elected mayor of Tennia. His current position—"

"Wait!" That name—*Kjus*—she knew that name! Aliaa had mentioned him in her story by the cave. The Goddess had chosen him to lead humanity to safety the day Solos became angry, when the sun ravaged the world ages ago. Kjus lived in Ilmarinen, founded the Keepers and the Monastery of Alashiya in the Ukko Mountains. "Simqua, could you tell me more about Kjus, please?"

"Would you like me to contact Mayor K'lon for you?"

"C-Could you?"

"The mayor strongly advocates person-to-person communication. If he is not preoccupied, he may speak with you directly." Simqua lowered her arms to her hips and steadily started to rise. Her bare toes pointed a foot above the floor, yet her weightless posture posed no mystery. Simqua was nothing but a trick of the light, like a rainbow that forms in the sky still hazy from the rain. Only her glass heart had any real substance to it, but how that managed to fly, she could not guess.

Translucent lids closed over her blue-flame pupils, and the ghostly woman adopted a trancelike appearance as though she were slipping into a dream journey of her own. A moment later, the pattern quavered like the plucked chord of an olol, and when the image settled into focus, Simqua had gone. The person manifesting in her spot stood taller but was just as insubstantial, a quivering phantom barely holding to its form. She looked him over incredulously, studied his bearded face, and deep-set eyes. His body, from the neck down, he kept hidden. He wore the traditional *gown* of the mayor, the buried part of her mind informed her. This man could not be who she hoped, could not be the Kjus from the songs, songs she had heard since she was old enough to listen.

"Citizen Tel'na, you appear distressed. How may I be of service?"

"Y-You're Kjus? *You?*"

"The one and the same."

The prominence in his voice, and the way he carried himself, were enough to quiet her doubts. His eyes were so like her father's, possessing the same hard qualities, black and glinting and burdened with too many hardships. She could see the troubled storm behind those eyes, the thoughts mulled over until the mind is ground to powder, the torment of things that can never be shared. Many truths became apparent to her, and the sudden impact, the weight of that awful epiphany, threatened to turn her knees to mush. The most important figure in history, the man immortalized by her people in song, the savior of their world, stood before her in the garb of an Outsider.

"Your mental patterns are highly erratic," Kjus said. "They seem to be doubling up, creating a kind of feedback loop." He grew silent, contemplative, adding, finally, "You're not—You're not from here. Who are you, really?"

"Me? . . . I am . . . I'm . . ." She strained to remember herself, to fish her identity from the deep well of Time but came up empty. "I'm from Ilmarinen, from the Braid River Valley. I know that much, at least." She felt completely inept. How could she remember all that and not her name? Did the place she was raised in mean more than who she was? Or could it be that home and self are intrinsically linked? One and the same?

His face beamed like an overeager child with a new toy. "A dreamer!" he exclaimed. "The soul is a nimble thing, indeed! Smaller than the smallest lepton, beyond the bounds of time and space."

"I'm sorry," she said. "I do not know where I am or how I got here. But some task nags at me, something I am supposed to do, but I am just so confused and, well . . . afraid."

He strolled away, and the orb emitting his form followed. "Walk with me, girl. You're not the first to seek me out in this manner, but

you are by far the most present. Voices come
to me like ripples, echoing from the past—
sometimes even the future—but they're just
echoes, you see, and I sometimes have trouble
separating what I hear, or think I hear, from
my own thoughts. I'm lucky to catch a phrase
here and there, decipher any meaning at all,
really, much less carry on a conversation. Of
course, some days, I thought my imagination
was getting the better of me, that maybe I was
just going insane. But *you*, you, my dear, are
altogether *here*! Clear evidence that old
polymath, Eldin, was right!"

His words were stupefying. She felt like a
two-year-old, possessing only a rudimentary
grasp of language, with a brain like unshaped
clay. She stood awkwardly attired in fabrics
she did not recognize on a balcony
overlooking sights her faculties could scarcely
process, knowing only that a projection
calling itself Kjus wished her to follow him.

"You said you were from Ilmarinen, is that
right?"

She nodded.

"That name—it didn't exist in my time.
When I first encountered your people, you
were entirely unaware of the wider world. You
believed all of Aenya was the mountains
above, the forests below, and the river in-
between. But you did have a name for the *ilm*,
that remarkable flower that can't be found
anywhere else but in your country. So I
named the land after that. What I didn't know
at the time is that *ilma*, in your tongue, also

meant *human*, which is only fitting, I suppose. You are truly the 'people of the flower.'"

She sensed a tremendous melancholy welling up from within him. "I fought desperately to save your people, I truly did, but the senior rank in the Ascendency was loath to listen. They couldn't see anything worth preserving. 'No intellectual value,' is how they put it, 'remnants of a bygone age,' 'holdouts to modernity,' 'lingering vestiges of prehistoric man,' and all that nonsense. Hours of debate and it all amounted to the same old rhetoric. They said to act with mercy was to force you out of the woods, adopt you to *our* society, teach you *proper* ways to live." Kjus uttered this last part with disdain. "But I saw through them and their insincere protests, for I know—and I may be the only one who knows—the great folly of the human mind. Do you want to hear what it is?"

She considered answering, but he went on before she could open her mouth. Evidently, he was speaking more to himself than to her, offering his impassioned plea before some imaginary tribunal.

"Let me tell you! *Humans insist they are anything but animals, divine beings driven by reason*, but we follow our instincts like every other animal. We act on our *feelings* and then, and only then, does anyone consider the critical faculties of their brains. Reason is rarely ever used to decide what matters, but to win arguments, to justify whatever horrible actions our passions lead us to."

She wanted to ask what he meant by this and what it might have to do with her and Ilmarinen. But Kjus did not seem interested in holding a discussion, carried away, as he was, by his own passion.

"So they voted me down, and that's when they showed their true faces, the greed driving all their reasons. Special interest groups lobbied to raze the forest down. They were willing to cut every tree in the Wildwood, rip out every plant, displace thousands of species on the brink of extinction, and to what end? To make room for agriculture and housing, and let's not forget . . . the never-ending pursuit of money."

He uttered the last word, *money*, with such despondency, she assumed there was no greater evil in the world.

"We are a wretched species, a sickness plaguing this planet, but what I discovered in the wild restored my faith, my hope, that human evolution was not in vain. In your people, I saw a kind of cultural innocence, an escape from corruption, from the ugly influences of civilization. But the plutocrats scoffed. They could not see the beauty I had found . . .

"So, I campaigned for mayor of Tennia, and after winning the election, I halted the logging, reined in the pollution, and created new legislation to safeguard the Wildwood and the indigenous races dwelling within it.

And when the end came . . . the doom that visits every civilization in its time, well . . . I like to think the best of humanity was salvaged."

Kjus was telling a story, she realized, not how the Ilmar would tell it, not as a ballad, but in his own meandering way. The pieces were slowly coming together. From what she understood, there had been a great contest of words between Kjus and the Outsiders bent on destroying her homeland. He stood against them and became the Goddess's champion, and while not born of her people, he eventually came to see himself as one of them.

"So the story is true . . ." she said at last. "Except, when we sing it, you were chosen by Alashiya to protect us from the sun when Solos turned angry."

He looked over the parapet as daylight washed across the silhouetted skyline. The sun shone brighter and more yellow than she remembered it, and in the dim avenues below, the windows in the towers flickered to life like waking fireflies.

"Truth can be found in every story. Sometimes, it can be literal truth, but more often, it's metaphorical. The sun, as you say, did get angry. It was swelling into a new phase, turning from a white medium star into a yellow giant. The process normally takes billions of years, and our scientists pinpointed the exact day the corona would consume us, the instance of our end. And do you know what we did about it? What our noble leaders did?"

She could only shake her head.

"*Nothing.* Oh, we had meetings, grand speeches galore. I penned one myself, I'm proud to say, brought the crowds to tears. But it all amounted to nothing. When the time came, we could not overcome human nature, couldn't bring ourselves to sacrifice our most basic wants for the greater good." He sighed. It was a long, hopeless, exasperated sound. "I really shouldn't be so judgmental. We evolved to think only about ourselves and those dearest to us. Humanity is ill-equipped to handle scales way beyond himself, to worry about an entire planet or the fates of his great-great-grandchildren."

She shielded her eyes from the burrowing yellow blaze in the sky. The searing heat was like a furnace against her pale cheeks, and she sensed a kind of menace in that light, wondering how such nourishing warmth—the source of all life—could turn against them. "It still doesn't make sense," she said. "If you knew the end was coming and could do something to prevent it, how could you let it happen?" Her eyes never strayed from the masses below. They went about their daily lives oblivious to the dreadful future awaiting them, and her heart ached with a sick and twisting horror. Every man, woman, and child, souls beyond reckoning, was doomed to burn. "You say we are animals . . ." she continued, ".

. . but animals fight to survive, don't they? All living things do."

He reached for her like a mentor comforting his pupil, his arm heavy in its sleeve, before pulling away. She would not have felt his touch because he was only a projection. "Your people would have found the will to do something, I don't doubt it. But we've been blinded for ages. Blinded by our excesses, our comforts, our craving for power and control.

"I see that you pity them, but we are already lost. Dead centuries before your time. Our fate, I believe, was decided long before any of us were born.

"We had shelter and food in abundance, everything anyone could want to survive. But still, our lives felt meaningless. So we sought distractions, ways to imitate the life our ancestors had. This technology you're so impressed by, well . . . it impressed us just the same. But what did our brilliant inventions amount to? Just a false and hollow existence. The orb granted every dream you could wish for, sated the emptiness and isolation growing within us until family, friendship, and love became nothing more than commodities, products to be sold and paid for. But it was not enough, never enough, because none of it was real.

"When the disaster came, when the sun turned so bright we couldn't lift our eyes to see it, we were too late to stop it. The wealthy managed to save their hides, of course, some of them merging into golems, others jumping through Fantastigates to get to alien worlds. But for the lower castes, there was no escape. The plutocrats had long seen to it, driven by their need for consumption, never thinking about the generations coming after them. The people fed on the orb's lies, and in all that senseless noise, our warnings went unheeded. I did what I could, railed against the *information plague* eating away at our humanity, and they called me an idealist, a luddite, a madman! The orb comforted them with delusions even as the forests burned and plumes of ash blackened the sky. We were lost, unable to distinguish between what we wanted to believe and what we needed to believe."

Her head felt too heavy for her neck. Overburdened with ideas. The particulars of the matter eluded her. But his zeal, combined with her own experience exploring the ruined city, instilled in her the spirit of what he was trying to say.

An uncomfortable silence grew between them then, and she knew he was waiting for her to offer some rebuttal, some perspective about a situation she had only glimpsed and could scarcely fathom. "If you are here now . . ." she said, carefully choosing her words, "then how can you know what will happen later?"

His face beamed with pride, surprised, she imagined, by what she managed to grasp of his story. "I've taken my own journeys, searched past and future myself. But all I ever saw were impressions, fragmentary moments of things to come. Of course, I had my doubts, never sure it wasn't just a dream, or the delusions of an addled brain, like my detractors keep claiming. I needed hard evidence. Needed to prove my predictions to show the Ascendency the folly of their ways. But I never managed it and never did sway them."

"If you thought you might be dreaming, why were you so convinced?"

He moved to speak, then hesitated. He did not have all the answers, she knew, and her question caught him without a ready reply. "You're right," he admitted. "I did not know for certain. I had only conjectures. Was the sun expanding? Yes. Every scientist could agree on that. But what was to be done about it? How were we to summon the commitment to avert the coming cataclysm? Oh, there were many suggestions, too many, but mine was deemed the most radical.

"It hit me during my time with your people. How could I have known we had lost our humanity before finding humanity for the first time? We had to take a step back before we could move forward. Find the will to preserve life by learning to *live it*. But the Ascendency couldn't see through to my way of thinking. They could not make the connection between the loss of our humanity and saving our future, refusing to accept that a primitive people—a people who went about naked, of all things—had anything of value to teach them." He looked wistfully over the railing. It was clear to her that the city would never accept him or his views, yet his convictions remained inviolable. "They'd never met you, so they couldn't know. A lifetime of philosophizing cannot replace an instance of experience."

Three metallic birds roared overhead like a gaggle of geese in formation, blue flame gushing from their tail fins, leaving a trail of hot shimmering air in their wake. She could feel the power of their engines in her ears, in her skin. They passed so closely that she could peer into the openings in their sides— see the passengers seated in the bellies of those monstrous birds. They should be amazed, she thought, in a perpetual state of awe. But she supposed that, in a world where wonders are commonplace, where sights and sounds can be delivered effortlessly across vast distances, even flight can become tedious.

"You've heard my prattling long enough," Kjus said. "Now then, tell me, why are *you* here?"

"Me?" A slow panic started to rise in her. She could not remember anything about herself, how and why she had arrived, her purpose, or even her name. Everything was gone. And the longer she mulled it over, the more the answers seemed to slip away. Her brain felt like a sieve and all of her memories were leaking out of it.

"Are you having trouble remembering?"
She nodded.

"I feared this might happen. The longer
you inhabit another's physical form, the more
your true self, your wandering spirit, is
consumed by it. The brain is a part of the
body you are occupying, and the brain holds
everything we think we understand of the
self. This is why dreams fade so quickly when
you wake. If you do not return to your future
soon, your Ilmarin persona will seem like it
never existed, and you will remain here
forever. Live as Tel'na, a citizen of Tennia,
until the end of this era. Until the sun burns
up the world."

She felt a slight tug at the core of her
being, and when she lifted her palm to her
cheek, she found a tear there. It ran down
over her lip and chin, but she could not see it.
Her shoulders were beginning to feel wet
now, like mist gathering over her skin, and
then the droplets started to fall. She could
hear them, the pitter-patter of steady falling
water echoing through the ages, drumming in
her ears like the memory of a song.

"Thelana," she said triumphantly, wiping
the raindrops from her brow, the raindrops
that were not there. "My name is Thelana."

"You've found the way to return then,
Thelana." He looked pained, aged before his
time, drained of hope but glad to have met
her. "Your name is the key. Now go before it's
too late."

"No!" she cried. "I can't go back! I am . . . trapped. Trapped in the ruins of this city. Dying."

"Where are you, exactly? In the city?"

"It's hard to say. Everything is so different . . . except . . . there is a door." She directed his gaze to the wall beside the electrical panel and the ilm emblazoned upon it. "But the door doesn't look out from here. I think it's below us. Below ground."

"In the slums," he offered matter-of-factly. "The lower levels."

"Yes. I am buried and can't get out. Please, tell me what I must do."

For a time, he stood without speaking, shimmering in his incorporeal form, until she began to fear that the orb had lost its connection to him. But when he opened his eyes again, she knew he had only been working the problem.

"You know what to do, Thelana. You only needed a little help from me. Ten years from now, when the city evacuates, I will make certain to shut every door in the slums. I will seal up every entrance and exit and all the drainage ports. So that when the rains come, the city will flood. Do you understand what you must do now?"

She thought, hoped, that she did, but her hold on the past was beginning to falter. The pull of the future was growing too great for her to resist. She could no longer make out the citizens below. They were turning into ghosts, into elongated, glowing wisps. Every window and door in Tennia became less and less substantial until disappearing altogether. The great domes and bridges and towers followed, becoming abstractions, cloudy brushstrokes, a painter's impression of what a city might look like. Only Kjus persisted, a solid image in a white void, yet he was also willowing away, not merely from her eyes and ears, but the very notion of him.

Surely, she had only dreamed of this fatherly figure, only imagined the impossible story he had to tell, a story she could now scarcely recall. He could not have been real . . . could not have been . . . and yet she needed him to be. Her consciousness was drowning in the traumatic events of a girl named Thelana and she still needed his counsel.

"I don't want to go. I don't want to forget you."

"If you listen carefully, you will hear your ancestors speak to you. Their voices are encoded in the essence of your blood. They share their wisdom when you are at your lowest, when you need it most, when you open yourself to them. I've no doubt you will live to do great things, Thelana, and the things you will see and do will trigger memories of the time we've shared together. You may not remember the when or the where, but the spirit of our talks will endure."

She opened her eyes to the hard, grimy surfaces of the future, to the chill of pounding rain, but could still make out his spectral form, the lingering vision overlapping her present. She wanted desperately to hold fast to his words, certain no greater wisdom existed in all the cosmos and, as if in answer to her thoughts, a lasting reply came drifting back through the ages.

"It was you who taught me what it means to live. The wisdom is yours to carry forward. Guard it well."

DAY 210

Kabira strolled into the main room with a yawn and an aching back. Morning had come too soon, intruding on her sleep through the dusty slats of her window, casting her meager furnishings in a pale light. Her eyes were filmy, the bottom rims still sticking to her lashes. But it did not much matter, for there was nothing worth looking at, all the same stuff for decades on end. The main room—and only room besides her bed space—consisted of a cabinet, a table worn to the pulp with a few equally worn chairs, and a chiminea neatly set in an alcove. But she was not one to complain, for all of it was hers, and she did what she could to keep it tidy.

A besom leaned in a corner by the door, where she placed it every afternoon and where it waited for her sandpaper fingers to begin the day. The broom had been a wedding gift, her mother-in-law's subtle suggestion that her son's new bride keep a clean house. Kabira's husband had never been one to splurge on items of a practical nature, least of all, anything that might help a wife tend to her chores. He spent the little money they earned tossing dice and watching prettier, younger girls gyrate their hips.

They found her husband in a bed of grass with his arms splayed apart. An empty bottle teetered from his palm and the morning dew glistened from his eyelashes. He had slept soundly through the night, so soundly in his drunkenness that he neglected the growing chill, and his embattled heart gave up the fight. *Coldest night on record*, the watchmen assured her. But that was of no consolation to a newly made widow, neither mitigating the blow when they first told her nor easing the lifetime of drudgery that followed. Kabira's husband had gone out and gotten himself dead, leaving her with two children she could not afford, a beat-up shack of a house worth *fishies*, and a dilapidated besom fraying at the ends. Perhaps, if she had been a more comely woman, with a fair face and a more shapely figure, she might have snagged herself a second suitor, a man with a heavy coin purse this time and better habits. But that was not to be.

As her thirties rolled into her forties, Kabira lost hope that a wealthy stranger might see in her something worth wanting, and so she turned her daydreaming to her children's futures.

Her son was conscripted early. He had just been a boy, really, a day over fourteen when the recruiters came marching into town. They sent him packing off to a place called Narth to battle bogren hordes. She would never learn whether he still lived or was taken by the Taker, but she never saw her son again.

But the gods were not entirely unkind, for Kabira had also been blessed with a girl, and the Kratan legion did not steal daughters for their wars. The child was comely enough for marriage, more than she had any right to be, and if Kabira could manage to keep her from the brothels, she might have attracted the eye of a suitor. Even a well-to-do merchant would have sufficed, a vendor with a proper kiosk and respectable wares brought in from exotic, faraway places. Rugs stitched in Shemselinihar. Pots fashioned in Hedonia. Fabrics woven in Yefira. A husband like that could afford her a new broom, or two brooms, or better yet, a serving girl to do the sweeping for them. But that was not to be.

Sometime after turning fifty—she could not be sure of the date, for she had long stopped counting—Kabira's daughter went to bed complaining of a sharp pain in her belly. The pain worsened as the night wore on. Simple teas did little to alleviate the symptoms, and they had no coin to pay the apothecary. By morning, Kabira found her only child cold and white, and deathly still.

When everyone that mattered to her was gone, Kabira was left with nothing but her chores and a smattering of belongings: a larder stocked with a cycle's worth of goods; some meager cooking supplies; a clothesline of rough spun tunics that once belonged to her parents; a few cots; a tub for washing and bathing; a fancy mirror from Hedonia, given as part of her dowry; and a single beat-up besom.

She did not mind the work. Never once complained of it. Despite her aging body, Kabira found solace in routine, a respite from the thoughts that kept her turning in the night. Her past and inevitable future could not trouble her so long as she kept the dust from the floors, the chiminea clean of ash, and the stains scrubbed from her clothes.

The only door in or out of the house stood on a tilt on rusting hinges, allowing bands of daylight to poke between the seams. Climbing the few steps of her ladder, Kabira threw open the hatch leading to the balcony. She slept on the roof under pleasant weather, and in the daytime, the hatch let in more of the sun until the main room was awash with light, a blessing for someone whose vision was beginning to fail. Her only trouble involved the shoddy state of the floor. The boards were coming apart, and weeds sprouted continually through the cracks, despite her every attempt to pry them from their roots. Now, whenever she went to sweep, the bundle of twigs in her hands got caught up in the prickly stems growing out of the floor, which made her back ache and tore apart her only besom.

Sweeping will just have to wait, she decided, setting the broomstick aside. What she needed now was a good pot of boiling

Nick Alimonos

water. Why waste so fine a day doing menial
tasks when she could sit and enjoy her tea?
Besides, her nag of a mother-in-law was dead
and unable to chastise her, nor was her
husband alive with his usual excuses for
hitting her.

Her kettle sat on the mantle, no bigger
than her head. It possessed an abnormally
long, looping grip, which she believed was of
Shemite design, but she could not be sure. She
would need to carry it outside to the pump,
but as she lifted the latch from her front door,
a somewhat familiar sound turned her ears,
stirring up feelings of annoyance and rage.

A plot of soil lay to the rear of the house,
two paces wide and a single step deep, set
between the back wall and a billowing line of
sheets. Kabira could expect to collect
basketfuls of carrots, turnips, napshins,
cabbages, eggplants, and leeks during a good
season. When she could not afford seeds, she
relied on whatever the birds pilfered from the
neighbor's gardens. The vegetables provided
for soups and trading for other goods. But
thieves abounded where the earth was
bountiful.

The kettle clanged to the floor as she
snatched up her besom and hurried out the
door. She regularly defended her crop from
rabbits, groundhogs, and the occasional
coyote. But the beast digging up her carrots
looked like no animal she had ever seen. It
bent over her small plot of vegetables, as big
as a hog, with splotches of dirt—or could it be

manure?—caking its hairless body, with a knobby spine raised in an elegant curve like the frill of a lizard.

Kabira edged closer, tightening her grip on her broom, focusing her ailing eyes on the creature, uncertain whether she should be afraid or angry. A wild hog could be dangerous.

"Hey!" she bellowed. "Hey there! You get out of my garden!"

The beast stood to its full height and her poor vision settled upon it, and what she saw nibbling on her carrot so voraciously was no animal but a young girl, her face muddied, loose skin peeling off her lips. Kabira thought she might be a beggar or some orphan child robbed of her clothes, but she was quickly dissuaded of the notion by the graceful way the girl moved, by her sinewy physique and the intense focus of her shimmering eyes, eyes that glowed like bright green algae under a running stream.

The girl vanished, crossing from the garden to the front of the house and toward the town square. Despite her limp, she moved with frightful speed, like a hare running from a fox, her disheveled braid snapping over her exposed buttocks. Dozens of shopkeepers would be setting up their tents, awaiting the daily bustle of customers. If the girl were to continue on as she was, every eye would fall upon her and take in every bit of her. Kabira could not fathom herself in such a situation. If she were to be seen out in the open like that, she would undoubtedly die of embarrassment. Even the brothel girls had sense enough to keep themselves covered and their proclivities discreet. But the poor girl did not seem to know any better. She was surely a *wilding*, some child abandoned in the woods as an infant, left alone to fend for herself. *A feral girl.*

Kabira snatched a white sheet from her clothesline, wound it tightly around her forearm, and started for the square. Her knees were not what they once were. She could not recall when she last attempted anything more than a brisk stroll. Perhaps, she had not broken into a full sprint since childhood. But she was gripped by a sense of purpose. The feral girl was close to her daughter's age, and Kabira could easily imagine the ridicule, the condemnation, the cruel jests made at her daughter's expense.

The people were just beginning to gather, drifting from their homes to the striped tents lining the cobbled center of town, when the girl arrived, wandering hither and thither without a care. They saw her but did not laugh—that reaction would come later—there was only an intense intrigue. Kabira could feel it thick in the air. Every merchant turned from the customers browsing their wares. Pots were hung up, baskets put back, smoked meats dropped in place. A watermelon rolled from a counter and smashed into a juicy pulp, but nobody seemed to care. For a time, all the goods in the market lessened in value. A young mother, with a babe in the crook of her arm, inquired as to what was happening. And even the youngsters broke from their games of catch and hide to look.

The feral girl stood in the square like an animal caught in a trap. She made no attempt to hide herself, to cover her bosom with her forearms, or shield the privacy adjoining her thighs. Her brazen disregard for decency was mesmerizing, stupefying the mass of onlookers. And still, Kabira heard no laughter nor any jeering remarks. She saw only pointing fingers and wide, wondering glances.

The white sheet she had brought undulated like a cloud as she lifted it over the feral girl's head. Kabira pictured herself on a boat, casting a wide net to ensnare a human-sized fish. Only, the wilding child did not wish to be caught, dashing from under the cascading fabric. And then the laughter started. Round and round the town square, she chased the feral girl, and the hoots and the hollers followed.

Catching the girl was like trying to nab a wild chicken with one hand. She moved with animal swiftness, her bare feet skimming the ground, and it was not long before Kabira dropped to one knee, her heavy frame heaving with every tortured breath, the fresh linen from her clothesline yellowing in the dirt.

"Get back here, child! Can't you see you're embarrassing yourself?"

The crowd roared in reply, and Kabira realized they were not laughing at the feral girl but at her. In her effort to save a stranger from shame, she had brought it upon herself, become the butt of the joke.

"Is that one yours, Kabira?" She could hear the mockery in his tone, someone who knew her by name. *Oh, will this nightmare never cease!*

She searched the sea of grinning faces, their shining eyes, their lips barely containing their mirth, but could not determine who had spoken. Her embarrassment was growing by the instant, but she could think of no way to extricate herself without looking even more the fool. If only she had let the girl go off alone.

"She's . . . She's my sister's child . . ." Kabira admitted. "She's very unwell, as you can see, not altogether there . . . in the head, I mean."

Despite her savage, unkempt appearance, the girl displayed an unexpected depth of curiosity. Kabira could see how she studied the townsfolk, their clothing, and their interactions.

The crowd began to murmur. Kabira could only hear snatches of what they were saying, theories mostly, regarding the strange naked child and who she might belong to. And with her attention drawn away, the feral girl crept closer, snatching the hem from Kabira's grasp. The sheet caught in the gale and sailed up, rippling broadly overhead.

The feral girl stood fascinated by the interplay between the wind and the fabric, and Kabira took the chance to grab the ends and fold her into it. The wilding child punched and kicked and whirled about, but Kabira held on, wrestling the girl into an awkward embrace as peals of laughter rang out across the square.

"I'm only doing what's best for you!" she cried. "You can't go running around like that!"

Once caught, she assumed the girl would be easy to subdue. Kabira was a sizable woman with brawny arms that could pull a plow across a track of upturned soil. Her own daughter had never been able to escape her grasp. But the girl fought to free herself as if the sheet were on fire, with a strength belying her emaciated appearance.

Kabira's patience had run out. She was prepared to leave her "niece" alone with the mob, to whatever awful fate they might think up. Girls without homes did not fare well in Makria. They usually turned into beggars or brothel workers. But before she could go, an arm from within the tented fabric went flying in a blind arc. Kabira recoiled from the blow, and the watchful crowd hushed. Her face throbbed, and the tender area about her left eye started to swell. She wanted to weep, return to the sanctity of her home and never leave again.

The girl pulled the sheet from her head but did not run away. Seeing what she had done gave her pause. She looked saddened by it, remorseful even. But Kabira was less mindful of the pain. Bruises healed. Bones could be mended. Reputations could not.

If the rumpled sheet had ever been white, only Kabira would have known. The girl knelt beside it, carefully examining the makeshift garment, prodding at it with a look of distaste as the townsfolk watched. Some of them were still chuckling. Others leered.

At last, she gathered up the fabric, turning the white-stained length like a puzzle, something she needed to figure out. She then wrapped herself in it, like an ill-fitted mattress, round and round like a child playing at dress-up.

DAY 214

The girl followed her home from the town square only to collapse in the cot her daughter once slept in. When she did not wake the following day, pity stayed Kabira's hand. "Poor thing . . . She must be so tired after all she's been through." She said this aloud to herself, despite only being able to imagine what horrors the girl may have been through.

"You poor, poor thing . . ." She muttered those words over and over throughout the day, stopping to repeat them while doing her chores, whether sweeping or preparing her meals.

Kabira let the child sleep for another three days, checking on her occasionally, like a mother making certain her newborn was breathing, when she decided the time had come to wake her.

It did not go as pleasantly as she imagined it would. The girl shot up with fright, so suddenly, Kabira stumbled backward on her heels. She then leapt into a crouch, like a cat readying to pounce, her mouth twisted into a snarl, her wild green eyes flashing. Kabira had to remind herself that she was only a child, not some wild animal that might hurt her.

The feral girl slowly took stock of the room, seeing the cot, the mirror, and Kabira standing there with her hands knotted together, and her dirt-caked face eased into a look of befuddlement, and her body adopted a less threatening demeanor.

The sheets will need a good scrubbing after today, Kabira thought. *And those feet are black!* But first, she would need to draw a bath.

She went out to the pump, and the wilding child followed. The sun had yet to fully crest the horizon and the early sky lay heavy with moonlight. Only the neighbors would be out to spy on their doings, but washing children in the open was a common practice and unlikely to draw much attention.

The pump had once been a pastel green, like a freshly plucked lime, but only muted patches of color remained. The girl squatted over the mechanism with fascination, poking orange flakes of rust from its edges. Kabira brushed her aside and went to work, an awful squeaking erupting from the metallic throat as she primed the handle. The pump was in poor condition without a man around to maintain it. But she made do with what she had, leaning her weight into every stroke. The spout rumbled and coughed until water sputtered out into the shallow basin below. And the girl gasped with amazement. Kabira's children had had a similar reaction once, when they were very little and the world was still new to them.

She took less kindly to the bath. Kabira had wanted to warm the water first, but that would have taken half the morning, and the child was filthy. Wrestling her into the tub was no easy feat, but Kabira managed it, forcing her to sit after a good quarter-passing. The more difficult challenge lay ahead, scrubbing the grime baked into the girl's skin. Kabira could not imagine anyone living in so squalid a manner. Street urchins who slept nightly in the grass would not have stomached the stench, she thought. Yet she was determined to rectify the situation. Kabira would break her back at the task, waste every bar of soap if necessary until this adopted child of hers was made presentable.

She labored well into the day, peeling layer after sooty layer, watching the tub turn from a milky hue to a clumpy black froth. The girl showed no signs of protest, having grown accustomed to the water, lulled by the revolving motion of Kabira's palms. But there were parts of the feral creature too stubborn to come clean. Ridges of hardened flesh, unsightly pink markings, discolored welts of purple and blue. *Great Sargonus! She's all beat up! These will never heal . . . How will she ever find a husband looking like this?*

"You poor, poor thing . . ."

When Kabira felt the girl was as clean as she would ever be, at least as anyone could

manage for the day, she turned her attention
to her hair. The girl's auburn locks, though
somewhat disheveled, were woven into a
lovely braid, and Kabira could not help
wondering how she could have managed it. If
she were abandoned as an infant in the wild,
if she had never even learned to wear clothes,
it did not seem possible.

She started in on the braid, tugging at the
knots with her fingertips to wash and wrap it
more neatly, when the girl lurched from the
tub, spilling half the water and nearly
knocking them both to their knees. Kabira
was taken aback. She had not seen her react
so violently since the town square.

The girl noticed her fear, drawing her
soapy forefinger tenderly over Kabira's
bruised eye, and a calm came over her. "No,"
she said, reaching around to the back of her
head.

"Y-You know how to talk?"

She offered no reply, but when her hand
appeared again, Kabira saw the browning
remnants of a strange looking flower resting
in her palm. The girl then stood from the tub,
carefully setting the petals aside before
undoing the braid herself. She seemed
unusually sensitive about her hair for
someone who insisted on running around
naked.

Kabira led her back into the house, and
the girl waited patiently by the door, her wet
body glistening, her hair running with soapy
water. *How different she looks after a bath!*

she thought, admiring her handiwork. *She's like a new person! Who would have thought it? She's almost . . . pretty.*

Her instinct was to offer the girl something to wear. Her daughter's clothes would likely fit, even if they were a bit baggy around the middle, but she reconsidered. The child would need to learn to wear clothes eventually, but would have difficulty understanding the need, and Kabira dreaded another violent altercation like the one they had in the town square. Besides, all that vigorous washing made her hungry, and the girl had to be starved after three days in bed.

She opened her cabinet, drawing out a bowl and a couple of jars from the shelves. Her supplies were limited, but it had to be more than the child was accustomed to eating. The vegetables in the garden were not yet ripe, so Kabira settled on sorghum in goat's milk. She made two bowls, one for each of them, then gathered a pair of wooden spoons and moved to set them on the table.

The girl's watchful gaze never strayed from her shoulders. But as Kabira rounded from the larder, they came nose-to-nose, and everything nearly fell to the floor. Those piercing green eyes never failed to startle her.

She has the self-awareness of a toddler, Kabira thought, like a three-year-old who hasn't yet learned how to behave around other people. But a keen intellect lay hidden behind that savage demeanor. Kabira saw it in the careful way the girl watched her prepare their meal. She seemed to want to know how everything worked and what it was used for. Perhaps, with some help, she could be taught to live a normal life. With proper manners, a little weight gain, and a lot of makeup to hide her scars, she might even someday make for a wife.

She set the bowls on the table, and the girl leapt into her chair, squatting with her feet planted into the seat.

"No! Not like that! Sit yourself down! Sit—" she patted her own posterior, "—with this, see? With your backside." She demonstrated by taking up a chair, and the girl slipped into her own. "Good!" Kabira said. "Now, be a good girl and eat your food."

She clasped the spoon in her fist like a spear, examined it closely, and started drumming the table.

"Great Sargonus, child, no! Must I teach you everything?"

Kabira demonstrated the basics of utensil use, spooning the sorghum from the bowl, and the girl expertly followed her example. "That's very good! Very good—" she was about to say 'girl' again, but hesitated. The child needed a name if she was ever going to be adopted into society. "Goodness! We haven't even been introduced, have we? Your name?" she asked. "Do you have a *name*?" Before she could answer, Kabira tapped her breastbone with her palm. "Ka-bee-ra!" she exclaimed. "I am Ka-bee-ra! And you are?"

"Thelana."

"Well, my, that is . . . That is quite pretty."
She had expected something more simple,
like a grunting noise. Who could have given
her such a name, if the girl was indeed feral, if
she had been left to fend for herself since she
was an infant? She started to think then that
perhaps she had been wrong about the child's
upbringing, and about many other things
also. Could she possibly know enough of their
language to carry on a conversation, she
wondered?

Kabira gestured to the floor, the walls, and
the solitary window, her arms encompassing
their surroundings. "This here . . . This is
Makria. What about you? Where are *you*
from?" she went on, overemphasizing the
'you.'

Without a word, Thelana left her chair
and strolled from the house, and Kabira
started to fret. Had she said something to
upset the girl? Was she running away again?
And what might the neighbors think if they
were to catch sight of her? Most townsfolk
lived far away, closer to the center of town,
and the only road leading to her home
consisted of dirt. Still, she did not wish to risk
further embarrassment.

The door creaked as she held it open. For
years, she had wanted to repair the hinges,
but there was no man in her life to do it, and
now it swung freely, a captive to the wind. She
found the girl just beyond the opening, her
eyes turned wistfully northward.

"There," she murmured. "I come from there."

Kabira had been right about one thing; the girl was native to the forest. But the untamed woods enveloped their small town on three sides. She could have found her way into Makria from any direction, but where she pointed to made Kabira's hair bristle. A host of invisible terrors seized her mind as she thought of that place, and a sickening wail rose up in her throat.

"No . . .! You don't say!"

From what she knew, the northern frontier was entirely impassable, bordered for days by sharp granite walls, thorny brambles, and a mass of gnarled trees. Whoever dared cross through that part of the world never returned. Even if the hills could be climbed and a path found through the foliage, worse things awaiting would-be adventurers. Ghosts haunted the woods to the north, which is why the people of Makria called it *The Land of the Dead*. She could not imagine anyone coming down from there, let alone someone her daughter's age. But it helped explain the girl's odd behavior, her injuries, and even her uncleanliness. Who had time to wash up in The Land of the Dead?

Kabira stared at her for an uncomfortably long time, reading the girl's striking green eyes, and knew she was being truthful.

"You poor, poor thing . . ." she said.

317

DAY 215

Thelana rocked from side to side until she found herself awake. Her cot did little to cushion the bumps in the warped floor, and the sheet the crazy old woman insisted on spreading over her made her sweat profusely.

She missed the subtle swaying of the branches, the wind flowing freely in her pores, the straw and beard moss packed under her spine and neck. But here, at least, she could feel safe. There were no sounds to be afraid of, only the chirping of the lovesick insects, the warbling of nesting birds, and the old woman's incessant snoring.

Sleep came coupled with exhaustion but was dreamless, empty, and for that, she could be grateful.

An open doorway led to the only other room in the house, where the nightly cacophony emanating from the woman's mouth and nostrils came and went in sudden spurts and stops. If Thelana were to have made such a racket in the Wildwood, she would have surely attracted every predator within a day's hike. But why the woman removed her cot to sleep by a cold hearth, leaving her alone in the room, Thelana could only guess. Could Kabira still be afraid? Or was it due to some custom?

Darkness reigned over the world, the light of morning having yet to emerge from the lone window above her cot. It might be passings before the day could begin, but Thelana was weary of sleep. She slowly managed her way to her feet, her ankle still aching from the voorgaven's bite, but she would forget the pain by midday. It would never go away entirely, she knew, yet she felt no resentment. Every morning, and for the rest of her life, her ankle would remind her of all she had endured. But the reminder would come as a whisper instead of a scream.

In the dimness of the Greater Moon, Thelana discovered that she was not alone. Another person occupied her bower, a girl of about the same age and height.

Britannia.

It could not be another hallucination; Thelana was neither starved nor injured. Her sister stood in the room as solid as the plaster peeling from the walls, as real as the cot at her heels and the grains in the floor. Britannia, it had to have been Britannia, watching her sleep without saying a word. She was now mimicking Thelana's every move, like she did when they played smacks.

The twin girls reached for one another until her fingers pushed against a cold, unyielding surface. *Glass*. She suddenly remembered the aged mirror with the whittled frame made to resemble waves. *Mirror*, another new word, for a device no less magical than the water pump.

Thelana peered into the mirror but could no longer see her sister nor anyone else she recognized. She touched the silvered glass again, examining her sallow face, her rough-jutting cheekbones, the knobs of her hips, the hollows of her ribbed bosom, the rivets of muscle weaving beneath her burnt and beaten hide. She was far from the girl who set out from home. That girl had been a waif. Life in the Wildwood had made her a stranger to herself, hardened her like calcified bone. But she did not know if she liked this new Thelana, and in fact, she knew that she didn't.

This girl no longer belonged, not among her family, not in the outside world, not anywhere.

DAY 246

*N**ew life. This is my new life . . .* And it was, without a doubt, a good one. *The Outside world*, no, she had to stop thinking of it that way; *the town of Makria*, rather, had everything she could ever want or need. She could drink from the magical pump paces from her door, and eat from Kabira's garden now that the vegetables were ripe.

Kabira's house was simple and small but had its charms. The clay chiminea, so much like her mother's, provided adequate warmth during cold nights—and nights in Makria were colder than she could have imagined in Ilmarinen—and the walls, decrepit as they were, kept away the pests. Thelana could not remember waking in the Wildwood without a single bug bite. Here, she expected no less.

Her chores were the only downsides to her new existence, but the work could not compare to gathering kindling, building fires, or searching for shelter. Nor did pulling weeds over so meager a plot as Kabira's bother her, not after putting in a hundredfold the effort on her father's farm. The old woman never insisted Thelana do anything more than help, but Kabira was too feeble to carry out her duties alone. She would have been an elder to the Ilmar, and elders did not busy themselves with the responsibilities of the youth. The Makrian woman had brought her into her home, shared her roof and food, and the gods demanded Thelana show gratitude.

Sweeping, she loathed, but Kabira complained about her back whenever she bent over to do it. Even after strapping new twigs to the frayed ends of her besom, removing every bit of debris from the house proved an impossible task. Dirt had never been an issue in the woods—the Goddess possessed her own restorative methods—but in tight spaces, where nature did not flow, there was a tendency for things to settle and stifle Thelana's breathing.

Back and forth and back again, she glided the bundle of sticks over the uneven floor as Kabira sipped her morning tea. Some days, the dust billowed into a hazy cloud to make Thelana's eyes water and her throat turn dry. But despite her sincerest efforts, the house never much improved, and she often questioned whether she was not just rearranging the dirt, moving it from one corner to the other. It seemed that nature abhorred cleanliness, and Thelana felt—knew rather—she was fighting a losing battle.

Washing the small ceramic dishes from the larder proved easier. Thelana could even say she enjoyed it. She and Kabira knelt together by the tub—the same one they used for bathing—to soak and rinse the plates, bowls, and cups.

Soap was another marvel for Thelana to discover. The bubbles produced by the squishy pale blocks were like magic, and the way they floated through the air brought to mind a dream she once had, a dream she could only hazily recall involving flying orbs.

The workings of the pump also mystified her, how it conjured water from stores hidden deep within the earth. Kabira could not explain it. But squandering so much water on containers for food and drink offended her sensibilities. She could not understand the reasoning for such waste, not when she had consumed so many impurities in the wilderness without ever falling ill. Spoiled meat and fruits with parasites she knew to discard, but a soiled pot could never harm her.

The greater offense was using the pump for what Kabira called *laundry*. Clothing had to be scrubbed with smooth stones and blocks of soap until they turned more white than yellow, cleansed of sweat and the grime that naturally accrued to discolor the fabric. Yet she found the lice nesting in the threads far more of a hassle. The hairs from her noumena could be shaved to the nub, at least, but the infested garment had to be beaten and hung out to bake in the sun, sometimes for days. Moths posed another problem. They liked to eat holes in the stitching, which had to be mended with needle and thread, a task Thelana found more tedious than making fire or weaving baskets.

She had always assumed that the people of the outside world belonged to a more delicate subspecies, that their hides were more prone to injury, and that they could be harmed by changes in the weather. But after living among them, she became convinced that the Ilmar and the Face People were equally human. Only their customs set them apart.

The townsfolk were protected from the ravages of nature by their sturdy walls, yet even indoors, they could never go about without their second skins. She may have welcomed slippers in the Wildwood, but the cobblestone streets posed no risks to her feet, no worms to burrow into her soles, no black thorns to savage her steps. Kabira wore shoes around the house, but Thelana could not ignore the maladies of her age, the skein of blood vessels climbing like ivy across her lower legs.

Still, Thelana adopted the customs of the townsfolk, learning the habit of clothing not for Kabira's sake but for the people in the square. When she first arrived in Makria, they had shown her no welcome, no hospitality, and no concern for her wellbeing. Their reactions had been altogether foreign, a greeting without counterpart in Ilmarinen. Baba had tried to warn her the day she left home, had tried to explain the attitudes of the wider world, but she had not listened.

If you reveal yourself, at the very least, they will shun you. Hidden by clothing, they will not know you are Ilmar.

It was as her father said, but worse than she could have understood at the time. The intensity in their faces, their quirky, surprised expressions, made the blood rush to her head, numbing her extremities. She had never experienced such an acute feeling of discomfort, an emotion welling up from within her like guilt or regret, or fear. A few of the women turned their faces away, but the men, and the boys, in particular, stared with roving eyes that seemed to glom to her flesh like leeches, the way Brutus regarded Anja. Had they wanted her in the same way?

When she found the courage to ask Kabira about that day, the old woman called it *shame*. "Do your people have no word for 'shame'?"

"No," Thelana admitted, while later that same afternoon, when she inquired, "What good is shame?" Kabira tripped over her tongue, only remarking, "Well . . . It helps you to behave. To know how to be a proper lady."

"What does that mean?" Thelana pressed her. "How is a lady not proper?"

Again, the old woman could only toss up her hands in frustration. "Just do as I tell you.

And if you see those boys again, stay away from them. They're nothing but trouble."

At Kabira's insistence, Thelana wore clothing about the house. Her head went through a hole in the top and the fabric draped over her knees, leaving her arms and calves exposed. The tunic was popular among unmarried women, but she hated how it made her sweat, how the stitching made her scratch and grow irritated. The townsfolk came in many shapes and colors, donning tunics and djellabas and chitons, but to Thelana, they were all just *clothes*, which to her Ilmarin ears sounded like "close," which was apt, she supposed. In clothes, she felt closed off from the world. She hated the sameness of the texture against her skin, even when the material was silky or otherwise pleasant to the touch. That sameness often dulled her mind until she could no longer sense anything at all.

But for the old woman, a simple outer garment would not suffice. She insisted Thelana wrap herself—the womanly parts of her that did not show—in a loincloth.

"It isn't decent," Kabira argued.

For the Ilmar, the noumena was sacred—*the source of all life*—and to bind it was to offend the Goddess, or so Thelana thought. And even if she were to agree to wear such a thing, how would she have relieved herself when the need arose?

"It isn't clean," Kabira went on.

But Thelana had not bled for the better
part of a year, and what she shed from her
body belonged to the River, and the Goddess.
They argued throughout the day until, sensing
her stubbornness, Kabira did not press the
matter further.

Thelana loved to visit the market despite
the shaming she experienced cycles before.
All washed up and dressed, none of the
shoppers or vendors seemed to remember
her, and she had gained so much weight in
Kabira's house that Thelana doubted even her
family would have known her. When she
looked into her bedroom mirror, she could
hardly count her ribs nor see where the bones
of her knees came together.

She helped Kabira barter vegetables for
cuts of meat, or the day's catch of fish, or
dairy products like cheeses and milk. Mounds
of salt and pepper climbed to her waist.
Spices abounded in great big sacks to
captivate her sense of smell. She perused
offerings of basil and bay leaves and browsed
foreign wares she did not know, like cumin,
paprika, and mustard seed. The square
tantalized her with colors and smells and
flavors. Even on festival days in Ilmarinen,
she could not have enjoyed such a variety of
sensations.

Three cycles after arriving in the town, the
rains began. It started timidly, water tapping
on cobblestones, drumming tent posts,
rattling the leaves from the trees. Then it
grew, intensifying into a sweeping, ghostly

howl. The sky rumbled and shook—an angry sound made by angry gods—their clashing arms exploding in a blinding blaze of purple.

Thelana found herself cowering in the corner of the house, bundled in the sheets of her cot. She did not know why.

A sudden gust blew the latch from the windowsill beside her head, nearly tearing off the hinges, leaving the shutter to rattle and smack the clay surface of the wall. She stood to steady the mirror, carefully lowering the polished pane to the floor, and retreated to her corner.

The dome of the sky ruptured like a giant egg, blinding her with lightning. She got up again and latched the window to keep the house from flooding, her cheeks sodden, rain spilling from her lips and chin. But she could still hear the storm fighting to get in, threatening to tear away the roof, to expose and drown her.

My new life . . . This is my new life . . . She wanted to scream it aloud, assert her new reality to whatever gods might be listening, but her old life came thundering back to haunt her. The Tyrant's serrated teeth flashed into the room with every stroke, the shadow of its enormous, meat-threshing jaws silhouetting her bedroom walls.

The storm did not let up, falling in relentless sheets atop her shoulders and brow and in chilling runnels along her shivering spine and down the crack of her backside. It gushed from the windows and doorways and cascaded in white foaming falls from the towering rims of the terraces above. A sudden stream formed in the alleyways. Water flowed over the bridges of her feet, rising to her ankles, knees, and now to her waist. How long had she been dreaming? Her body was emaciated, barely strong enough to stand, yet the torrent lifted her away.

She drank. Drank fully and deeply, and a modicum of strength surged into her veins, making the blood flow again and the knots of her joints unravel. She needed only the stamina to wade through it, keep her chin above the undulating waves until the flooding carried her over the walls to freedom.

DAY 252

The door came alive with an intense thumping sound, and Thelana turned from her sweeping. The echoing rattle from outside the house felt vaguely familiar, disquieting even, but she did not know how best to respond. Kabira still lay by the hearth snoring, and she did not wish to disturb the woman.

She decided to wait until Kabira could instruct her in the proper habit of greeting visitors. And she hated doors. Before famine spread over Ilmarinen, her family had only partitions in their home, precious stones threaded together to keep out the wind and the insects, to beautify their surroundings the way henna embellished their bodies. A door kept Mana from seeing her off the day she left for the woods, imprisoned her in the city ruins, and let strangers into her home to steal away her brother.

The knocking grew louder.

She considered looking out to see who or what it could be. But the only window to the main room faced east, while the front of the house led north into the Wildwood. She could also pull the hatch and climb to the roof. All Makria could be seen from the balcony. But the sun would fall directly into Kabira's eyes, tearing the old woman from her sleep.

The banging persisted, causing the panels in the door to warp and wobble, the brass ring to clang against the plate, and the latch to tug at the nails secured to the wall. But she was most annoyed by the dust falling from the lintel to mess the spot she had just finished sweeping.

Something or someone wanted desperately to get in, but Thelana resisted the cacophonous summons. The latch stubbornly held, and so would she. Whoever it was could want nothing good from them. Even in the marketplace, she took care never to speak to anyone but the shopkeepers. And besides, Kabira had instructed her to clean out the chiminea after finishing with the floor. The charred remains would blacken her hands and tunic, and she would need to wash up.

The intrusion did not cease, intensifying to a repeated hammering. Even Kabira, in her deathly state of slumber, could not help but wake to the noise, sitting up on her elbow with a puzzled expression. "Thelana, dear, aren't you going to answer it?"

"Should I?"

"Never you mind, child. I'll do it." She threw off her covers, tucked her hair into her scarf, and slid her veiny feet into her slippers. The door shuddered like an angry beast as

The Feral Girl

Kabira sleepily made her way to the front of the house. To Thelana's ears, the danger was overtly apparent. Two hundred days in the Wildwood had sharpened her senses to a fine edge. Only a fool would go to such a call. But Kabira was a creature of habit, unused to violence, helplessly bound by custom. And yet she retained a modicum of self-preservation, carefully pulling the latch and the brass ring, allowing only a seam of light to break into the room.

Kabira shaded her face, her eyes rheumy with sleep, as Thelana rushed to her side to stare through the narrow opening. All she could see were faces, men's faces by the look of stubble on their chins.

"Whatever do you want?" she said, more irritated than afraid.

"We want to see the girl." They were not men, Thelana could see. Just boys, no older than Borz had been when he left.

Kabira hesitated. "I don't . . ." She sounded uncertain, groggy, and half-asleep. Whatever the purpose of the visit, Thelana knew it was not customary.

"Come on!" another boy said. "We know she's in there. We just want to see."

Thelana backed slowly into the recess of the house, her hands turning clammy, tightening her grip on her besom. The boy, whoever he was, had not shouted, made no threats, but his words were laced with an undercurrent of menace. How could the old woman not hear it?

"You'll have to forgive me," she answered after a moment. "But if you're asking after my daughter, you'll have to come back some other time. She's gone out for the day."

Suddenly, the door bulged, forced inward from the outside. Kabira pressed her shoulder against it, trying to hold back the intruders, but was overpowered. The struggle tore the hinges away, leaving rusting nails, shreds of wood, and clumps of plaster to litter the floor. She stood rooted to the spot, shocked and holding desperately to the brass ring and the door like a shield.

The boy on the other side apologized. He was young, perhaps younger than Thelana, with a stock of curly red hair and the beginning wisps of a beard below his ears. "I am so sorry," he said. "I didn't mean to do that. Let me help you with that."

In her frazzled state, Kabira seemed to believe him, surrendering the barricade to the boy, who carefully pulled it aside and into the gravelly path. His companions appeared through the opening, the morning sun rising over their heads.

"I'll fix that later. I swear." He sounded sincere enough, regretful even to Thelana's ears. But the other two could only smirk, and the taller boy with the yellow hair started to laugh. They were dressed in hide sandals, studded leather skirts, and woven shirts like metallic fish scales, bringing to mind the Face People. One of them carried a helmet under his arm, another a sword looped through the belt at his hip. Their accoutrements were mismatched and in shoddy condition, bits and pieces collected at different times from different donors.

"Now, where are you boys off to?"

"The war," the red-headed boy answered. "My buddies and I, well, we've been conscripted, and well . . . they're waiting for us at the edge of town."

Kabira sighed. It was a long, drawn-out note. "I understand, my dears. Believe me, I do. But what do you want with me?"

"Well, nothing, really." He peeped through the doorway, and the others he called his buddies did the same. Thelana did not think to hide from them. She could not abandon Kabira to whatever they had in mind to do. "We only wanted to see the girl, you know, before we were sent out. Heard she was a real beauty, tramping all over town and all . . . And my friend here, Sev, well, he's never seen a girl before."

"What do you mean?" Kabira said, flustered. "*Never seen* a girl? How has he never seen a girl?" She did not know what the boy meant. Even Thelana could not be sure exactly. But then, with sudden dismay, the old woman understood. "How dare you come here asking such a thing!" she cried. "Have you no decency? Get out! Get out of here this instant! This is no brothel!"

"Aww . . ." He made an exasperated noise, like a petulant child pleading with his mother. "I didn't mean it like that!"

The older pair, whose beards were more grown in, poked their necks into the house. The one with the yellow hair falling against his broad shoulders locked eyes with Thelana and smiled—it was a greedy, hungering expression that made her shiver. "Hello!" he said, lingering on the "L", his lips pulling back from his ears to reveal a gleaming set of molars. "There she is, Sev. Didn't I tell you? I told you, didn't I? I told you."

"She's a real beauty," the boy called Sev agreed.

Kabira was having none of it. Her face flushed with rage, the gray hairs of her scalp bristling like a cat's, and she shook her meaty fist at them. "Be gone with you!" she bellowed. "Or I'll call to my husband. He's asleep in the other room, and he's got his ax."

It was a bold ploy, but they could not avert their gaze from the young girl standing in the room. Seeing that words alone had no power over them, Kabira wedged herself before the entrance, replacing the door with her body. Sev tugged aggressively at her wrist as the yellow-haired boy shoved his hands into her pillowy bosom. They were not simply moving her out of the way, Thelana could see, but toying with her, tossing the old woman back and forth between them like a sack of potatoes.

"Stop it!" Thelana screamed. "For the Goddess's sake, leave her alone!"

Kabira lifted her face to say something, but no words came out. She could only shake her head with disapproval. Telling Thelana to let things be.

"She's feisty!" Sev said. "I think I like that . . ." He released his captive, and the old woman spun to the ground, falling hard on her rump.

"I want to see what she's got under there," the yellow-haired boy suggested. "I wasn't there that day and didn't get to see." He reached for the hem of her tunic, but she swatted him away. For the first time in her life, Thelana was grateful for clothing, wanting only to hide from their hungering eyes.

"Take it easy," the red-haired boy implored. "No need to get rough."

"Well, if she won't play nice . . ." said Sev, as if that was argument enough. "Besides, she can't be *too* shy. She let everyone see—the whole town see—and we just wanted a look. No harm in that, is there?"

Thelana knew their intentions were anything but amicable, yet she did not know what to do. The situation was entirely foreign, as surreal as the day she first wandered into the market. Men did not say such things in Ilmarinen.

Kabira found her bearings, at last, rolling into a seated position, crying out, "Get back in the house, Thelana!"

The yellow-haired boy leaned over the woman, reaching his arm with a slap. "Shut it, you old bat!"

Something awakened in her then, a visceral response born of the Wildwood. She acted before she knew what was happening, the besom still in her hand, no longer a tool for cleaning but a weapon, a spear without an edge. The youngest of the trio, with the red stubble beard, stood within striking distance, entirely by chance. He had expressed remorse for the treatment of the old woman by his friends, and Thelana was sure to remember that fact in the coming days. But at that moment, he was no longer human. In him, she could only see the snarling halfman, the all-devouring Tyrant, a creature hurting someone she loved. The butt of her broomstick flew up in her fists—she did not hold back her strength—driving directly into his throat. An instant later, he lay flat on his back, gasping for air, a large swelling welt radiating from his neck, alternating between sickly shades of violet and crimson.

Sev bent over him with a panicked look. "What happened?" he cried, too stunned to process what he had just witnessed. "What just happened!"

The yellow-haired boy rounded on her, his mouth contorting with hatred, his bloodshot eyes keen as a killer's. "What'd you do? What'd you do to him!"

The boy on the ground clawed at his throat now as if trying to open a hole in it—a hole to take in air. Sev knelt beside him. "I don't think he can breathe! Gil, for Sargonus's sake, get over here and help me. He can't breathe!"

But Gil, entirely preoccupied, offered no reply. A short blade appeared in his hand. He slowly advanced, closing the distance between himself and Thelana. "I'm gonna kill this bitch-whore."

Her nerves tensed, but her heart remained steady, even as he continued to approach. She did not step from his path, made no motion to retreat. Instead, she welcomed him, the broom firm in her hands, her heels raised and ready. She did not doubt his willingness to harm her. But she could no more fear the boy than a voorgaven would a gazelle. Fate had not seen to her survival through the Wildwood only to die at the hands of some pubescent man-child. And seeing her steely resolve gave him pause, made him question with whom or what he was about to engage. But as the boy called Gil raised his blade to strike, a great sense of distress prevailed upon her, fearing not for her own sake but for his. There could be no turning back from what she was about to do. But what choice did she have? She had grown to care for the old woman, and those boys would never leave them alone. Hatred existed even in Ilmarinen. And the need for vengeance.

Gil's sword came down clumsily, and she realized he had not held a weapon in battle before nor slain anything more significant than an insect. For all his bluster, the boy had never been hunting, never eaten flesh from a creature someone else had not slaughtered for him. She moved effortlessly from his path, and her broom caught in his knees, sweeping him to the ground. He rolled forward in a cloud of dust, cursing, his sword tumbling from his grasp. But before he could regain his footing, she was over him, her feet planted into his sternum. He reached for her ankle, but she slashed at his wrist with his own sword.

"I am going to kill you!" he bellowed.

The weapon was a lot heftier than she was used to. *Hammered iron*, she thought, a perfect killing tool, with an edge she now directed into his neck.

"I'll do it!" Gil threatened. He twisted and turned, foam flying from his lips with every frenzied syllable. "I'll kill you! And I'll kill your mother too!"

She could not hold back the moisture from building in her eyes. "I don't want to do this," she murmured. "Promise me you'll go away. Promise me you'll leave us alone, and I won't hurt you . . ."

He made a sudden jerking motion to toss her from him, but she quickly asserted her balance, pushing him hard to the ground.

"Please . . ." She was begging with him now, her tears falling freely over his scowling face.

He spat up at her again, most of it landing on him. "I'll promise to come back when you're sleeping and slit your throats. That's all I'll promise, you ugly quim." His glaring eyes told the truth of it. He had every intention of committing to his threats. And Thelana was taken aback. She had never experienced such wanton cruelty in another of her species, would not have believed humans capable of what Gil proposed to do—the Ilmar did not have a word for *murder*—and this distressed her most of all.

Sev sat watching from afar, as did the red-haired boy alongside him, who was now sitting upright and breathing normally. They seemed a lot younger than they had been, little more than children, and the dread in their eyes was awfully apparent. "Come on, Gil," Sev said. "Let's get out of here. They're waiting for us." Kabira stood next to them, and if Thelana had not known otherwise, she might have mistaken them for her sons.

"I'm not going anywhere!" Gil cried, wrestling away with such unexpected power, Thelana was forced to her knees. The sword warbled as it hit the ground, bouncing once before coming down again to rest. Kabira, Sev, and the red-haired boy gasped in unison. The pommel lay an arm's length from the two of them, but Thelana moved more swiftly, scrambling over him to grab hold of it. Dust clouded the air as they fought for control, and then, a terrible wailing rang out across the town.

She heard her own tortured voice as she stumbled from the yellow-haired boy, her empty hands glistening and crimson. Turning away, she could see the horrified expression in Kabira's eyes. *They've killed my daughter! The bastards went and killed her!* What else could the poor old woman have been thinking?

But it was not so.

The Ilmar were forbidden from doing three things. The first was for man and woman to merge before the Solstice. The second was to take the dream journey when one has not been initiated. Thelana had already violated one of these dictates, and now, she had committed a second.

"I wanted no part in this . . ." she whispered.

Gil lay on his back twitching, his neck quartered like a melon, the sword wedged in his flesh protruding from the ground like an iron sapling. Sev and his red-headed friend rushed to the fallen boy. They were already sobbing. Weeping as the blood gushed from the wound in Gil's throat like a blossoming rose.

Thelana could only stare, paralyzed by the grisly scene. *How many friends did he know? How many brothers? Sisters? What will his mother and father say when they learn he is dead? That someone killed their son? Oh, Alashiya . . . How many lives have I just destroyed?*

The boys did not notice her departure, but Kabira's attention never strayed. "Where do you think you're rushing off to, young lady?"

Thelana could not face her. She and the townsfolk stood united in her mind, like one family, one people. Thelana was the oddity, the piece that did not belong. She could only think to walk, tearing a seam in her tunic to free her legs, and she would continue walking, far from the town and everything in it.

Kabira kept shouting, pleading for her to stop, but Thelana hurried further and further away, until she could scarcely make out the old woman's despondent voice.

The great turquoise disc wheeled up into the eastern sky, and only then did she dare look back. Makria appeared as she first saw it, a sand-colored discoloration against the horizon. Her salvation, her place of sanctuary, had been little more than that. A shape she could blot out with her forefinger.

The woods beckoned with the music of the insects and the chorus of the birds. Cypress trees mingled with palm fronds and olive heavy branches, their conjoined limbs greeting her, swaying over the forest's edge to embrace her. Beyond the leaves, she glimpsed the white elk dashing between the trees, gone before she could be sure he was ever there. Was the Goddess directing the course of her life again? Or did the avatar with its magnificent antlers affirm what she had already decided?

Thelana longed to run freely, far from the roving, judgmental eyes of other people. But in Makria, she would never again suffer from hunger, cold, or hungering predators. Still, the comforts of civilization could be a prison, like the sweet-smelling nectar of the flower that

lures the bee to its death. And in the coming
years, her courage could only wane as her
body aged and grew tired, until she was
buried as one of them, only knowing what
Kabira taught her, a life of chores, of
sameness.

Loneliness.

She had spent a little over four cycles
lodging with the old woman. But Kabira was
still *someone*, an ear to listen when she
wished to talk, a face to greet her in the
morning. Loneliness was what Thelana most
feared.

As if thinking upon a thing could make it
appear, she spotted the old woman steadily
cresting the slope, her dirndl hiked to her
knees. She had to stop and rest every few
paces before reaching the top, and as she
came within sight of Thelana, her lined face
lost much of its color.

"Thank Sargonus . . . I caught . . . up with
you . . ." She bent over her knees to steady
herself, and Thelana rushed to take her arm,
fearing the old woman might collapse.

"Why did you follow me?"

Kabira brushed the gray curls from her
face. Her scarf sat lopsided, drenched with
sweat and sticking to her brow. "How can you
ask such a thing? We're . . . We're family,
Thelana."

"I had family," she said. "They're gone,
now."

"Nonsense, girl. I've come to take you
home. Home with me," she added, not as a

mother but as a lonely old woman. A woman lost and afraid.

"I can't." She wanted to apologize but could not remember how. A simple *sorry* would not suffice.

"But you belong here." Kabira was pleading with her again. "You belong here with us."

But that's just the thing, the deciding factor, the reason she could not stay despite every reason she should. An Ilmarin girl did not belong in Makria. "I can't," she said again, and there was a finality to her tone suggesting no more discussion could be had.

"It's those boys, isn't it? Those wicked curs! I know it . . . But don't you fret about them. We all saw what happened. We can say you were just . . . defending yourself. Defending me!"

"No!" Thelana shoved the woman away. In Ilmarinen, there were no excuses for taking a human life. "I killed him!" she declared, fresh tears washing over the stains of the old. "I killed *ilma*. Ilma don't kill ilma!"

"But you didn't have a choice, my dear . . ." Kabira insisted.

Shame. Kabira worried a great deal about shame, and being judged, but did not seem to know what truly warranted judgment. None of them did. She stared over the old woman, seeing the town with all its fancy walls and doors, and the haunted hills looming beyond it, the remnants of the forgotten, ancient city.

"Can't you see? You ruined it!" Thelana cried.

"Ruined what, my dear? What did I ruin?"

"All of you! Your people. You ruined it!" The words came unbidden to her tongue, ideas welling up from another time and place, from a dream. But it seemed to mean everything. *It's all starting again, the greed, the lies, the willful blindness.*

"I don't think I understand, dear."

Despair consumed her rage, leaving her empty, drained. "You take a beautiful thing . . ." she said, her lips quavering, "and make it *ugly*." Thelana did not entirely know what she meant by this either, but the words felt right.

Kabira took up her braid, securing the fold and tamping down the loose strands. Making things presentable is what she knew best. "You're not coming back," she said. "Are you?"

Thelana shook her head. And to prove her decision was final, she tugged at the collar of her tunic until it lay crumpled in her hands.

"Take it with you," Kabira said.

"I won't need it." *Not where I'm going.*

"Then . . . Won't you take *me* with you?"

Thelana stood dumbfounded. After all Kabira had taught her about being a proper lady, she was prepared to leave it behind for her—for a daughter she hardly knew. But the wild was no place for someone nearing the end of their lives. Even if she had been young enough to take the journey, a human born to excess could never hope to survive it. Thelana could only pull the woman into a tight embrace, knowing that some customs—customs of affection—are universal. It was the kindest way she knew to say "no."

The old woman moved slowly away. She seemed to accept her determination to go, yet came forward again, delicately opening Thelana's tattered fingers to place a small pouch in her palm. "Well, you can't go without your flower, dear. I know how much this means to you."

She remembered. She knew . . . Thelana did not speak. Could not even look at her, unable to bear the sight of the old woman's caring, maternal face. If she were to return to Makria, even for a day, she would never leave it.

"See? We're not *all* bad. Now, you run along, dear. Be safe. And don't you worry about me. I'll be just fine . . ."

Thelana knew Kabira would not be fine, and wanted to say something more, to explain at least that she had, however briefly, found family in Makria. But she could only turn and step into the forest, having not the words.

DAY 600

"Just keep going as you are," they informed her, "holding the Moon to your left, and you shouldn't miss it." When she asked for directions, the villagers had not hesitated. But how much of a fool did they think her to not know her north from south?

She heard the subtle call from afar, rounding in her ears like the rumbling of an impending storm, and knew she was near.

Soldiers native to the coast spoke of the Sea with longing, the way she described her home. "She's like a lover," the fishmonger told her one night over the campfire. "She can be cruel, or she can be kind. Just like people. It all depends on how you treat her."

But nothing could have prepared her for what she was about to see.

The sky appeared like a dull iron sheet, a suit of armor after a day's battle, and a forlorn light penetrated through the chinks to settle upon the sand. She sighed, having hoped for better weather after dreaming of this day for years.

She skipped down from the bluff, her sandals sinking through the soft bed of pebbles until she came to the place called *beach*, where the world ended.

Waves swelled beneath the clouds, rising like giants to hammer the rocky shore. *The One Sea.* She could not help but be awed by its power, the destructive tide breaking from one form to the next, smashing into countless white specks before falling and reforming and breaking again.

The wind whipped through her hair, tugging at the fine jade cloak about her shoulders, carrying a briny scent to drown her other senses. She pressed her face into the gusting air, and it pushed back like a forbidding hand. A little way ahead, the gnarled stump of a dying olive tree marked the base of the slope, the pebbles diminishing in size as the ground turned smooth with the sand.

The beach was a dark slate gray, nearly black in color. She watched her sandaled feet form impressions across the ebony surface, creating a distinct, meandering line from the olive stump to the shore. She knelt to pinch the sand, rubbing the granules between her thumb and forefinger. It was much finer than what collected by the banks of the Braid.

Boulders shot up from the beach like petrified wings, their irregular peaks cutting sharply across the hazy sky like obsidian fragments. She stopped to unbuckle the belt at her waist, gently laying her sword beside the rock. The quiver clipped to her side came next, followed by the gold fibula fastened to her collar. She was relieved to lose the weight, still unaccustomed to the habit of clothing. But she treasured the loose-fitting cloak. It had been a gift from her captain and called to mind the rich green fields of her homeland. Her sandals, however, were standard issue footwear, what every infantryman was expected to wear. These she hated most of all. The boiled straps cut across the skin, forming lines of irritation across her calves.

She trudged across the sand in her bare feet, euphoric, her steps growing heavier and wetter and colder, yet she still held fast to her suit of gambeson and the leggings fitted to her thighs.

Aenya did not end as she imagined it. She expected a vast drop, the world's crust vanishing sharply into nothing, like peering over the edge of a canyon only to see an expanse of puffy white clouds and, come nightfall, a dark void littered with stars. Instead, endless gray water met her eyes in every direction she looked.

The Sea was nothing like the tranquil lake, the Eyes of Alashiya, where Borz had taught her to swim, but wild and terrible like the rapids of the Braid. Only, here the waters of Ukko—the lifeblood of Ilmarinen—emptied away.

The tide thundered and crashed, spraying her with mist, but she continued across the slate-dark sand, daring the incoming waves.

Tiny shelled creatures, green and yellow and spotted, skittered sideways from her footsteps. If she still lived in the Wildwood, she would have scooped them up for a meal.

She arrived at the shoreline, where the water met the land, staining the knees of her garment. The collapsing Sea flattened into long oval streams as it rushed toward her, swirling into a pitted reef, filling the hollows and draining away before refilling again. She cupped her hands into the hole, drawing the clear liquid to her lips, and immediately spat it out. *Yech!* The saltiness stung her tongue and throat and made her eyes itch.

So much water . . . and all of it undrinkable.

She sat in the sand with her back against a flat rock. As the tide came tumbling down in a fresh dazzle of white, the water raced like a gleaming sheet across the beach to douse her feet and muddy her skirt. The constant roaring rhythm lulled her troubled mind like the chorus of a ballad. The Sea sang to the Land, whom it loved, asserting its name over and over and over again.

Beauty was everywhere to be found in the Outside, even here, at the southern edge of Aenya where the wind lashed at her with icy fingers, where her journey came to its unsatisfying conclusion.

She used a conical mollusk to draw the Ilmarin sign for "six," followed by a second symbol indicating "hundred." The marks showed distinctly against the dark sand until the tide hurried to wash them away.

Six hundred days since she departed from her father's door. Thelana crossed through woods and savannah during that time, lived as a native in Makria, circled back into halfman territory, and became a warrior and later a thief. Yet she never managed to discover any clue as to her brother's whereabouts.

Borz . . . I never could find you . . .

"It was never about me."

He stood on the beach, his torso as plain as the rocks on the sand, the muscles of his abdomen as evident as the mountains exploding and reforming along the coastline. If he had been attired in any way, decked out in the panoply of the Kratan soldier as she was, she would not have known him. She could only imagine him in his skin.

"You know that, don't you?"

"But I wanted to bring you home," she answered. "That's where you belong. Where we belong, Borz. Mana and Baba were wrong to sell you. I wouldn't have let them do it if I could have stopped them . . ."

"They did what they thought best, Thelana. What was best for their family. As did you."

"No!" She became furious with him, with this phantom from the past. "They could have found another way. I *would* have found another way! There's always another way . . ." She resisted the urge to weep. It was unbecoming of a warrior, a survivor, a show of weakness. "If only I'd been a bit older. Stronger. I could have saved you . . ."

"That doesn't matter anymore," he said. "It only matters that they made the right decision *with you*, by giving you a chance at life."

The wind coursed over the waters, churning the crests of the waves to froth, snapping her braid and raising her cloak like a sail. But his dark cropped hair did not change, remaining as it had always been in her mind. "Oh, what do you know?" She waved him off. "You're not even here. I'm just talking to myself."

"Even if you were to have found me, slaving away in some rich man's court, I would not be who I was. At least, not who I was to you. The Outside has a way of changing people. We all adapt to survive, just like a girl I know, who braved the worst of the woods and came out stronger. But the man you remember isn't gone entirely. He helped you survive the Wildwood, and now, he is helping you move past it."

"I have moved past it. I'm here, aren't I?"

"Your body is here, yes, but your spirit remains where you left it. In Ilmarinen. That isn't what Baba hoped for you. Not what Mana wanted either."

"They didn't care about me . . ." She brushed a knuckle over her eyes, her hand trembling with the effort, and the moisture caught in her lashes like dewdrops. "They sent me away to *die* . . ." She could scarcely speak above the din of the tide—the Sea drowning the last of her words.

"No, Thelana, you couldn't be more wrong." She could hear him distinctly in her head. As always, his voice was reassuring, calmly teaching her how to survive the world. "You convinced yourself they didn't care, so losing them wouldn't matter. But you're here now, because Baba and Mana knew how strong you could be. The others were too young or sick and would have been a burden. It was never an easy decision, Thelana. Sending you away was the hardest thing our parents ever had to do. But they did it because they loved you. *Because they loved you most.*"

She shut her eyes to keep from seeing him as warm tears washed over her cheeks, adding to the runnel of the Sea. *Was this real? Could anything be real?* Perhaps that was the wrong question.

A rush of air prickled against the exposed hairs of her arms. Such weather was not known to Ilmarinen or the Wildwood. This land called beach belonged to different gods, indifferent to human hardship.

Borz strolled across the sand, his feet making no mark, and took up her hand. She could feel the rough textures of his palms in hers, the scabs at the base of his fingers formed from a childhood of chopping wood.

"You have to let me go," he murmured. "So long as you cling to my memory, so long as you blame yourself for what happened that day, you'll never be free. You'll never be out of the woods."

"B-But . . ." Her heart quailed, and she felt paralyzed, powerless to argue or think. "But I don't want to let you go."

"It's never easy, but this is the way of the Goddess, the cycle of death and rebirth. It is as true for memories as it is for the body, and civilizations, and the whole world. But you have a great more living to do, sister, and your family would not want you to waste it—*I* would not want you to."

A gentle kiss touched her forehead, and he was gone. Gone with the mist and the crashing waves.

She gathered up her sword and quiver, hooking them to the baldric at her waist, and took up her cloak, clasping it by the fibula to her collar. Her sandals she would carry in her hands, wanting to feel the wet sand gush between her toes a little while longer.

The weather shifted, the iron-gray sheet of sky drawing steadily away to reveal the blue dome of Aenya. To the south, the roiling Sea quieted to a jabber, and the mountain-high waves subsided into hills, and the wind's grip on her cloak turned playful, frolicking along the hemline at her heels.

A great fishlike shape emerged from the haze, riding over the water's surface. She watched it come in, a boat of sorts, like what her people might use to ford the broader parts of the Braid. But it was far sleeker in design. Her people could never have constructed such a thing.

The water-going vessel advanced upon the shoreline, rising and falling with the rhythm of the Sea, as dozens of oars dipped in unison to battle the waves. And Thelana found herself drawn by the uncanny feeling that she was meant to go out and greet it.

She stood in her sandals atop a long, glassy reef, the natural outcropping reaching across the water like a bridge to nowhere. Waves broke against her on every side, falling like cold, heavy rain. And as the long wooden barge slid into view, she could not help but marvel at its size.

So big a vessel could house ten of my family!

A ramp touched upon the reef, and a man rushed from behind a railing, carrying a thick braid of rope. He coiled the tether about an iron knot at the base of the outcropping. Other men followed in his steps, shouldering wooden crates and metal-ringed barrels, trundling down the ramp in a parade of dour expressions. All of them looked hungry and restless, their beards long and disheveled. If she had to guess, they were just returning from a long, arduous journey.

"My, you're a fine sight to see! I've been cooped up so long with none but smelly sailors about, I'm doubting you're even real." The man with the rope had a face like boiled leather, a burnt brow a blister shade of red, and nearly colorless eyes—pupils as white as the scraggly hairs coating his neck.

"Pardon me," she said. "These are all strange sights to me. What exactly is—" she pointed to where the men continued to disembark, "—that?"

"Oh," he said. "You mean our ship? That there, missy, is the *Trident.* We bring goods from all across The Imperial Coast."

"But . . ." she stammered, trying not to sound like a child. "Where is it you come from, exactly?"

"From?" He laughed. "From everywhere! We hit every port from here to, well . . . Graton Town."

"But I thought . . . Well, what I mean to say is . . . This isn't the end? Of . . . the world, I mean?"

She feared he would laugh at her again, derisively this time, embarrass her as she often was when asking questions about the world she did not know. "No, miss," he said, looking on her kindly. "The world goes on and on. In fact, I just so happen to be captain of this here ship. Captain Joba's the name, and I can show you aboard if you'd like."

She sensed no malice in his voice—if anything, he reminded her a bit of her father.

"We're scheduled for Thetis, after we unload all this stuff, and then we're headed for Hedonia. And if you never laid eyes on Hedonia, you've not seen a thing yet. *Jewel of the Sea.* That's what they call her."

"Is it . . .?" She turned back from whence she came. Ilmarinen was so very far away. She could see no hint of it, the Mountains of Ukko, on the horizon. "Is it to the south? You see, I've been going south a while, and I'd like to go on. I've been searching for . . . something." *Maybe someone else like me.*

"Well, you've certainly found yourself *something*," Joba remarked. "I can assure you that." He bowed. "Now come right this way, my lady."

The sun sailed from beyond the clouds, dappling the *Trident* in gold. And Thelana looked back once more, her cloak rippling from her shoulders across the ramp and over the Sea.

They loved me most, she thought, and did not look back again.

Where does Thelana go from here? Find out
in . . .

AGES
of
AENYA

NOW AVAILABLE

Made in the USA
Columbia, SC
17 May 2022

60535036R00221